DOPEHEAD

A NOVEL

EMANUELLE ELLISON

Production by eBookPro Publishing
www.ebook-pro.com

DOPEHEAD
Emanuelle Ellison
Copyright © 2024 Emanuelle Ellison

All rights reserved; No parts of this book may be reproduced or transmitted in any form or by any means, electronic or mechanical, including photocopying, recording, taping, or by any information retrieval system, without the permission, in writing, of the author.

Translated from Hebrew: Maya Thomas
Edited: Evan Gordon

Contact: ellisonemanuelle@gmail.com
ISBN 9798343256871

*I'm not afraid of death, but I won't let it take me
until I've exhausted life to the fullest!*

– Emanuelle Ellison

CHAPTER 1

It all started on New Year's Eve, 1987. My girlfriend Angie and I were sorting out a few things before leaving the house. The plan was to go hang out at Andy's basement and then move on to Shine, our local club. I was waiting for her by the front door, ready to make a move, but she'd locked herself in the bog, as usual, retching all of the pizza we'd eaten.

"Come on, love," I tried to urge her.

"Two minutes," she replied.

I knew that it would be more like twenty, but I had to keep it to myself. If anyone dared to even hint at Angie's bulimia, things would end very badly. So, I sifted through my pocket, took out a bit of MD, lined it up neatly and snorted it. It burns like mad, but it kicks in after ten minutes and the high's way more intense.

"What are you doing?" she asked from the other end of the door.

"Sorting myself out a bit, waiting for you to come out… Want some too?"

Angie fell silent. I assumed that she was just getting everything out, so I ignored the silence and chopped a couple of neat little lines for her.

"What's the crack, love? I'm starting to feel lonely … longing … bursting with love…" Still no reply, which seemed odd to me. "Babe, what's happening?" I asked as I approached the bathroom door. "Angie, what is it? Why aren't you answering, darling? Is everything okay…? Angie? Angie?!" I shouted as I burst through the door.

She was sprawled on the floor. I lifted her up to the sink in a panic, washed her face and then laid her on the bed. I ran to my mum's room, grabbed a bottle of rubbing alcohol from the shelf by the bed, then placed it under Angie's nose. I patted her cheeks a few times and she started coming around. I ran to the sink and got a glass of water, and forced her to sip some. And then she smiled at me, as though nothing had even happened.

"What happened in there?" I asked.

"Dunno, maybe I put too much effort into it, I felt this strange pressure in my head and I must have fainted…"

"You had me worried sick! Enough already … you have to put an end to this. I don't understand why you have to throw up."

"Why do you have to do drugs?" she retorted defiantly.

"You do drugs too."

"Yeah, but you do loads more."

"What does that have to do with anything?"

"I'm trying to say that it comes from the same place…"

"But the retching nearly killed you!"

"And drugs can't?"

"We're talking about you, why do you block everything and just toss it back at me?"

"Because you hate it when people stick their noses in your addiction, so I don't like it when you stick your nose in my addiction! Basically, don't try and play doctor when you're a fucking patient yourself!"

"Fine, you're right, keeping my nose well away. Are you all right?"

"Yeah, all good."

"Then can we get ready and go? We can talk about everything when we get back from the party."

"No! We need to talk about it now!"

"But they're waiting for us! And I'm fucking high, babe, it's not the right time… We'll talk about it when we get back."

"I'm tired of you fobbing me off every time and then nothing ever happens," she insisted on bringing me down, "Do you even realize that if your mum kicks us out, we'll be fucking homeless? And then we'll definitely OD or catch some disease that'll kill us."

"What?! How on earth do you figure that? No one's kicking us out!" I fought back, "We're doing what we're supposed to be doing at our age, doing drugs and enjoying life!"

"We're not enjoying life, we're ruining it! We haven't seen anything yet and that's how it'll stay if we keep at it. Show me one person on our block that actually amounted to something."

"Listen to me, I swear that when we get back, first of all you'll put an end to the purges, and then we'll get off the drugs, together, and we'll get an escape plan going and get out of here."

"You're talking bollocks," she fumed. "There's no such thing – rehab from the one addiction and only then from the other? It all goes together; do I look like an idiot to you?"

"No, of course not," I got defensive. "I'm just not thinking straight, I'm high."

"That's precisely it, don't you get it?!"

Of course I got it. Deep down, I knew that she was right and that we had to make some serious changes to our lives. I also knew that I just kept making excuses, mainly about the timing being shit. But I wasn't where she was at. I wasn't fully ripe for the change, it scared me. I was worried about coping with an unfamiliar challenge. I was scared by the thought of us sobering up and realizing that this life's too intense for us, that we won't be able to make it the way we'd dreamed of. I preferred to dream that I'd make it, rather than actually try to do something with the chances of success being slim to none.

I took the baggie out and chopped a few lines on a plate. But she stared right into me, waiting for my reply.

"Well, what do we do now? Right now?" I asked as I snorted a line, "It's a bit too late to get clean today, and what would we do with all the stuff anyway? I got loads for the party."

"Then give it back."

"Angie, this ain't a Tesco's, why are you stressing me out right now?"

"Calm down," she said in a childlike tone and softly stroked my face, "I love you! Let's celebrate New Year's together and start the change right now. Trust me!"

She loosened me within a second. The combination of drugs together with her touch and infantile tone made me surrender to her instantly.

"Okay..." I replied and she went ballistic. I'd just meant 'Okay, let me take this all in, let me get my head around it for a sec,' but she took it as 'Okay, I'm going for it,' so I didn't even manage to react before she pounced on me and kissed me passionately.

"You're the best, you're the fucking best! You're the smartest man alive!"

Of course, it felt good to get all that flattery, and I really didn't feel like rewinding back into the argument with her. I wanted to keep going and hear about how great I am, so I just stared at her, smiling like a kid watching a magic trick.

"Well?" she said, her look reminding me of my younger self eagerly awaiting something my mum had promised me.

"Right now, just like that?" I asked.

"Yeah, exactly," she answered, buzzing, "You said 'okay.'"

I said, 'okay'... Of all the words that came out of my mouth, the way she clung onto my 'okay,' staring at me with her glimmering eyes... She looked so beautiful and happy, and I felt like a full-on hero ... I was mesmerized.

"I'm going to chuck it all down the bog," I said, giving her an Elvis Presley look. She blurted out a joyous shriek and jumped onto my back. That was funny.

I stood over the toilet, Angie still hanging on my back, tightly grabbing onto me. I flipped the plate over and all of the stuff plummeted into the toilet. Naturally, I immediately regretted it. "I can't believe I just did that, you're completely bonkers!"

She wiggled on my back, ecstatic and horny. "I love you," she whispered.

"Back at you, times a thousand!" I replied and we kissed for a long while.

We got into bed and cuddled. A second before taking my trousers off, I quickly reached my hand down to pull the second baggie out of my pants. It had all sorts of pills, acid, and coke. I chucked it behind the bed so that Angie wouldn't notice.

We hugged and had a giggle and talked about life, me, her, and us. I loved talking to Angie about everything, but most of all I loved hearing what she thought about me. She saw me as the king of the world, fucking Hercules! She always told me that I was smart and that I had the kind of potential and ideas that no one else in the world could ever have. She'd compare me to all the stars and claim that they only got to where they were by pure luck. "Take Prince for example, looks-wise he ain't got nothing on you, not to mention brains. And I swear that sometimes, when I hear you sing, you really move me. Then why him and not you?! Because he lucked out. He must have been in the right place at the right time, and he became a megastar. One day we'll luck out too, and you'll be a thousand times greater than him!"

"Prince? Come on, who doesn't look better than him?" I challenged her, "And I don't even want to be a singer."

"I just used him as an example, it applies to anyone really," she explained, "The point is that timing's the most crucial thing in life. I believe that one day, we'll be the ones in the right place at the right time, and it'll happen to us too!"

"And what do you want to be?" I asked.

"A great writer, like Ernest Hemingway."

"Ah wicked! And I want to be a great writer's husband, so we're already halfway there."

CHAPTER 2

We made love. But a few hours later, the stuff was already wearing off, so at that point, I started doubting our ability – or more like my ability – to make a real change in life. To be fair, the only time I could genuinely believe that it was possible was when I was proper stoned. Actually, I was pretty pissed at Angie for making me promise things I couldn't keep when I wasn't sober enough to know any better. What was she doing clinging onto a word that had an entirely different intention behind it and choosing her own preferred interpretation?!

"Angie, I'm starting to feel unwell, I'm not sure I can do this."

"Of course you can! You're not feeling unwell, you're just finally starting to feel, so it crept up on you. I wanted to purge too, but I stopped myself, don't want to run away from my emotions anymore. Let's start planning things, go get a pen and paper for us…"

"You go get it! And you're not getting things right! I can't be bothered with changes right now!"

Angie looked at me. I hoped she'd get angry at what I'd said, and then we could fight and I could get the fuck out of the house without feeling guilty. But she swallowed her pride and got up to get a pen and paper.

"I'm writing this all down, we'll look for jobs in the papers, maybe even ask your mum. She always talks about trying to get you this job or that job."

"Why are you bringing up my mum right now? Out of the question, that's the last thing I need," I replied agitatedly. The mere thought of the woman who gave birth to me was enough to make me want to get completely and utterly smashed.

They say that a parent's love for their child is the building block of life, the strongest sort of influence on their personality. But my mum ... she didn't really see me. The way she saw it, I was the biggest obstacle she had, the little critter she could never get rid of, the one who'd made her life stop. If she'd had the opportunity to get rid of me without anyone knowing, then she would have definitely done it.

It was so blatant. All of her usual lines proved exactly what she really thought of me. "You're the spawn of Satan, that's what you are, just like your dad!" That was a nice little line she used to tell me. There was also that polite enquiry to God as to why she'd been blessed with a child like me. To be honest, I could have provided her with numerous answers to that question, but her retort of – "I have a feeling that you were swapped in the hospital, there's no way you came out of me!" always managed to bring me down.

During parent-teacher meetings at school, she'd sit there with a stubbed-out fag between her fingers, her foot twitching restlessly, as though she couldn't wait for the nightmare to end. During one of those meetings, my teacher, Miss Alice, showered me with praises and told her how good I was at grammar, literature, and even history. "He's a genius in a workshop and one of our most talented footballers," she went on excitedly, "The coach has got his eye on him. But he is having difficulty in math."

That's when mum suddenly switched on, as though she'd just been waiting for that one thing I wasn't good at so that she could charge. "Math, of all things? Are you serious? He's better off not being good at literature! And what'll he get out of history? It always repeats itself anyway! But math's the most important subject, and that's the one he's bad at?! He's just like his father, he was always best at all the things that didn't matter."

Miss Alice seemed embarrassed as she retorted, "Oh, come now, I'm sure his father had a few good traits, and I'm certain he's got some of your best features too…"

"Of course he does, he took my finest years, my joy, and the air out of my bloody lungs! Those are the very best features he's gotten out of me! Anything else I need to know?" My teacher shook her head. "I hope that next year, you'll invest some more time into teaching him the subjects that actually matter," my mother summarized and left the classroom.

And me? Like a stupid git, all I ever did was try to prove to her that I was the best thing that had ever happened to her. But nothing worked, she viewed everything I did as an absolute failure. What does a kid want if not for his mum to care? For his mum to forgive him and say he's the greatest, no matter how many mistakes he's made. Even if some of the other kids are better looking or more talented, a mum should still tell her kid that he's the best looking and that he's better than all the rest.

A kid needs his mother's touch, and he, in turn, needs her to need him, he needs to know that she couldn't live without him. That's what kids grow up with, and that's what they go searching for in the world and in the people they choose to let into their lives.

Well then, fuck my mum, who only ever loved herself and her booze.

That's what it's like growing up in a neighborhood full of people who only know the concept of love through the telly, the kind of people who work morning till night and still don't get through the month. Either they're on the dole or they're yardies and junkies, it's as though our area's a factory for defects. The only ones who dared to dream were us, the kids. We always said we'd never turn out like our parents. We planned to make it big one day and finally burst the scummy bubble we were living in, we'd be millionaires! It was clear to us that something big was going to happen to us one day.

But none of us wanted to work hard or study for it. The boys dreamed about winning the lottery, getting into a premier league football team, or finding a suitcase full of dosh by the riverbank. The bolder lads fantasized about a good old bank robbery. The birds dreamed about some bigshot producer flying them over to Hollywood, or some rich bloke falling for them, love at first sight, like in Cinderella.

I remember this one time, during a ceremony at school, our headmaster lectured us about having to work hard if we want to succeed in life. Naturally, we didn't believe him. After all, everyone we knew who'd worked hard just stayed poor and frustrated. All of the posh people, however, were driving lush cars, flying out on holidays, sitting in restaurants and shopping all day long, so how much spare time would they even have left to work?!

Even my mate Andy's parents said they earned pretty good wages but that the country just kept taking all of their money in taxes, theirs and everyone else's. We didn't fully get what they meant by 'country' – what kind of country would do that to so many people, and why wasn't anyone stopping it?! Our plan was that one day, when we're rich, we'd find that country and return the money back to the people that it took from them!

We were a tight crew, Tommy, Andy, Manu, Smiley, and me. We grew up and went through our entire adolescence together. We even started doing drugs in that forum.

Drugs weren't a big deal in our area, we even had a substitute teacher who was an ecstasy dealer. In fact, the first pills he gave us were on the house. He supplied them for us for a short while until he was arrested, and we found our way to other dealers and other drugs.

Each of us came with his own heavy emotional baggage from home, and we always helped one another out when things went rough. But as we got older, there was something very basic suddenly lacking, something that we couldn't provide for one another, being an all-male crew.

And then Angie came along. She loved me and she was the best shag ever! I became addicted to how I felt when I was with her. I never got tired of her, mainly because I constantly lived in a state of fear that she'd suddenly get over me and walk out.

CHAPTER 3

I paced back and forth around the house like a lunatic, thinking about our mates waiting for us. I felt caged and stifled. I was itching to chop a few lines, just a few lines to calm me down. I couldn't stop thinking about how to get to the baggie I'd tossed behind the bed without Angie noticing.

"What's up with you?" she asked, "Come here, sit down for a minute, we can't do any planning like this."

"I can't sit down! Stop stressing me!"

"Okay," her eyes softened, "I only mentioned your mum because I thought she'd be glad to finally have us out of the house. But if you're not up for it, that's cool, I get it."

"No, I'm not up for it, Angie!"

"Chill, Iggy."

"I don't want to chill!" I replied in a furious tone when the phone suddenly rang. I rushed over to pick it up, of course. "Hello?"

"Are you two still home?!" That was Tommy, my closest mate.

"Well, there's been a change of plans and we might not make it," I said, glancing at Angie agitatedly. "I'm in a bit of a bind, mate," I then whispered into the phone.

"Seriously mate, does this seem legit to you?" he raised his voice, "Now you listen here, if it's not a pregnancy, a terminal illness, or an emergency appendicitis, then you better get your asses over here and be quick about it, we're already at the club, is that clear?"

Even with my nerves on edge, he still managed to make me chuckle. Once Tommy gets something in his head, then nothing can make him budge. He had serious charisma and some of the world's finest persuasion skills. No matter what the argument was about, he'd always manage to convince you that he was a hundred percent right, or at least make you think that his point was just as valid as yours. The guy was a proper bookworm and maintained an active infatuation with anything to do with spirituality and the universe. He always had these crazy, fascinating theories about the afterlife.

Birds would fall for him in a second. Actually, everyone loved hanging out with him. Except for his dad. The way he saw it, his son was the man who'd stolen his wife from him, and it drove him mad. Instead of treating Tommy as his kid, he treated him like the competition. Needless to say, it's hard for a kid to compete with a grown man. But to compete with your dad over your mum, now that's plain bonkers, and Tommy's dad did it by any means necessary: punishments, beatings, and screaming. But his son was strong; it didn't break him. He was also a serial fall-in-lover, fancying a new girl every week.

We had quite a few chats about that. I was intrigued to know how he got all that energy to fall in love with someone new every few days.

"Iggy, that's just what God intended for me to be," he used to say, "After all, everyone's built differently. He didn't make us all different for nothing. Do you realize that each and every person on this earth has a different DNA? So he made me the Columbus of women..."

"Iggy, you there? Hello...?!" Tommy's voice broke through the receiver, shaking me out of my daydream.

"What? Mate, I think ... I can't make it..." I replied gloomily. I could feel Angie's threatening stare piercing into me, even though I wasn't looking at her.

"Listen here, if you bail on me today then just bear in mind that it'll be the start of a very serious crisis in our friendship!"

"Ring me in a few minutes," I said and hung up. I looked at Angie as she sat on the bed and then approached her.

"No, Iggy, you're not doing this…" she flinched away.

"I can't get clean right now, babe. I love you, I'm crazy about you. But I can't do what you want me to do, it has to come from me in order to work."

"Then do it for me, if you care about me. And in a few days' time, I promise that it'll change and you'll feel that you're doing it for yourself."

"But I can't…"

"You can!"

"Then I don't want to!" I was proper fuming at that point.

"You're a coward! And you don't love me! Because you care more about partying than you do about me."

"Is that right?" I raged, "Then you care more about getting clean than you do about me."

"You're such a manipulative wanker!"

"Thanks, love you too."

"You don't even know what love is!" she said, tears streaming down her cheeks.

I shocked myself. I knew that she was a hundred percent right. I realized how sad and despaired she was. But my urge to leave the house and do more drugs was simply stronger at that point. My fucked-up head was telling me, like it always did, 'Break it now, fix it later.'

At that moment, it hit me – I was acting just like my mum, and that alone was enough to make me empty out the entire baggie.

I approached Angie and tried to stroke her hair, even though my hands were already trembling. But she moved away.

"Stop it, Iggy, I can't handle what you're doing, it's not fair."

The phone rang. I knew that it was Tommy and that he wouldn't stop.

"What do you want then?" I asked Angie.

"I want you to piss off!"

"Didn't drink enough to piss…" I tried a pun in an attempt to make her laugh, but she was fuming and crying. And then the phone rang again.

I stood there facing her, tucked my shirt into my trousers in a standoffish way that wasn't like me, and then leaned down.

Angie was sure that I was trying to get close to her and shouted, "No! Don't touch me! If you leave now, then we're through, is that clear?"

But I just quickly picked up the baggie from behind the bed and straightened up nonchalantly. "Just remember, you're the one giving up on us," I said and then went out, shutting the door to my room behind me.

CHAPTER 4

I immediately took two hits from the little bottle of coke in the baggie, then hid it all in my pants and left the house. I walked all the way to the club, I was itching to get to my mates and get proper wasted. The scenario I ran through my mind was that when I'd eventually get back home, Angie wouldn't talk to me, we'd act like a couple of strangers for a few days, but then I'd end up apologizing and ingratiating her, tell her a few cheesy lines and she'd end up giving in, we'd shag like crazy and go back to our daily routine.

I reached the club. They were standing at the entrance waiting for me – Tommy, Manu, Smiley and Andy – who spotted me before the others, walked towards me with his arms spread out to the sides, and then gave me a loving, chemical-filled cuddle.

"I'm on three ecstasies already, Iggy, I'm like a blazing fire, this is how the sun feels, no wonder it's so filled with love that it burns."

Tommy peered from behind me and pushed me down by the neck. "I'm not well," I whispered to him.

"You snorted your cake, now eat it! You're here now! Don't leave your mind back there. This is New Year's Eve, we'll party hard and everything will be fine," he said and winked at Smiley, who approached me and stuck two pills in my mouth, nothing to down them with. I almost choked on them.

Tommy stopped someone and grabbed the bottle he was holding, handing it to me, "Sorry old chum, my mate's choking, it's a matter of life and death," he told the bloke.

I gulped down the vodka cranberry drink and almost emptied the bottle. "Sorry mate, I'll get you a new one once we're inside," I promised as the bloke looked at me suspiciously, eventually nodding his head and going back inside the club.

"Are we going in or what?" I asked.

They all gave me this strange grin, and Manu started talking with a spliff in his mouth. "Today, bruv, we won't be celebrating the way we usually do. This time, we're doing it in style…"

Smiley couldn't help himself and interrupted him. "We're going to Amsterdam!"

"Amsterdam?" I asked, baffled, "Why? What's wrong with celebrating here? We've already got everything we need." I then pulled out the baggie that was tucked away under my sack in an attempt to illustrate my statement.

Manu pounced on me. "Mate, over here we have to worry about getting caught with the gear, over there it's all legal, the drugs, the birds, the bash!"

"Plus I've got a little job I said I'd do for a Dutch fella over there," Andy added, "Get some dosh for us."

"Okay," I said.

"Okay – you're in?" Tommy immediately asked.

I felt like hugging him right there and then. He instantly knew that the fact I'd said 'okay' didn't mean I agreed, but could rather be a means of saying 'I see.'

"Okay – understood and approved," I replied as I took out the little bottle from the baggie. I snorted a bit of the coke and passed it around. "What about Angie, should I call and tell her?"

"Mate, you two had a row," Tommy piped up, "You just got a get-out-of-jail card! So allow it, what does it matter if you're at a club or in the Dam?"

"Dunno," I replied.

"Iggy, you'll just come out a right cunt! What she doesn't know can't hurt her," Smiley declared. He was our crew's jokester, full of ideas, with a wild mind and loony style. He'd concoct all sorts of makeshift costumes with the kind of creativity that would put the world's greatest fashion designers to shame. The best was when he'd arrived at a bash wearing a suede and fur boot over his head. It even looked pretty dapper, believe it or not.

Smiley's full name was Samuel Glick. His parents – Matthew and Cherie – were hippies on the dole who'd lived at his nan's place, whose name was Golda. A few months after he was born, they went to visit mates up north and had never been heard from since. Any attempt at getting in touch with them failed miserably. Smiley stayed with his nan, who showed him a lot of love drenched in a lot of booze, and Smiley loved her back, no doubt about it, but he never stopped dreaming about the day he'd meet his parents – even though he always made sure to claim he hoped something terrible happened to them and that they were no longer alive. "Otherwise," he'd explain, "It means that they just abandoned me, and that'll kill me."

We took a train to the pier and got on the deck, already stoned off our asses. There was a festive atmosphere all around with loads of people, and we almost stepped on one another. Tommy chatted up some gorgeous bird, as usual, and within a few minutes they were kissing passionately like one of those erotic novels. I was a little jealous of that ability of his – there was something so brave about that absolute surrender within such a short span of time. He wasn't scared of rejection and he'd approach girls with the confidence of a true Casanova, making them feel like the whole world was made just for them. Of course, they'd give in to him in no time. That's the power of love – it's addictive within seconds.

I stared at them from the side and then noticed Manu from the corner of my eye, that horny fucker. He was so fascinated by some bird's bum that he must have forgotten all common courtesy and just clung onto her. The poor bloke looked like a right perv, just like he always did when he got too stoned, especially on ecstasy. By the time I'd noticed, it was too late. The bird turned around and smacked him so hard his head flung to the side.

At that point we leaped onto him and pulled him away from there, trying to avoid the kind of commotion that would bring the coppers round. We really didn't feel like spending New Year's in the nick. This wasn't the first time Manu got smacked around for harassing birds, and we'd often find ourselves in huge fights which ended in arrests – all because he couldn't control his lust. What can you do, eh? It must have been genetic. He was scared he'd inherited the trait from his dad, Jose, who used to cheat on his mum left, right and center. Everyone in the neighborhood used to laugh at Jose because his fly was always undone. If I had a quid for the number of times he'd get told about it in one day, then I'd never have to work a day in my life. We assumed that he did it on purpose so that people – and especially women – would always look at his crotch. The thing that was exceptional about Jose was that every convo with him somehow led to the subject of sex. Didn't matter if he was talking to the rabbi about the Torah, or to some random kid asking about the meaning of the universe. It made his son go mental and refuse to be seen with him out in public.

Manu's family belonged to a small community of Christians living in our Jewish neighborhood, and we all lived peacefully alongside one another. Our community's rabbi was mates with their priest; whenever they'd bump into each other on the street they'd stop for a chat. Their convos always revolved around religious insights. Whenever that happened, anyone in the vicinity would stop and listen. During one of these convos, the rabbi told the priest that there was no actual difference between the Jewish, Christian, and Muslim religions.

"After all, everyone agrees that there's only one God," he explained, "And that if a man desires something, he needs to pray to God every night for his wish to come true."

From that day on, Manu prayed to God every night asking for his dad's cock to fall off, or for his dad to just stop being so bloody horny. And, miraculously, after a short period of time, it came true. Jose's fly was shut for business, he never spoke about sex again, and he seemed to be particularly chuffed. At first, we were sure that God had answered Manu's prayers, but we very quickly realized what had really happened. Jose had fallen in love with a new bird who'd moved into the neighborhood, and he only had eyes for her. Every quid he'd made at work was spent on taking her out and buying her jewelry and such. Manu's mum was fuming, she turned from a pleasant woman to a bitter, aggressive old hag, and that really damaged her relationship with her son, so he developed a kind of obsessive hatred towards his dad's new lover. He used to stalk her, steal her clothes off the clothesline and then burn them. When his dad bought her a used car, Manu painted her windows and mirrors black time and time again, until she gave up and went back to commuting on the tube. He even made sure that her boss's wife heard the rumors about her affair and got her sacked. Jose was well pissed off with Manu for the way he treated his lover, and after a few intense rows, they ended up severing all contact with each other.

Manu straightened back up and touched his bruised cheek. "You cunt," he muttered under his breath as he assessed the commotion around him, then lowered his head in humiliation and wandered off, looking for somewhere to hide.

We followed him. "Manu, wait a minute, stop," we called out.

"Look at how they're all staring at me," he moaned, "I don't understand why this is happening to me, why can't I just be like you?!"

"Come on, mate, you're no different from us, you're just stoned and horny," I told him.

"I am different! I differ from you in horniness and in skin color too! And I can't be bothered with you chatting shit right now, either be real with me or leave me the fuck alone!"

"Mate, you do realize we're Jewish, right?" Tommy said, "We're the most hated minority in the whole world! But that's the world's problem! Doesn't matter what group you belong to, there'll always be another group that hates your guts."

"Yeah," Manu replied, "But you lot don't go around with a sign over your head saying you're Jewish, and I get treated differently because of the color of my skin."

"Just be thankful that it doesn't hurt like circumcision does." We all nodded in agreement as Tommy continued. "Mate, the world's got everything on offer! We're at some chav's party tonight, tomorrow we can be in Mexico or in Africa with some dark-skinned lot. Humans are proper loopy, bruv, they'll always look for the difference that they can hate. Now, tell me, who is every woman's wet dream?"

"Julio Iglesias," Manu whispered.

"Ding, ding, ding, well done!" Tommy called out, "And you know what, at the end of the day, we all sit around for hours trying to get our tan to even come close to your color, and we just end up looking like bloody tomatoes."

Manu gave a slight smile and we all sighed in relief, but then a couple of random birds passed by and one of them called him a perv. His smile vanished within a second. "I can't take it anymore," he lashed out, "I'm scared that the drugs just amplify things that already exist in my DNA. If my dad's like that then I must have gotten it from him."

"You're nothing like him," I tried to pacify him again, "Your dad can't control himself even when he's sober, and you can. Don't forget, you haven't gotten off with a bird yet, and you're soaking in ecstasy."

"Smiley and Andy are on ecstasy too and they haven't gotten off either, but this doesn't happen to them, does it!"

"I got off!" Andy piped up.

"Stalking your mum's mate when she changed clothes and wanking over it doesn't count!" Smiley roared at him.

"Back to business, lads!" I shushed them, otherwise it would have turned into a messy row.

"Leave it out," Tommy told Manu ingratiatingly, "Let's just say that you don't do anymore ecstasy outdoors until you find a bird to shag. Keep the highs for home sessions only. Are we clear?"

Manu took a moment to think it through and then nodded his head, "Crystal."

"I hope that every time you see a bird when you're stoned and get a raging boner, all you'll be able to think about is your nan's face," Smiley told him, and we all cracked up.

"My nan was as fit as fuck when she was younger," Manu tried to retort.

We all grimaced with disgust and unanimously shouted, "Fuck off you perv!"

By that point, the atmosphere was more relaxed and we sat down in a corner of the deck, fantasizing about what we'd do once we got to Amsterdam. To be honest, I spent the whole time thinking about Angie … my conscience was killing me.

We finally made it to the Dam. The moment we got off the ferry, we hailed a cab and drove straight to the Dutch bloke that Andy was doing business with, hoping he'd get it done quickly and have some dosh for us to spend. We arrived at a shabby building block with a buzzer that seemed to cost more than the entire complex. Andy said it would take him around an hour and for us to stay outside and wait for him.

It was freezing cold, and we weren't getting to any of the clubs before midnight, so I decided to pass the time wisely and took out my baggie, handing out acid to everyone.

"Least we can do is trip on our trip," I said.

We started feeling it after about twenty minutes, speed rushing through our system, making us all jittery and jumpy like a bunch of fleas, and we no longer felt the cold or even our bodies.

When you're on acid you disassemble, as though your soul, mind, and body suddenly become separate entities to one another. The soul feels free, the mind shows you what it can really do and how much wasted potential it possesses. The body, however, is nothing but a constant reminder that in a few hours' time, once the acid wears off, you'll go right back to being trapped inside it. After all, at the end of the day, it's the only thing connecting you to this fucked-up world.

CHAPTER 5

We suddenly heard a voice calling out to us, "I'll finish up and come down in a bit, lads."

That was Andy speaking through the intercom, but to me it sounded like God was addressing us out of nowhere, which made me burst out laughing, infecting Tommy, and then Smiley and Manu too. We all laughed at the same time, but each one was laughing about something else. That's what happens when you're on acid.

By the time we started calming down, Andy spoke to us through the intercom again and started singing Roc Ocasek's *Keep On Laughin',* which drove us straight into another bout of laughter.

Andy was the type to always flow with things, as easy-going as they come. He was a genius and extremely talented at copying any sort of document or picture with a 99.9% accuracy rate. He was in charge of forging sick notes for the headmaster whenever we ditched school, and once we were older, he forged some IDs for us, too; that way we could get into eighteen and over clubs. But his best work by far was forging report cards for us and for a few others from our class.

The night before the graduation ceremony where the report cards were to be handed out, we broke into the headmaster's office and swapped the originals for them, so that our parents could see the headmaster handing them to us the following day. After we got off the stage at the ceremony, they were shocked by 'our' superb grades.

The rumors of Andy's abilities traveled far, and with time he'd gained enough experience to become some of the neighborhood's heavier lot's forger. They paid him pretty decently, which contributed to our partying since he'd always spend his money on us.

"Lads, am I seeing right? Is someone approaching?" I asked.

"Let's be quiet," Smiley suggested, "Let him talk and we'll all just repeat everything he says. If we all say the same thing then it'll mean he's real."

"Hi guys, want to buy some gear?" the bloke asked.

We all fell silent and looked at Smiley, who'd forgotten what he was supposed to do and just stared back at us sheepishly. We burst out laughing again. Even the random bloke started laughing along, and then he said, "I guess you guys are already sorted… You should hit a club called Blacktown, it's right up the street."

A few minutes later, we heard people all around us shouting, "Happy New Year!" and realized that it was midnight. Andy appeared through the building's front door and showed us the dosh he'd earned. We all hugged and screamed, "Happy New Year!"

We were buzzing as we marched up the street towards Blacktown, each to his own thoughts. I was in a pensive loop about Angie. I couldn't stop feeling bad about having lied to her when I'd promised to flush all the drugs down the bog.

I think that everyone, without exception, lies. Anyone who says he never lies is definitely a liar. No one remembers their first lie, as though it's part of our nature, from the day we were born. Some parents document everything their child has ever done – first tooth, first poo, first steps. Shame that no one ever films the first lie.

People can testify to being lazy, arrogant, or selfish, but no one in this world ever admits that they're a liar. Everyone hates liars and everyone lies. I wonder what it was that made us think we needed to lie at some point in our lives.

People only admit to a lie if they get caught, or if they're scared of getting caught. We hate the ones who lie in order to gain something, but forgive the ones who lie because they have something to lose. I reckon that a lie's a lie. For example, I tried telling myself that I lied because I didn't want to lose Angie, but the truth is I also did it to gain some quality time with my mates and my drugs.

All of a sudden, Angie's face surfaced in front of my eyes and said, "At your house, lying is a sort of power, as though hiding things and keeping the cards close to you gives you an advantage over whoever it is you're facing. Your parents never trusted each other. That's why you can't trust them, or anyone else for that matter, even yourself. Otherwise, you wouldn't be so scared of being with me and making the change. So how much more weight are you going to carry in order to get rid of me?"

"As much as possible," I replied out loud. I then pulled out the blue pills from my pocket and swallowed two of them immediately, with no water to down them with.

"As much as possible of what?!" Tommy exclaimed, "Are you talking to yourself now? You're going well overboard mate, don't want you dying on me here! You're soaked as it is, how far are you trying to get?"

"Dunno," I said, "It's like there's a lump in my chest that won't let loose."

"Is it because of Angie? What makes this time any different?"

"Look, I'm not just thinking about my row with her," I explained, "I'm thinking about all the moves rushing through my fucked-up head, and about life in general. What the fuck are we doing here? What is this world about, even? And why are we acting the way we do? I have a feeling that I'm going straight to hell!"

"And what if I told you that everything we'd ever been sold since we were kids was just a load of bollocks?" Tommy chuckled, "That there is no heaven or hell, and that this universe is just a huge slammer for souls."

"Okay…" I replied cautiously, trying to keep track of what he was saying.

"For argument's sake, let's just say that every soul that gets here had been arraigned and sent to this universe to serve time and learn something," he continued, "To make amends, as it were. Some people's sins were major, so they go through a process of weighty punishments and lessons, like in third-world countries. Some people's sins were so ghastly that they have to die young and come back a few times, and only then do they start the process. Some's sins were only medium-sized, so every once in a while they get smacked down and rise back up, and some only came with lightweight sins so their lives are pretty cushy – as much as can be expected in the nick... Each soul makes their own amends according to their sins' severity."

"Then what about all the people in the world who turn out successful?" I asked.

"Ah!" Tommy proclaimed, "Some are regulars who keep coming back – souls who were sentenced to life in the slammer. They signed a contract with the warden, and the contract states that they keep coming back in different bodies, giving hope to all the rest of the souls about the possibility of success and happiness. Take Marilyn Monroe for example. We know that she started at the bottom and became a superstar. So the fact that she came from nothing and managed to succeed makes you hopeful, right?"

"Right."

"And when Marylin died, her soul immediately moved into another body – Madonna's," Tommy continued lecturing confidently, "Madonna is Marylin's soul, and she's taking the same route from the bottom to the top. And that's what it's like with all the stars. That's what makes all the other souls think that they can succeed too so that they keep at it... But what they don't know is that if they haven't signed the contract, they'll never truly make it big."

"Do the souls that signed the contract know about it?"

"They're not supposed to, but... Remember what Rossa told us about reincarnation?"

"Yeah, about that little boy who remembered growing up with a different family in the same city…" I mumbled.

"Precisely! So I read up about it, and turns out there's a fair bit of stories about people who remember their previous lives."

"And are they famous now?" I asked.

"Well, if I've read about them then they obviously are, innit? But they can just as well be souls who'd sinned and died young a few times until they finally reached the long process phase… Someone upstairs must have mucked up with wiping out their memories. Mistakes happen in all the realms, Iggy. That's why they give souls a period of adjustment where they can't speak for a few years. Babies only start talking when they're about three, and by that time, any memories they've had are long gone. From the very first moment in this universe, you start going through a change of good and evil, fear, hope, and dependency. You're born with people's help, but you start by getting smacked into tears, and only then do you get a cuddle."

Tommy was clearly enthused by his own statement. "All the souls that descend on Earth possess a divine spark and a psychic memory of the happiness that remained where they came from – a place that must have been incredible, full of love and kindness. That's why they never stop searching for it, all through their lives and up to their deaths. But it's just like mice running inside a spinning wheel, because there's no such thing in this world – there's no real happiness. We're bestowed with the sparks every now and then to keep our hopes up – that's why you get to experience moments of joy, of love, and of happiness. But most of the time, it's harsh here. Generally speaking, there's more suffering, more poverty, more wars than peace, and more broken hearts than love. They line up the conflicts for us all the time. Tell me this – do you know one couple in this world that stayed in love forever? Have you ever heard of such a thing?"

"No… But I hope that's what'll happen to Angie and me," I replied, baffled.

"Precisely, bruv, you have the hope and the faith, even though it's not realistic! It never happened to anyone you know, but you still believe that it can happen. Ever met or heard of anyone who found true happiness?"

"No," I said.

"And yet, generation after generation, we all ceaselessly search for it," Tommy explained. "This universe is filled with the fantasy dust that they keep sprinkling over us, because it's a well-known fact that if we dream, then we'll continue living here, even if the challenges become unbearable ... do you get me? They're constantly deceiving us and feeding our hopes."

"Wait, if we came here just in order to make amends and leave, then why are we making such an effort while we're here?" I asked.

"Education, bruv, brainwashing, peer pressure – they're all much stronger than common sense," Tommy laughed, "You just told me you'd never met anyone who stayed in love forever, or reached the ultimate form of happiness. But we still have hope about being able to change things so that we can make it. We're fucked up! Whoever's running this world is a bloody genius! Otherwise, God wouldn't let him run it. If people knew that they were in a prison and that somewhere out there is a better place, most of humanity would surely commit suicide, or never have kids, and then the world wouldn't continue existing."

"Wait... So you believe in God?"

"Of course! All of this is God's work. There are guards and instructors, and rewards for good behavior, just like in prison. God's employed a CEO for us here – call him the devil for argument's sake. He has to account for everything to his superior – meaning the Lord. He's in charge of all the worlds, including the slammer for the souls. We also have souls who belong to the light, sort of like angels sent by God, and they keep coming back here too in order to help the souls make amends, maybe we're actually them."

"Nah, mate, I really don't fancy coming back here," I declared, "The way I see it, one day, I'll get out of here for good."

"Wicked," he said, "You'll only know that once you die and reach the sky. The only thing for certain is that this world's corrupt as fuck! Play the game, and maintain the kind of conscience that doesn't let you harm all the other souls who are trying to make amends ... but don't be hard on yourself if you make mistakes or cut corners, or do things that aren't cool. You're in prison and you don't have a choice! You have to get your hands dirty every so often in order to survive. In this world, even saints get tainted. And you're one of the good guys, bruv, you feel that, don't you?"

"Fuck yeah," I said.

"Well then, if everything's sweet then let's start partying!" he announced as we all picked up our walking pace. I felt a kind of relief. I was one of the good guys. I turned back to look at Manu, Smiley, and Andy as they walked behind us, and felt like such a lucky bugger for having them.

"Welcome to Blacktown!" we heard someone call out as we entered the club. The vibe was wicked, everyone was cheery and the music was spot on. You could see all these unique-looking people everywhere.

Smiley jumped up and hugged me. He told me to stop being greedy and said I didn't look well. All of a sudden, I could feel my stomach cramping, and before I even managed to say something, I felt everything coming up and trying to burst out. I shut my mouth and blocked it with my hand so that I wouldn't spray the vom across the dance floor. I shoved Smiley aside and ran to the loo. The heat, the smell, the crowdedness, and all the speed rushing through my body – I felt flooded, genuinely stifled. I pushed through the people queuing and they shouted at me and tried to shove me back but I persevered, unapologetically. The second someone opened the door, I leaped into the cubicle and everything came out, in and around the toilet bowl. I pushed the door shut with my leg and continued retching until there was nothing left, and my body kept cramping until it finally calmed down. I wanted to wash my mouth out and clean my face, but I wasn't ready to go out and queue again. I locked the cubicle door and flushed the toilet. Once the vom went down the drain and the water was fresh, I shoved my hand in and washed my face. I then popped the lid down and sat on it, allowing a sigh of relief to come out. After a few seconds of feeling physically better, I lit a fag.

A pleasant sort of current flooded through my body, and my mood was getting better. That convo with Tommy really did my head in. I felt that this was precisely the right time to come out of the loo and head back to the dance floor, and I immediately found Tommy. I pounced on him and held him tightly.

"I fucking love you, bruv!" I shouted at him.

He laughed and said, "I'm getting a drink from the bar, you want a pint?"

"Oh yeah, please, I'm just going to get some fresh air and I'll be right back!" I replied as I headed out.

There were loads of people outside. The air was clean and crisp and I could breathe easily. I started walking and turned up the pace until I found myself running. My body was as light as a feather, and the run became a glide. Joy flooded through me, I felt like Peter Pan, as though I'd merged with the wind and was looking down during my flight. I couldn't fully fathom the sensation. It was like moving through fireworks as they exploded through the air.

'Don't want this to end, doesn't have to be temporary,' I thought, 'Gotta hold on a little longer. Actually – why a little longer? Why not forever and ever?' I tried my best to maintain that heavenly sensation, but my brain kept bringing me down.

"Please, God, just a little bit longer," I mumbled, but the universe's CEO insisted on landing me back down. He'd only afforded me a touch of happiness, and after that, everything crashed. That's the kind of life I had – whenever things went well, instead of enjoying it, I focused on being scared of it ending.

And it did end. Just like Tommy said – "everything's temporary." But the sensation was so good that I wasn't going to forgo trying to feel it again.

I landed with a sense of frustration and looked around helplessly. I sat on the pavement and tried to figure out where I was and how to get back to the club. I have no idea why, but I suddenly decided to do some more acid and I immediately popped it in my mouth. Within minutes, everything was swirling inside my mind. I only had a few little flickers of sanity, during which I realized that I was completely out of focus. I decided to head back, but in my confusion, I must have constantly changed direction. At some point, I reached a wicked street with loads of illuminated shop windows. At first, I thought they were lingerie shops, but the mannequins were moving and it seemed odd to me, when all of a sudden it hit me – I was at the famous Red Light District.

The street was beautiful and had a unique vibe to it. I have no idea why people were worried about going there, or felt ashamed to admit they'd been. What's there to be ashamed of? After all, in our world, the body is a vessel for the soul. It serves all of the materialistic needs of this creature called man. So what's so bad about it? Who says that sex is dirty? And who says that anyone can decide on what's right and what's wrong? Not only is sex the most natural thing, it's also fun and pleasuring, and yet we act like prudes when it comes to it – just like we do with lying. Can't live without lying and can't live without sex. But we sweep it all under the rug because we want to present ourselves as educated.

I slowed down and curiously inspected each and every window. The girls were different, each one was interesting, and each had her own unique backdrop and theme.

'These ladies are so strong,' I thought, 'It takes a ton of courage to do what they do without hiding it. It's like they're declaring – This is me, this is my body, and this is what I choose to do with it.'

And yeah, it is their prerogative to do whatever feels right for them. Women have the strongest vessel in the world, but someone did a fab job at confusing all of humanity and shushing their vessel in all sorts of ways, so much so that they're ashamed to use it. But the funny thing is that everyone else uses it unabashedly. I'm not even sure if that feminist lot really are trying to empower women and not the opposite. I guess that the developing world had a surge in population and not enough hands on deck, so they founded a movement to start a revolution and get women out there and working while getting paid much less than men, making them feel like there's equality. In short, giving them a lolly but taking their teeth away.

I could have continued this stoned philosophizing session forever, but one of the windows made me stop. The woman behind it seemed familiar. She looked at me seductively, but I felt repelled since she was a spitting image of my mum. She did all sorts of gestures with her hands and gave me a smile that looked as fake as my mum's. I got as close to the window as I could and carefully examined her. I thought I was hallucinating. She obviously had no idea what I was doing and motioned at me that she was calling the coppers, but I just couldn't stop looking at her until I felt a pat on the back which made me jump.

I turned around and there was a girl standing in front of me. "Are you going in there or what?"

I was embarrassed. "No, she just looks exactly like my mum."

The girl's eyes gaped open and I quickly explained, "But that's not to say that my mum and I... eww..."

"It's all right," she interrupted me, "I can tell you're pretty out; you don't need to explain anything. After all, you're a tourist, and all the tourists come here at some point. Where are you from?"

"London," I replied, "But just to be clear, she really does look like my mum, and that's doing my head in, do you understand?"

"Yes, you're stoned and freaking out!"

"Exactly! And you?"

"What? Freaking out?"
"No, where are you from?"
"I live here, in Amsterdam."
"And what are you doing here?" I asked.
"They have men here too, you know…"
"For real?" I was surprised. "And you're here for that?"
"What is it, are you the only ones allowed? There are still a few of us lonely women looking for momentary love, just until our knight in shining armor finally shows up."
"Is that right?" I was still stunned, "I just never thought that men do it too, or that women would even need it, because a woman can get with anyone she wants to, and for free." She burst out laughing.
"Wait," I had an idea, "Maybe you're not even real?"
"Maybe you're way too stoned?"
"Oh yeah, defo," I replied.
"So you're saying I can get with anyone?"
"Anyone!" I said confidently.
"Does that include you?"
I was so shocked that I couldn't think of a reply. We just stood there facing each other for a long while. It felt like forever.
"Well, are you coming?" she asked as she started walking away.
That turned me on. I felt like a cat who'd suddenly seen the peering end of a ball of yarn, so I followed her, filled with curiosity, not even asking where we were going or why she'd chosen me of all people.
Eventually, the girl stopped in front of a posh-looking building and turned to face me. "I live here, top floor, shall we?"
"After you," I replied.
She smiled and continued walking, and I followed her. She punched in the code to get in, and we climbed up a winding staircase that seemed endless.
She suddenly turned towards me. I'd been climbing really fast, so I unintentionally pressed against her. Then she leaned in to kiss

me, and I instinctively turned my head to the side. I felt embarrassed. "I'm sorry," I mumbled.

That threw me back to this one evening when we were kids and sat on the benches by the park. Manu ran up to us, he was upset, and almost crying. He told us that Michaela, a bird from our year at school, had tried to kiss him and he shoved her away. We didn't see what the fuss was about and we gave him a hard time, calling him a pussy. It was only now, when this girl was trying to kiss me and I flinched, that I realized how men are no different to women. I have no idea where that whole idea came from, that when a woman kisses a man it means she's bold, but when a man kisses a girl, he's a perv.

Maybe that's just what we were raised to believe, that men always have to make the first move. So when a girl breaks that convention it really is bold, but it's also awkward and confusing. We can all get stressed by someone invading our personal space without warning.

"Listen," I told her, "I'm not sure that I'm the man you wanted to spend the night with, I really am too stoned to communicate and this is all kind of confusing."

"Don't worry," she smiled, "It wasn't sexual, it's just that it's New Year's Eve and I'm a bit lonely and a bit high … and you looked cute and lost, but if you don't want to then I get it."

What's the worst that could happen, I thought, *I'll do a good deed for someone else and be on my way in an hour or two.*

"After you," I said, and we continued climbing up until we reached the top floor.

"Here we are," she opened the door to her flat and turned on some dimmed lighting. The flat looked spot on. It had these huge glass windows and you could see all of Amsterdam through them. She chucked her bag on the sofa and quickly put some music on. She chose Lenny Kravitz, Angie's favorite singer.

"Is that all right?" she asked.

"As good as it can get," I replied and pulled her towards me. I closed my eyes and imagined that I was with Angie. We danced, embracing as tightly as possible as my arm wrapped around her and my hand stroked her hair.

"You having fun?" she asked.

My heart was pounding so wildly that I felt like pulling it out of my body and putting it into hers. That way she'd have two hearts, just to be on the safe side. "You have no idea, gorgeous."

"Fancy trying something really good?" she whispered.

"You're the best thing that's ever happened to me!"

She laughed, handed me a rolled-up note, and pointed at the table. I sniffed the beautiful lines she'd so lustfully chopped, and quickly hugged her. And then I let it slip. "Angie, I love you."

She shoved me onto the sofa. "Now, we dance!"

I got up and we continued dancing. I closed my eyes. I have no idea how much time had passed, but when I opened them again, I realized that I was dancing on my own and the music was only playing in my head. I looked around and saw her lying on her stomach, totally out. This was a stranger who'd gotten the love of a lifetime out of me in the course of a single night, while the girl that I loved was somewhere out there crying about her own life.

I grabbed my coat and rushed out. I was determined to run off and get back to my mates. It was dawn, and I was knackered. The drugs were wearing off, and my baggie was empty.

I started marching through the streets, nothing but my gut leading me. I had no idea where I was, so I just walked in whatever direction felt right. I asked a few passers-by, but no one knew where Blacktown was. All of a sudden, I noticed these two blokes approaching me very quickly. I have no idea why but they gave me a bad feeling, so I turned around and started quickly walking the other way, but then they did the same thing and increased their pace. I veered into an alleyway and they continued following me. Even when I started running, I could still hear them chasing me.

CHAPTER 6

I was scared witless and ran as fast as I could without stopping and without looking back. Even though I didn't hear them anymore, I was scared they'd ambush me, so I didn't stop. I guess that the chemicals in my system helped me go on without my legs cramping. There was no one in the streets, and I thought to myself, 'I'm not stopping until I see some people or find an open venue.'

Then I finally heard some voices. I rushed over in their direction, reached the entrance to a club and stopped. I caught my breath and looked back for the first time. There was no one there, so I calmed down and approached a group of people standing at the entrance. "Pardon, do you happen to know how to get to … Blacktown?"

They all chuckled, and then one of the blokes told me, "Yeah, a little nudge to the right, two to three steps, and you're in."

It was only then that I realized I was standing at the entrance to Blacktown. That was odd. I stood there for a few seconds, trying to figure out how I'd managed to get there. 'Could it be that the blokes chasing me were actually angels sent to help me find my way?'

I went in. The place was nearly empty. I found my mates sprawling in a pile on one of the sofas. My first instinct was to wake them up, but I decided to sit down for a few minutes, and collect myself. I closed my eyes and surrendered to the beautiful film rushing through my mind, starring me and Angie. We were running together, hands held, towards the lottery building. I was holding the winning numbers in my other hand and I told her, "We've got it all now, Angie."

"Shhh, quiet! Don't say a word until the money's in the bank, don't jinx it!"

"Jinx? What are you talking about babe? We're the good guys, we're protected, you're so boldly lit. Now I get that saying – fortune favors the bold."

"Oh yeah? You know what's funny?"

"What?" I asked.

"This is all we needed, money, it's that simple. Got money – got happiness. This is so wild! What is it that David the greengrocer always says?"

And we both recited in unison, "Ain't no problem that a million quid can't fix."

We entered the building. I was tightly holding onto the ticket, didn't want it falling out of my hand. We stood there, excited and smiling, facing a counter with a little window and a nice clerk sitting behind it.

"Hello," he welcomed us with a smile.

"Hello!" We both replied excitedly, giggling. "We're the winners…!" I said and handed him the card.

The clerk grabbed it, fed it into a machine, and then lifted his head and looked at us. "Listen, young man, there are winners and there are losers in life, and I've got news for you, you two are now…"

Before he even finished his sentence, I felt something heavy landing on my face, which instantly brought me back to the literally painful reality. Tommy's foot kicked me in my sleep and shattered my dream. 'Why did it have to happen right before that clerk gave me the news?' I thought.

But Tommy had no idea, he just continued snoring like a bloody donkey. I looked around, my body felt beat and weak. The drugs had worn off, and in the daylight, the club looked like just another dirty, minging warehouse. I was disgusted by the place, and mainly by myself. I felt empty and my stomach was aching like mad. I had no air and was panting heavily. I was consumed by a great sadness, and then, without warning, my eyes filled with tears, so I decided to go get some fresh air.

It was cold outside. My throat froze and my tears dried but the wheels in my mind wouldn't stop spinning and my thoughts were tormenting me. 'I left Angie just so I could take drugs that would make me hallucinate that I was actually with her,' I pondered pensively. 'What kind of fucked-up coward am I? Why do I hate being sober? How much longer can I run away from just being me?'

In reality, I was Iggy, an unemployed junkie living with his mum. And I was the only one who could change that. After all, the drugs and the mental escapes wouldn't change me into anything except the worst version of myself. 'I want to make a change, I have to make it and as fast as possible, and become a millionaire!' But first, I needed to get back into the club and wake my mates up.

"Come on, you lot, get up already!" I shook them, "Look at yourselves! We look like shit; I just want to get back home already!"

We came out into the street despondently, looking like the Garbage Pail Kids, disheveled and dirty. Once we got on the ferry, we all huddled up together, each with his own thoughts, each staring blankly at a different spot far into the horizon.

My knees hurt so I lifted my legs and placed my feet between Tommy and Smiley who were sitting in front of me. An old lady behind us whispered to someone, "It's not right, putting their feet on the seats, no consideration whatsoever, those hooligans, punks, they should be locked away, they shouldn't be allowed to roam freely!"

She was talking about us, obviously, but we just looked at one another and stayed quiet until she suddenly turned to me and said in a self-righteous tone, "That's not nice you know, how would you feel if your mother suddenly showed up and sat down right where your feet have just been?!"

I didn't bother answering her as I shifted my legs aside theatrically, making sure she noticed the scum on my shoes being spread across the entire bench's frame. I only did it because of the way she'd spoken to me, that horrible woman! Why couldn't she have just asked me politely to take my feet off? People treat us like monsters and then expect us to act like humans. I think that generally speaking, this world is made up of hypocrites! No one genuinely respects anyone else because deep down, at our core, we are not respectful beings. If we were internally built to show and maintain mutual respect, then surely we wouldn't have to be taught about it.

"Did you see that? See what he did, that savage?!" I heard her blabbering on through my cloud of thoughts.

I started collecting all the snot I had in the back of my throat in the most vocal manner possible, but Andy put his hand on me and stopped me. "Let it go, bruv, she's not worth it, and she's old and all…"

So that annoying woman was spared a juicy lump of snot to the face only because I had more respect for Andy than I did for her. According to Tommy's theory, you shouldn't respect people simply because of their age or social status. The young ones learn from the older ones, that's the convention, not the other way around! Then how come it's always the grown-ups disrespecting the youth, and then having the audacity to complain about it?

The older people get, the meaner they become. But then, what's the point of life experience?! Everyone loves kids because they're pure, honest, creative, imaginative, and fearless, and they nurture these big dreams. In fact, they're the epitome of everything that adults want and search for. And if that's what we're like when we're young then why do adults interfere and "educate" us? If the world were run by children, it would turn into a kind of members' club. It's this "education" thing that adults force us into that fucks us up.

Our "educators" are the ones betraying us each and every time, over and over again. The first ones to do it are parents – they tell us how special we are and how wonderful it is that we want to go to kindergarten wearing a costume, and they get excited when we want to be astronauts or lion tamers in the circus, but then, at the age of six, everything suddenly flips! We get sent to an educational facility, where we're expected to dress like everyone else and they make us compete against one another, they only assess us according to grades, and we get punished for individuality. Instead of opening our minds, they cage us both physically and mentally. Twelve years of our lives are wasted on studies that don't help us for shit as adults, but we do internalize the idea of obedience to authority. That's why I think children deserve respect more than adults, who turn meaner and meaner as time goes by.

I wonder how badly my mum was oppressed as a child, considering that as far as I know, no one could ever stomach her except for my dad and Angie.

I can't say much about my dad. He left us when I was four or five years old. My mum made sure that nothing of his would remain, not even a measly photo. All I have left is a vague recollection of his silhouette, and even that has faded with time. I remember states of obsession and various forms of abuse, not just him towards her, but also her towards him. How can two people hug each other one moment and then hurt each other the next? And how can it be that people who love can just get up one day and disconnect, never to see each other again?

Angie, on the other hand, was the only person on earth to make my mum act humanely. Maybe it's because she reminded my mum of herself when she was young, or maybe it's her tormented life story, so bad that even a hag such as my mum couldn't ignore it.

Angie was an only child. Her parents were the neighborhood's Romeo and Juliet, Joel and Mia, a proper cinematic love story. They were beautiful and likeable, and even successful compared to the other neighbors. Mia was a kindergarten teacher, and Joel was a diligent, hardworking construction laborer, but they couldn't have any kids. They tried for eight years, but to no avail. Mia went through countless agonizing treatments that made her gain weight and lose weight; her hair even started shedding at some point. She also had two miscarriages, both of them pretty early on, and that really shattered her and made her want to give up, but Joel convinced her to go for one last try at some specialist doctor he'd heard about through a workmate.

The last time was a charm and Mia was finally pregnant. The whole neighborhood eagerly followed her pregnancy, and everyone prayed for it to work. A miracle happened and she gave birth to a healthy little girl and called her Angel. This all happened during the summer, and the entire neighborhood joined in the celebrations. All the women baked cakes for the occasion and the high street was filled with stalls, balloons, and music. Everyone partied until the late-night hours, but it didn't even take a week for it all to go to shit. See, Mia got postnatal depression, really badly. She refused to go anywhere near Angel, she even expressed blatant hatred towards her. The concerned family and worried neighbors wouldn't leave her alone with the baby for a single minute for fear that she'd harm her. She was sent to dozens of treatments, but nothing helped. Joel had to quit his job and stay at home to care for both Mia and the baby. Their finances were withering and Mia's mental health got worse by the day. Joel looked like he was about to collapse from the financial and emotional burden of it all, but he continued caring for his family as dedicatedly as possible. Everyone felt sorry for them and especially for him, with the entire neighborhood admiring him for everything he was doing for his girls.

When Angie was four years old, Joel threw her a birthday party at her kindergarten. They say that during that morning, Mia fervently refused to come and insisted on staying home alone. Joel pleaded with her to go to the kindergarten with them but it was no use, and he ended up taking Angie there alone, heavy-heartedly. He must have sensed something, that's what everyone said. In any case, when the two came back home at noon and opened their front door, they found Mia hanging off the ceiling fan with the curtain tied around her neck, she was long gone. The people who'd arrived said that they saw Joel holding Mia's body and crying, and little Angie was standing behind him, a birthday crown on her head, hugging him from behind and weeping. From that day on, Joel dedicated his whole life to Angie and Angie alone. They say he was the best father anyone could ask for, that he'd completely coddled her. "My Princess," that's how he called her, and she was exceptionally close to him.

When Angie was about seven years old, Joel met a woman and fell madly in love with her. She moved in with them shortly after, and the atmosphere at home became really tense. She and Angie couldn't stand each other and they fought over Joel's attention all the time. It seemed like Angie always won, but one morning she woke up and ran over to her father's room as she always did, only to find it vacant. There was a letter on the bed which read, "*I truly believe that this is best for us all. Love, Dad.*"

CHAPTER 7

The day her dad left, Angie dragged a chair outside and sat by the door without budging. She didn't cry, didn't speak, didn't eat. She just sat there and looked up at the sky, and whenever anyone tried to come near her, she screamed so loud that the whole neighborhood trembled. Even when her nan showed up, she didn't allow her to come close. Everyone was worried and just waited for her to eventually fall asleep, but she didn't close her eyes, not even for a second. It was only after two days that she got up and dragged the chair back into the house, got into her bed and fell asleep. When she woke up, she just went about her day as she always did.

Joel never came back or tried to get in touch, and Angie never mentioned him, she refused to even hear his name. Her nan moved in and raised her. She was a bored, obese woman who used to spend her days doing nothing but eat, but when she moved in with Angie, she decided to get her life in order for both their sakes. She had surgery to get a gastric band in place, and she lost so much weight that her skin looked like it was seeping out, like one of those shar-Pei dogs.

One time, during a birthday party hosted by one of the kids from Angie's class, her nan stuffed herself with nearly half a chocolate cake without batting an eyelid. A second later, she retched it all over the lounge floor. All the mums rushed over to help her, but she smiled embarrassedly and told them, "Serves me right. Make no mistake, inside this skinny body is a fat woman who has to burst out every now and again."

Ever since that time, whenever there was a social occasion in the neighborhood, they'd make sure that there'd always be a bucket at the ready next to Angie's nan, just in case the fat woman from within would suddenly reappear for a cameo.

Angie and I went to the same school. When we were still young kids, she was fat and pretty uncommunicative, so everyone thought she was odd, and it made her very unpopular. One day, Manu's mum and my mum were called over to the school after we fought some kids who'd called Manu a Paki. While we were sitting outside the headmaster's office, my mum went to get a glass of water from the teachers' lounge. Manu and I were shocked when she came back holding onto Angie's hand.

"Iggy, do you know this lovely girl?" she asked me.

I wanted the ground to swallow me, but at that very minute, the headmaster's door opened. I ran straight in, closed the door, and leaned onto it with all my might, trying to stop Angie from trying to come in. The headmaster got up from his seat and shouted at me to step away from the door immediately, but I refused to give in. They tried to open the door numerous times, but I pushed them back and used all the strength I had to keep it closed. The headmaster came over and forced me aside just as my mum pushed the door from the other end, so she fell straight into the office.

I was suspended for a week, but ever since then, Angie has been obsessed with me. Everyone was saying that she was in love with me, and I couldn't stand it. At first, she only stalked me in the school's hallways, but within no time, it extended to the after-school hours. I'd get home and she'd already be waiting for me there, having heart-to-hearts with my mum in the kitchen.

I was so angry at my mum for bonding with her, of all people. I couldn't figure out what she saw in that girl, and I was shocked by their newly formed bond. In a way, I was even jealous about it.

One day, I came back home and saw them in the kitchen. They were deep in conversation and didn't notice me coming in. I was curious to hear what it was they were talking about, so I hid behind the kitchen door and eavesdropped.

My mum was telling her that she'd been really fat too when she was young, and that back then the world was very cruel towards her. "Nothing helped!" she went on, "Until I started purging and finally lost some weight! And then, suddenly everyone was nice to me and tried to chat me up. You should know, Angie, that most of humanity is made up of hypocrites who give out contradicting messages! Everyone says that appearance doesn't matter and that success isn't measured by your finances, but the second a fit bird walks by, the blokes forget about everything, and if a fella drives by in a lush car, all the women just fall at his feet."

Mum continued her explanation by claiming that all of the fairy tales proved just that. "Take Cinderella for example," she continued philosophizing, "She was bloody miserable until that fairy of hers sewed her a gorgeous dress and gave her those glass slippers, and that was enough for her to catch the prince's eye. He went looking for her throughout the entire kingdom, and it was only because of her looks. And the ugly duckling, who had to go through agony and rejection until he finally transformed into a beautiful swan. And Hansel and Gretel too, they started out as miserable little kids, but once they killed the witch and took all her money, they became successful. So you, my dear, you do what you have to do in order to live the dream, if you see what I'm getting at."

At that point, I lost interest in the conversation and went over to my room, but within a few months, when we started Year 9, Angie suddenly showed up without all of the extra pounds she'd had. It was as though all of the fat had gone to the only places worthy of it – the lion's share in her breasts and the rest in her bum. Her boobs swiftly became the fantasy of every teenage boy at school. Everyone assumed she'd become addicted to workouts, but I knew that she was addicted to purging, and that she'd turned from a fat girl into a fit bird because of her conversations with my mum.

I never told Angie that I had listened in on their convo because, like everyone else, I was stoked by the transformation and hopelessly in love with her. Even though I knew that she was purging because of my mum's toxic speeches, and that her metamorphosis was unhealthy, I still kept my mouth shut. I was angry with myself for being as shallow as everyone else, but most of all, I was frustrated by the fact that my mum was right.

Everyone changed their attitude towards Angie once she'd changed, and no one ever stopped to think about how she'd made it happen – even her nan, who welcomed every opportunity to boast about her granddaughter's amazing transformation. In any case, ever since she'd changed, her obsession and attention towards me ceased. Unsurprisingly, it was then that I hoped to come out of a classroom and have her pounce on me. I tried to start a convo with some girls every time she passed by me in the hallway, but it didn't work. At night, I'd dream about coming out of class and into the schoolyard, and I'd see Angie wearing shorts and a tight top, joyfully jumping during PE. In the dream, she'd notice me and smile, and I'd be on cloud nine. I'd wake up from those dreams with my blanket damp, and my body loose and relaxed.

I often planned to gather up the courage to go talk to her, but I always chickened out in the moment of truth. I felt so exposed and stupid. Maybe I was scared that she'd reject me just like I'd rejected her when we were younger, and I felt bad for having been such a shit and not having noticed her potential earlier on.

One day, I heard my mum on the phone with her … she invited her over for lunch. The second she hung up the call, I stormed into the room and demanded she tell me exactly when that was going to happen.

"You're all the same," she said dismissively, "You should all be neutered the moment you're born, that way you'll grow up thinking with your head and not with your little fella. I don't know what she sees in you. If I were her mum, I'd kill her if she brought home someone like you."

"Well, she doesn't have a mum, so problem solved," I said and stormed away to my room.

That Friday, I was in the kitchen making myself some grub. My mum was in the lounge, talking on the phone and sounding exceptionally chipper. I paid no attention to it until I heard her saying, "I'm making you your favorite pie, Angie." My heart skipped a beat and I froze in my spot, waiting to hear when it was all meant to go down. "Of course! I know, love," I heard Mum continuing to talk affectionately, "We'll talk about it all when we meet. No, don't worry, he always goes out to meet his mates on Saturday at noon, so it'll just be the two of us. Don't be late."

I'll never forget that weekend for two reasons – first of all, because it was the first time in my life that I preferred spending the whole of Saturday at home rather than hanging out with my mates. And secondly – it was the first time I realized what a woman's power really is.

That Friday felt like the longest day of my life. When nighttime finally arrived, I hardly even managed to fall asleep, and woke up several times to check the clock. I was eagerly waiting for Angie to arrive and for our eyes to meet, just like in my dreams.

CHAPTER 8

It was finally morning and I hopped out of bed straight into the shower, trying to get myself ready and to look good for Angie's visit. My mum was already in the kitchen, cooking and drinking with a fag in hand. She did everything with a fag in her hand – making food, putting on her makeup, eating. She'd even go in the shower with a fag and just leave it leaning on the sink. When she washed the dishes, she'd leave her fag on the corner of the counter. Obviously, the house was full of yellow spots and burn marks all around. One time, she was so drunk that she stubbed her fag on the edge of my plate while I was still eating. Naturally, I got angry, and she screamed at me to stop being so dramatic. "It was nowhere near your grub; it was just in the corner of the plate!"

That Saturday, she set the table for Angie while I paced back and forth from the kitchen to the bathroom and back to the kitchen, utterly dazed.

"Iggy, will you stop whirling around like that?" she grumbled, "You're doing my head in! What are you even doing here? Aren't you supposed to be with your mates?"

"What's the matter? You having someone over?"

"Yeah, I've invited your dad for the last supper."

"Oh, wicked – two birds; one stone."

The doorbell saved me from her comeback. Angie was finally here!

"Iggy, go to your room," my mum said on her way to the front door, "I told her you weren't going to be here and now she'll see you, it's not right."

I went into my room and pressed my ear against the door, trying to listen in on them.

"Angie, you gorgeous thing, what a lovely dress!" I heard my mum call out, "You're showing off all the right stuff."

She was clearly saying that to torment me. I leaned down without hesitation and peered through my door's keyhole.

"Hiya, Sarah," I heard Angie's sweet voice and managed to see her long legs following Mum into the kitchen.

"Fuck's sake, why the kitchen of all places?!" I muttered in frustration and ran to the other end of the room, to the wall closest to the kitchen, pressing my ear tightly against it.

I could hear their voices but I couldn't make out what they were saying. My heartbeats and my stomach's growling interfered with my eavesdropping. They were laughing a lot when suddenly the phone rang. A moment later I heard my mum say, "Hello? Oh no, you don't say…?"

She then shouted, "Iggy, can you come here for a minute?!"

My mouth went dry and I couldn't speak. I was so unprepared for her to out me like that – after all, she was the one who'd asked me to hide in my room! I prayed for the ground to swallow me right there and then, but she shouted again, "Iggy, you better get here right now!"

I was genuinely distressed. I glanced at the mirror and realized that I looked like a ghost. I thought that the best solution would be to escape, so I quickly put my shoes on and opened the window. I already had one leg hanging out when I heard two quick knocks on the door and it immediately opened. Angie was standing there.

"What are you doing?" she asked.

"Just hanging out, looking at the view," I lied, sweating like an ice lolly on a radiator.

My mum then appeared, standing next to her and bursting out laughing, "What is it? Did you want to jump through the window?"

"What are you on about? What do you want?!" I shouted at her in embarrassment, but she just stared at me, her eyes reflecting how pathetic I must have looked. "Well? What do you want?" I raised my voice again.

"Something's come up and I need to pop out for an hour," my mum said, "Can you keep Angie company until I get back?"

"Okay," I replied, stunned.

"Go on then, get out of the window and serve the food I made," she said, then kissed Angie on the cheek and left.

The air was electrified. Angie stayed standing in the doorway. I lifted myself, my legs shaking, and stood up cumbersomely. "Wanna eat something?" I asked.

"I'm starving actually, haven't eaten nothing since this morning cuz I knew I was meant to have lunch with your mum."

Ever since then, I heard that line every day – "haven't eaten nothing since this morning." You see, Angie did eat, but then she'd purge at least three or four times a day.

I expected her to move as I neared the doorway, but she just stood there, as though waiting for us to collide. All of a sudden, we were pressed against each other. I could smell her body, and all of my senses went shaky. "Should we go to the kitchen?" I whispered, my voice quivering.

"After you," she said softly, causing a sharp and unexpected rise in my pants. I was so embarrassed that I swiftly walked around her and rushed to the kitchen.

'Can't believe this,' I thought. I stood in front of the pots and pans with my back to her, scared to turn around. I tried to find a way of reaching the table without freaking her out with my trouser snake.

"I'll bring the food over," I told her, "Can you just grab the salad out of the fridge?"

"Of course," she replied and turned to the fridge. I quickly ran to the table with the plates in my hands and immediately sat down.

"There's no salad in here," she said.

"No worries, my mum must have eaten it this morning," I blatantly lied.

Angie walked up to the table, neared her plate to mine, and sat right up against me. I could feel currents rushing through my whole body.

"Are we really gonna eat now?" I muttered embarrassedly as we lifted our heads and looked each other in the eye. It was so intense.

I tried to transmit all of the thoughts rushing through my mind, the ones I'd never be able to say out loud to her – that she was the most beautiful and smartest girl I'd ever met. I also tried to decipher her gaze and understand everything she wanted me to know but would never be able to tell me. My mind asked her, 'Why me, of all people?'

She was so fascinating that I was ready to die if it meant I could just get into her head for a minute and study everything inside it. *'How could I have been so blind? And why did I only notice her when she became physically attractive? I'm not worthy of you,'* my eyes tried to tell her. But her eyes convinced me that our bond was as right as anything could ever be, and that the combination of our flaws made the most complete thing that could ever exist in this world.

I have no idea how, considering I didn't even feel us moving, but all of a sudden our lips met, so softly. I couldn't breathe, but as she kissed me, I felt like she was putting oxygen inside my lungs, reviving me. "I love you," I whispered to her. "I love you too," she whispered back. Even the biggest spliff in the world couldn't make me feel as good as I did at that moment.

"Suits you two, all that romance. Go on, you lovebirds," Mum's voice suddenly echoed through the kitchen.

We didn't even jump in fright, or try to apologize. We just stayed pressed against each other, smiling and hazy-eyed, like two people in love. From that day on, we were inseparable.

CHAPTER 9

My thoughts were interrupted by a loud beeping noise, followed by Tommy's voice imitating a pilot, just like in a film, "Ladies and Gentlemen, we've now reached London, local time is 05:00 am and the temperature's minus ten degrees. We do hope you've dressed appropriately. On behalf of the captain and the crew on board, we thank you and hope you'll be sailing with us again soon."

Everyone except us was already on their feet and anxiously waiting for the ferry to dock so they could storm out of it – which is one of those things I literally can't stand! Would it kill you to wait ten more minutes and stay seated? Why's everyone always in such a panic to get out? Where are they all rushing to? People sit quietly throughout the whole journey and then all of a sudden, once they've reached their destination, it's as though someone announced that an atom bomb's about to hit and everyone just frantically pushes through the gates.

We stopped a cab and got on. Once we reached the neighborhood, I was the first to say goodbye and get off, and I knew that I wouldn't be seeing them for a good while. I knew that if I wanted to be with Angie and make a real change in my life, then I had to stay clear of them, at least until I'd stabilized. It made me really sad. I felt torn between one love and another. It seemed so cruel to put someone in that position, and I'd never ask Angie to make that sort of choice. But this time, I chose her, because I knew it would be impossible to get clean with that lot around, and mainly because

I could potentially lose her, but I'd never lose the lads. Even if I stayed away from them for a long while, once I returned, they'd take me back with open arms.

I went into the house quietly; it was dark and I didn't want to turn the lights on. I hoped to find Angie asleep in bed, but once I opened the front door, something felt empty, hollow. I walked into our room and felt the bed, but Angie wasn't there. I turned the light on and discovered a vacant room, no scent of fags in the air. I realized she must have left on New Year's Eve.

I was knackered, physically and emotionally. I missed her and I had to calm my mind and figure out what I wanted to do, so I went out into the lounge and sat down in front of the telly, feeling gloomy.

"Iggy?" I heard Mum's voice.

"What?" I replied.

"What do you mean, what?! You've only been back for two minutes and all the bloody lights are on, turn them off! Electricity costs money you know, I don't work for you!"

"You don't work at all. Dunno where you get the money from," I retorted, lifting myself off the sofa to go back to my room and sleep, but then she suddenly appeared in the lounge, barely managing to stand upright. She looked proper sloshed and her lips curled into a venomous smile. I plummeted back onto the sofa. "Oh hello, my darling boy, Happy New Year," I said mockingly, "Thank you, my darling mother, Happy New Year to you too."

"So Angie's finally come to her senses?" she laughed viciously, "Thank God you didn't get her pregnant, otherwise she'd be fucked for life, just like me."

She was doing my head in. I felt bad as it was, and that was the last thing I needed to hear. "I can't listen to you," I shouted, "Get out of here!"

"Hello?! You're in my house and I'll say whatever I bloody well like."

"Fine, then just don't talk to me, and you reek of booze!"

"And you reek of drugs! Sometimes when I look at you, I feel so disappointed that I just want to cry."

"You? Cry?" I laid into her, "You're literally the only person I know who wouldn't surprise me if you got fire bursting through your eyes instead of tears."

"All right, Ladies and Gents, give it up for Iggy, my successful son, currently studying medicine in Oxford!" she announced in a sarcastic tone, "Wake up, son, you're a junkie! And now that she's left you, you're only going to get worse! You're just like your dad, giving up the best thing that's ever happened to you for that shit!"

Her words enraged me. 'What does she want from me?' I thought, 'Why does she always drag me into these horrid rows? Why do we pick at each other's wounds every time, why did she even give birth to me? Wouldn't it be simpler to just put a rubber on?! After all, it was her decision to have me, she could have had an abortion instead!'

I waited for the day when she was old, lonely, and helpless, and there'd be no one around for her to talk to, so she'd have to try and talk to the fifty-quid notes I'd send her once I was a millionaire, because I sure as hell wasn't going to be there for her.

"Don't worry," I muttered under my breath, "I'll get a job soon and get out of your house."

"Brilliant, just make sure it happens in this lifetime, yeah?! I told you a thousand times already that I can sort you out with work at my mate's place, but you're not serious, are you?"

"Get me a meeting with him and I'll go!" I declared.

"You serious?" she looked at me in utter disbelief.

"Try me."

"Fine, I'll ring him in the morning," she said, "But let's be clear – if I set it up and you don't go there, then you're getting the hell out of my house and you never show your face here again. Are we clear?"

"Crystal," I shouted and went to my room.

I lay down on the bed and fell asleep within seconds. When I woke up, I started rewinding back to New Year's Eve and then fast-forwarded all the way to my shouting match with Mum. The thoughts were doing my head in and I was consumed with longing for Angie. I was itching for a line to sort myself out, but I didn't have any dosh left. My stomach burned with hunger so I got up to make something to eat, and I saw my mum talking on the phone in the lounge. I went into the kitchen to make a sandwich and noticed her bag hanging on the chair. I couldn't help myself so I made sure she was still on the phone and then quickly pulled out her purse, grabbed the first note my fingers found and stuffed it down my pants. I grabbed the sandwich I'd made and rushed back to my room, pulled the money out of my pants and saw that it was a fifty-quid note. 'Where does she get this kind of money?' I thought, 'And I wonder if she notices how she's always missing some dosh.'

Naturally, the moment my mum left the house, I rang my dealer, Cuba, told him to sort me out with a small amount, just to keep me sweet so I could function. Cuba said he was on his way and I decided that once he came, I'd do a few lines and call Angie. But I couldn't wait. I took a few deep breaths and dialed her number.

"Hello?" she picked up the phone.

"Angie, what's up?" I asked excitedly.

"I'm fine." She didn't ask me how I was doing, so I fell silent. "What do you want, Iggy?" she asked in an uncharacteristic tone.

"I'm ready, I want to go for it, the change we talked about."

"Great," she said.

I thought she'd be happy, but there wasn't a shred of emotion in her voice, and my heart started racing. "What about you? You still want us to go for it?" I asked. She didn't say anything, and that scared the hell out of me. "Angie, I know I hurt you," I said, "But I was high … and … I'm sorry, I was a proper dickhead, but I'm genuinely ready now. And I love you and I want us to do this together."

"Yeah," she still sounded cold and it made my heart freeze, "I knew that this would happen, that you'd come back all hero-like and feeling yourself, Iggy, that's what you always do, and I can't be with you when you take me for granted."
"I don't take you for granted!"
"Yes you do! You left me even though I begged you not to. You were so sure that I'd be waiting for you when you got back, and that's called taking someone for granted! But I'm not coming back!"
"Angie I'm sorry, I miss you, and I love you!"
"I hope this'll teach you that even the people who love you have lines that you can't cross. The only thing missing was a bloody letter waiting for me on the bed," she added in a stifled voice, "Bye Iggy!"
"Please don't hang up! I need you! You're the only one I need! Angie…?"

It was only after she hung up that it dawned on me. I'd hit her where it hurt the most! I did exactly what her dad had done! I wanted to die right there and then, and I vowed to do everything in my power for us to get back together, so that I could prove to her I was nothing like him!

After that day, I didn't leave the house at all, except for nicking our neighbor's paper in order to check the job listings. I didn't answer calls either, and I evaded any and all interactions with my mum. I only did a few lines here and there – just to keep my focus, not to get stoned or anything.

I finally got a job interview at an electrical supplies shop in Central, which was set for Thursday at ten in the morning. I wasn't really sure that I wanted to work as a salesman, but I told myself that I had to start somewhere, otherwise I'd never make it anywhere. I was determined to make the change and prove to Angie that we were destined to be together.

On Thursday morning, the alarm went off. Before I even managed to get out of bed, my mum stormed into the room, wearing a new black dress. "Iggy, you have a visitor."

"What visitor?" I asked, but she didn't say anything, just turned and left the room.

"Who could it be?" I mumbled to myself.

Suddenly, I saw this masculine figure in the doorway. He was wearing cowboy clothes, just like in those westerns. He was even dusty, as though he rode across the entire desert on a horse, just to get to my room. He was wearing a cowboy hat and clutching a stubbed cigar between his fingers.

"Hello, Iggy," he said in a coarse, manly voice.

"Howdy," I answered in jest, as befitting a couple of cowboys.

"Do you know who I am?" he asked.

"Clint Eastwood," I joked.

"My name's Blood," he said in a serious tone, ignoring my jokes, "And this might sound strange, but I've known you since the day you were born."

"Wow, that's a long while now… You my mum's mate?"

"No, son, I don't have any mates. I'm here for you, and you alone." He took a step in my direction. "I'm here to tell you that you're wasting your time trying to make a change and wanting to become some sort of millionaire. You see, son, the way the world works is that everyone is born with their own destiny, and there are all kinds of people. You belong to the kind that doesn't make it. Throughout your entire dynasty, no one's ever made it – your great-granddad didn't make it, your granddad Elijah didn't make it, your dad didn't make it, and you won't either." He gave me a chilling look.

His words made my blood boil, and all I wanted was to get out of bed and beat the shit out of him, but before I even managed to move, I suddenly felt something crawling on my throat. It was a huge snake, twisting and winding and slowly suffocating me until I hardly had any air left in my lungs and … I woke up.

That was one of the most surreal dreams I'd ever had. I was stunned by how real it felt, and I was worried that maybe some of that New Year's acid was still imploding inside me.

But then, just like in the dream, my mum opened the door without knocking, wearing the same black dress she wore in the dream. She started telling me that she'd spoken to her mate, the one who owned a delivery company, and got me a job interview with him. She gave me a little note with all the details and said, "Here's the address, he'll be at the office till noon today. If you don't make it, then you can go there next Thursday. Good luck!"

I was still shocked by the bizarre dream, so I just silently stared at her.

"Wakey-wakey, Iggy! What's the matter with you?" she asked.

"This is bonkers," I replied, "I just woke up from this dream where you were wearing the same dress you are now and … someone was telling me all sorts of things… What's your mate's name?"

"Rico," she said, "And now you'll be saying it's the same name from your dream!"

"No," I said.

"That's a shame, clairvoyants make good money," she joked as she left the room.

I got dressed and went to the kitchen to make some coffee before I left, recalling my dream and everything Blood had told me about my destiny. I wondered if it was a prophecy-type dream, and thought that maybe I needed to find out some details about my family's dynasty. I never knew my dad's parents, nor my mum's mum, who'd passed away when she was six. But I knew grandad Elijah well. He'd raised mum all on his own, and did a shitty job at it. I knew that he had been born in Israel, in the slums, and that he was Sephardic. He used to tell me that back when he'd lived in Israel, the Sephardic lot were considered a minority and a nuisance, just like the Afro-Americans were in the US, so they had a lot of hardships. He used to tell me that against all odds, he and his mates were the first Sephardics to be accepted to study economics at uni and to complete their degrees successfully, but no one gave them the chance they needed to get ahead because of their ethnicity. So, despite their efforts and all of their protests and strikes, they found themselves unemployed and desperate. They were well angry with the country and at the Ashkenazy lot who were running it, so they decided to move abroad where they could make it big time. Their plan was to move to England, where they thought that their ethnicity wouldn't be an obstacle and they'd be able to get into things and take over the stock market. After that, they planned to go back to Israel filled with knowledge, drive, and a ton of dosh, and instigate a major social change, but that never happened. Instead, they crashed and burned. There was no difference between their old lives in Israel and their new lives in England. That was the beginning of our neighborhood, and by the end of it, all that was left were their stories.

When I was little, I loved hearing old tales of the Holy Land and about how they'd duped everyone there and schemed in order to survive. By now, I already know they'd only duped themselves with all those stories of theirs – and us too, actually, the ones who'd listened to them. Because, after all, none of them ever made it.

I was ten years old when granddad Elijah died. He was such a loved man, and everyone came by to pay their last respects to him. The day of the funeral is still etched in my mind. Right after the ceremony, Oved came up to me – he was granddad's best mate. He leaned down towards me and the skin on his face drooped. He looks like an alien. "God rest that man's soul, his fierce soul," he said and tightened his hand into a fist, "It's still here, his soul, listening to us, so now you listen to me!" He took out a blue lolly from his pocket and put it in my hand. "Many of our lot are no longer alive, but I'll tell you one thing – they're all angels now, and they can help you out, if you want them to. Take some initiative, and never give up on what this world has to offer you… Look," Oved pointed up at the sky, "If you concentrate real hard and think of your granddad, he'll give you a sign to show he's with you." He patted my cheek and went on his way.

I stayed standing there in the middle of the cemetery, my eyes looking up at the heavens, trying my hardest to get a sign from Granddad, until my head started hurting and I decided to go home.

On the way, I took the lolly out of my pocket. It looked beautiful, the same color as the sky, and seemed tasty and enticing. I unwrapped it, but before I even managed to pop it in my mouth, it was snatched out of my hand by some dickhead kid, this bully who always nicked everything from the rest of us. He stuffed it in his mouth but then his face started contorting. "What is that, it tastes like shit!" he shouted, coughing and choking until he finally spewed it out. He was so embarrassed that he ran off hysterically, and I took it as a sign from Granddad Elijah.

CHAPTER 10

I finished my coffee and my fag, looked at the time, and saw that it was ten. I did a couple of little lines, just for some Dutch courage before the job interview. That was one of the reasons I loved drugs so much, they helped me handle all the stress and criticism around me.

As a kid, I used to need a good few hours to get ready and leave the house. I'd get anxious about people looking at me and laughing about how I was dressed or how I walked. Sometimes I'd stay at home for days just so I wouldn't have to deal with that stress. When I left for school or to meet up with friends, I'd run all the way to where I was going, and it would take me a good while to calm down. But all of the sweat, the trembles, the heart racing – it all just magically disappeared the first time I tried drugs.

'When I get my millions, I'll start treating my social anxiety,' I thought as I left the house.

I reached the electrical shop and immediately went up to the counter. Before even managing to introduce myself, I saw the manager, who had a name badge on his chest. He was talking to someone, who must have been one of his salesmen, and told him impatiently, "I don't care about any of your stories! I'm taking the difference out of your wages."

Then he turned to face me, instantly taking on a kind and professional expression. "Hi there, how can I help?"

"You can't!" I exclaimed and quickly left the shop.

I knew that I could never work for that sort of person. If he ever spoke to me the way he did to that salesman, I'd trash the place in a second. As I walked to the bus stop, gloomy and trying to figure out what to do, I pulled out the pack of fags from my pocket, and the little note my mum had given me was stuck to it. *"Rico's Deliveries – 17 Thomas More Street, Tower Hamlets, 2nd floor."* I knew that area, and I had nothing left to lose, so I decided to go there straight away and not waste any more of my time. I was out the house as it was, looking dapper, and I'd still make it there before noon. I continued walking until I finished my fag, then got on the bus and rode to Rico's Deliveries. I reached the building at noon on the dot and rushed inside, hoping not to miss him.

I was excited, the adrenaline was rushing through my body. I marched up to the lift and checked the note to see what floor Rico's office was on, but before I managed to press the button, a uniformed security officer stopped me. "Oi, where are you heading?"

"Rico's Deliveries, I have a meeting," I replied.

"With who?" he asked.

"With Rico."

"Name?"

"Iggy," I said impatiently, feeling the anxiety slowly surging within me.

"Why are you in a panic? Got any identification on you?"

"Bruv, I get stressed when people pester me," I said as I rummaged through my pockets looking for my card, "I don't have any identification on, but I do have a note from my mum… I mean… Rico knows my mum, just call him up and tell him Sarah's son has come to see him."

"Wait over here," he said and went up to the counter to make the call, "There's someone here who says he's got a note from his mum."

I wanted to die, the sheer embarrassment! That guy was such a knob-end!

"What's your mum's name?" he turned to me.

"Sarah," I said, my eyes trying to tell him he'd come out a real dickhead, but he didn't seem to care.

"Sarah," he said into the phone, then hung up. "Second floor, third door on the right," he pointed at the lift, which had remained open the whole time, but before I managed to get in, he planted himself in front of me and motioned for me to lift my arms.

"Seriously, bruv?" I asked.

"Routine check, nothing personal," he said as he felt me up.

"Should I take my shoes off too?" I asked in a cynical tone, "Maybe I hid a machete in them."

"You don't look the type," he muttered and let me go.

I got in the lift and quickly pushed the button. The doors closed and I let out a sigh of relief. They opened again on the second floor and I got out and reached the third door on the right. There was a sign on it that said, "*King Deliveries*" and another one beneath it, "*Rico King.*"

I knocked on the door and thought to myself, 'What a name! You have to make it if you're born with that name, Rico King.'

"Come in," I heard a woman's voice and walked in. It was a secretary sitting in front of the door. She looked like a model on a tea break during a shooting session for a Guess campaign. "Iggy, right?" she asked.

"That's right," I smiled in awe.

"Go on in, he's expecting you," she pointed at the door to the left.

I opened it and Rico got up and welcomed me with a smile. The first thing I thought was, 'Wow, what a handsome fella!' That's a very rare first thought for a man when meeting another man, but he was something special. He was wearing jeans and a short-sleeved white T-shirt which accentuated his muscles and his tan. His arms were covered in colorful snake tattoos. He had blue eyes, and his black hair was meticulously cropped. In fact, everything about him seemed meticulous, even his facial features. He was probably around my dad's age but he seemed a lot younger. He grinned as he passionately shook my hand and gestured for me to take a seat.

"Iggy, look at how you've grown!" He looked me up and down. "You probably don't remember me, you were so young, but look at you now!"

"I understand the disappointment," I jested, but his expression didn't budge. "I was joking," I tried to explain.

Rico smiled at me and nodded his head, "Yes, humor's important, testifies to one's wisdom and wit."

I liked what he said, it made me feel good about myself. "So you've been mates with my parents all these years?" I asked.

"Yonks! Your mum used to be one of the most beautiful women in the world – still is to be fair!" he declared, "And I'm not just talking about looks, beauty's a temporary thing. I've had as many beauties in my life as I've had socks, but your mum's like fine wine, she only gets better with the years!"

I didn't know what to say to that so I just nodded my head, stunned by what he was telling me about her, as though he'd gotten her confused with another woman. "Just to be clear," I mumbled in embarrassment, "My mum's Sarah Allely, yeah?"

Rico laughed. "You're funny, son! Yeah, Sarah Allely, you should know she's asked me to help you quite a few times already, but you never showed up until now. I'm glad you've finally decided to come. To be honest, I don't like taking people on who I don't know personally, but I know you, trust me."

"I trust you."

"With that in mind," he then went serious, "Let's be clear, if you don't keep to the standards that I demand, meaning stability, diligence, flexibility, and loyalty – which is the number one thing for me – then you can't work here. Keep to those four criteria or you and I will be in a real pickle!"

"Ain't no pickle in sight!" I joked confidently.

"Are you working anywhere else right now?" he ignored my joke yet again, "Need some time to get anything else sorted first? Because you should know that once you say yes, you're immediately an employee for all intents and purposes. Remember we said flexibility?"

"That's right," I replied.

"Want to take a few days to think about it?"

"Trust me, I've given it enough thought. I'm in."

"Brilliant, all right, glad to hear it," he said. He told me that Rico King had branches all around the world and that he worked with some major companies, some of which were even classified as top secret, so as far as his employees were concerned, everything was considered confidential, meaning I wouldn't always be able to get information about what I was delivering. Some deliveries would take whole days to complete, so I needed to prepare a change of clothes and personal equipment and have them ready at all times.

"All expenses are on the company card, and everything's given in advance," he added, "And the wages are an hourly rate of a hundred quid. You good with that?"

"How much?" I asked, stunned.

"How much did you hear me say? I don't like repeating things."

"A hundred quid an hour…" I replied hesitantly.

"You heard right!" he confirmed, "You need to understand that all of my employees have been here a good long while now. There's no turnover of staff here. Take Don for example, you must have met him downstairs. He joined us back when he was thirteen years old, two days after his dad, who was a bartender at one of my clubs, got sent away for thirty years for … some nonsense. So, like I said, these are people who I know personally."

"You said you didn't like to repeat yourself," I tried to jest again, but he stared at me with a severe expression and ignored my comment.

"You're getting a once-in-a-lifetime opportunity here, son," he told me, "And I hope you won't prove me wrong about you."

"I won't let you down, I promise," I said confidently.

His tone of voice and flattery made me feel like I was in the right place. This was the first time in my life that I felt like someone except for Angie was seeing my true potential and believing in me, and that really moved me.

Rico got up and said, "Welcome to the family, son."

I reached my hand out to him, but he grabbed it and pulled me in so forcefully that my arm nearly ripped out. He gave me a warm, fatherly hug.

"Handshakes are for strangers!" he declared, "And we're family! Here, take this for now, it's on the house," he added and handed me two fifty-pound notes. I was shocked, but I grabbed them immediately. Who could turn down that kind of dosh?!

I left his office feeling ecstatic, and with a thousand questions rushing through my mind – some of which I was too embarrassed to ask, and some I was just scared to. All I'd wanted was for him to take me on, and everything he said sounded fine. All that mattered was that he'd said yes to me.

'Welcome to the family, what a line!' I thought. 'What does it even mean? After all, the way I see it, family's the most destructive thing in the world... But when it came out of his mouth, with all of those compliments and that fatherly hug, it made me feel right at home.'

I then realized Tommy was right about what he'd said on the way to that Blacktown club – "Even though it doesn't make any sense and it's totally wrong, the idea of 'family' being a good thing is shoved so far into our brains that we genuinely believe it!"

I pressed the button for the lift and ran through the meeting with Rico in my mind. We barely spoke, but I was impressed by how he'd managed to make me feel confident about being part of a family I didn't yet know. Rico was precisely what I wanted to be. He reminded me of Tommy, but a much more refined version. That's when I realized why girls gave in to Tommy so easily. This bloke and Tommy, they just knew how to sell people dreams. It only took a few moments for this stranger to make me surrender everything to him – my stability, diligence, flexibility, and loyalty. I wasn't even bothered by that niggling suspicion that he'd had an affair with my mum and maybe even played a major part in my dad leaving us. The main thing was being a part of his "family." I'd sold myself and my dad within a mere few minutes.

CHAPTER 11

To be honest, it wasn't difficult to give up on my dad. As a kid, I prayed for him to disappear one day so that Mum and I could be free. He was never home during the day and only came back late at night, like a thief. I don't remember a single quiet night at home if the two of them were there at the same time. They'd always shout at each other about anything and everything, from the moment he set foot in the house until the moment he'd storm out and vanish for a few days.

I remember one night in particular; it was my mum's birthday. I was supposed to be asleep in bed by then – that's how night-time went when my dad was meant to turn up. Mum would rush me into my room and make me swear not to come out, because if my dad saw me awake at those hours then he'd get well upset. I was always scared of him getting angry with me, but I never really slept. I'd stay up and listen to whatever was going on in the house.

On that particular night, when he arrived, I heard him coming in and ran over to peer through the keyhole in my room. They seemed drunk, and Dad was holding a huge bouquet of flowers. "Happy birthday!" he called out and went over to give Mum a cuddle, but she pushed him away.

"You know I can't stand flowers," she said and continued walking around the lounge in a daze.

He followed her with the bouquet still in his hand and asked, "Don't you like the flowers?"

"No."

Dad planted himself in front of her and blocked her path as she continually pleaded with him, "Come on, let me through, I need to tidy up the house…"

"It doesn't need tidying, it's your birthday! Get a cleaning service to come in tomorrow, let's do something…"

"I don't feel like it," she replied and tried to evade him, but he wouldn't let her.

"What's wrong with you?" he asked, agitated.

"Nothing, what do you want?"

"Why the bitter face?"

"So I need to fake it just cuz it's my birthday? We haven't said a word in a week, and then you show up all of a sudden with a bloody bouquet?! Go give it to one of your slags!"

I remember his face's silhouette. He turned, and I thought that he noticed me through the keyhole and looked me right in the eye. My heart stopped, but then he turned to Mum again and I breathed in relief – until they started shouting at each other.

"Flowers, is that what you get me?" she screamed. "You bloody cheapskate! I should have stayed with him, you're a bigger shit than he ever was!"

"You didn't seem all that upset when we brought you flowers that day!" he screamed back, "Or maybe that's because we had a suitcase full of dosh?! You were so excited that you were ready to fuck us both right there and then, cuz you ain't nothing but a slag who loves money!"

"You cunt! You're the slag! I made sure nothing would happen to you! You don't deserve me; I wish they killed you when they had the chance!"

"He spat you out like yesterday's gum, you should be thankful I even agreed to keep you."

"If I could, I'd find him and beg him to take me away from here! You fucking loser!"

"I'm a loser, am I?!" He grabbed her and pulled her by the hair, beating her as he screamed, "Who's the loser now, eh?! Who's the bloody loser now?!"

Mum cried and screamed, and I closed my eyes tightly and prayed for him to stop. Then, all of a sudden, she wasn't making any noises anymore, so I opened my eyes and looked through the keyhole. He was standing there, staring at her as she lay sprawled across the floor, then turned around and laid down on the sofa, motionless. I waited for a few seconds and then opened the door a little, quietly walked over to my mum and stood next to her. I just wanted to make sure she was breathing. The second she moved, I rushed back to my room, closed the door, and resumed my position in front of the keyhole.

Mum slowly sat up and groaned with pain. Dad rose from the sofa, picked up the flowers from the floor and stood towering before her, like a huge, looming shadow. "Fuck's sake, Sarah, see what you make me do? What did I even ask for? All I wanted was to get you some flowers and make you happy."

She rose from the floor and stood in front of him silently, as though contemplating his words, but then, instead of keeping quiet and ending the row, she went on to say, "You don't scare me! I'm fully immune to your fists by now!"

"Haven't you listened to a word I've said?" he yelled, "What kind of masochist are you? All I'm saying is I got you some flowers, just some fucking flowers ... take the flowers already!"

"Fuck off!" she told him, and within a split second, he raised the bouquet high above her head. I was so stressed that I opened the door and shouted at her pleadingly, "Mum, just take the flowers!"

They both turned to look at me and Mum shouted, "You, get back in your room right now, before I..."

But before she managed to complete her sentence, he lifted the bouquet and hit her over the head with it, over and over again. My mum tried to shield herself with her hands, but then she started laughing for some reason. By that point he'd totally lost it, so he grabbed her head and lowered it down to the floor. "You fucking cunt, you're the devil incarnate! You don't like me when I'm nice, you didn't want no flowers, you wanted a beating for your birthday!"

I was scared he'd strangle her to death so I shouted, "Dad!"

All at once, he came to his senses, left my mum alone, and marched towards me. I was so frightened that I ran into my bed and pulled the duvet over my head. He came into the room and pulled it off me. I was sure he was about to do something terrible to me so I closed my eyes as tightly as I could, but he just mumbled, "I'm sorry, son, I didn't mean it."

I kept lying there motionless with my eyes closed, and then I heard my mum call out, "Sorry my ass, tell him the truth – tell him about the betraying bastard that you are, tell him what really happened, if you're so bloody sorry..."

Yet again, she didn't manage to finish her rant and he was already on top of her, cussing and smacking her frantically, like he'd lost his mind.

I don't know where I'd gotten the strength to do this, but I ran up to him and leaped onto his back, holding onto him for dear life. That got his attention and he let go of her, grabbed me, and turned me to face the other way, so that I wouldn't see him. 'He must be ashamed,' I thought at the time. He held me so tightly that I almost choked. Then he loosened his grip and collapsed onto me with tears, but he didn't let me turn around the entire time. I silently cried too, and Mum just lay on the floor and didn't move.

After a few moments, he got up, still holding onto me, and carried me back to my bedroom. He laid me on the bed, face down with my back to him, and hugged me tightly. *'Probably doesn't want me seeing him crying,'* I assumed and kept my mouth shut. I lay there with him without budging, until I fell asleep.

When I woke up during the early morning hours, Dad wasn't next to me anymore. I got out of bed and went to the loo, and I heard my mum on the phone. "Call me crazy, but I hate him so much that I can't stand Iggy either! He reminds me of him in so many ways, I look at the kid and all I see is that horrible man. I swear, I keep dreaming about him coming here one day and taking him as far away from here as possible, so I can go back to living my life in peace! Do you think that makes me a horrid person?"

I had no idea what her mate's reply was, but I certainly thought that she was horrid.

Once I left Rico's place, I decided to walk around for a bit. Despite the meeting having gone well, I felt uneasy. After all, I wasn't used to spending half a day without getting high, or spending such a long time without Angie and the lads. I missed them terribly. I tried to convince myself that I was strong enough to handle seeing the boys without regressing and getting high again – after all, I was starting a new job and needed to keep my mind sharp. I hoped that if I told them about the change I was undergoing and my new job, they'd keep me safe and wouldn't let me get high. I decided to call Tommy, when I suddenly passed by a nice-looking pub called Savages.

I went in for a pint, hoping to get some time to process everything I'd been through, but first I went into the loo and sniffed a couple of lines, just to calm myself a touch. When I came back out, I looked around for a phone and suddenly noticed Simon – a bloke who went to school with us and dreamed of being a stand-up comedian, even though no one ever laughed at his jokes except for him. He stood behind the bar and announced, "Would you look at that! Iggy, it's been ages! What brings you around this area?"

"I was just at a job interview; I'm starting work around here soon."

"Hallelujah, guess there's still hope for all the other lazy gits out there," he said.

"Yeah, too bad there ain't no hope for dimwits," I retorted.

"I don't get it…" he looked at me with a dumb gaze. "Hey, how about a pint on the house?" he then added.

"Wicked," I replied.

"Okay… but not today, all right?" he said and burst out laughing at his own joke. I couldn't see what was so funny.

"Say, where's the phone in here?" I asked.

"Over there," he said and pointed at it.

"And how are the tips round here?" I said.

"Great, no complaints here, mate," Simon replied and motioned for me to look to the side. There were six blokes sitting at the bar.

I wanted to let one rip and make a run for it, just to chase that lot away, but I overcame my childish impulse – which felt really satisfying. I could feel the change happening within me. Usually, at that time of day, I'd be stoned to my bollocks, and there I was, after a successful job interview, handling a twat like Simon in a mature manner.

I dialed Tommy's number. His mum picked up the phone and said he was at Andy's. I assumed that the rest of the boys would be there too, and that they'd most likely tried to get in touch with me by that point. Naturally, I left the pub and headed straight there.

I was right. Andy, Smiley, Manu, and Tommy were sprawled across the carpet, wasted and happy, as usual. The moment I walked through the door they pounced on me. "We've been ringing you! Where have you been?!"

"Did you get married, Iggy? Are you on the way to your first million?" Smiley asked.

"Still a way to go before the millions start coming in, but yeah, I went for an interview and got the job."

Tommy patted me on the back and congratulated me. Manu rose up from the carpet to the table and cut a few lovely-looking lines. "Here you go, mate," he said and handed me a rolled-up note, "Let's celebrate the occasion!"

"We love you, bruv," Andy piped up, "With or without your millions! As long as you're here!"

"Listen, I'm only going to do a little bit, I can't afford to get proper wasted, I'm starting a serious job!"

"All right, that's my boy!" Manu declared, still holding the rolled-up note in the air and trying to figure out if I was up for it or not. It all felt odd, and I didn't want to come off as patronizing or weird, so I grabbed the note.

"Just a touch, yeah?" I said, "I'll do one or two lines with you, but that's it!"

One thing led to another, and at some point, I suddenly realized that I was as stoned as fuck. I hadn't noticed how many lines I'd had as I told them about the whole Angie thing. After that, I felt so good that when Tommy suggested we do some ecstasy, I downed a pill without hesitation.

We partied all night long, doing what we did best. We had a wicked time together, and if Angie were there with me then, I'd have called it the perfect night.

At around five in the morning, once the comedown kicked in and my conscience started acting up, I decided it was time to get out. I didn't want to get sucked into the same place as before, and I was scared that my new workplace would ring me in the morning and I wouldn't be home to pick up the phone.

"I'm abandoning ship, lads, my career's waiting for me," I said.

Tommy hardly managed to open his eyes, but he wished me luck. He said he was genuinely happy for me, and that he was even a bit jealous of my conviction and drive.

I guess he too felt that it was time for a change in our lives – but my objective was fiercer than his. My love for Angie and my longing for our bond was my real drive. The way I saw it, there was nothing stronger than my desire to get back together with her. The faith that we could be together again drove me beyond just wanting it – it made me do everything within my power to make it happen.

"Mate, I'll get myself settled in and then I'll sort you out with a job there too, he doesn't employ anyone he doesn't know, but we'll make sure he gets to know you," I promised Tommy.

I got back home completely knackered. I collapsed onto my bed, my clothes still on, and immediately fell asleep.

The phone ring was doing my head in, it wouldn't stop. I picked it up and slammed it back down so I could get back to sleep, but then my mum stormed into my room and said that Rico was looking for me, and that I had to get up and talk to him.

"Hello?" I answered the call with a hoarse, tired voice.

"Iggy, it's Rico, wakey-wakey!"

"I'm awake!" I replied.

"Good, I need you here at nine o'clock."

"This evening?"

"No, son, this morning!"

"What time is it now?"

"Quarter to nine, wash your face and get down here, you can make it in time!"

"Right, see you in a bit," I said and quickly brushed my teeth, changed the clothes I'd slept in, and tossed a coat on. I managed to get ready in under five minutes, but my head was throbbing from all the drugs and lack of sleep, so I ran to the kitchen to find some headache tablets and found my mum there, reading the paper and having a cup of coffee. I opened one of the drawers and grabbed a tablet.

"You off to work?" she asked.

"Yeah," I replied, looking for a glass so I could get some water. I couldn't find any so I turned the tap on and drank straight from it.

"You're being naughty, and you won't last long if you keep at it," Mum said, "Rico won't have it! He hates junkies."

"I'll have you know that I only had one little drink and nothing else! We just hung out and chilled."

"Right, that's a lovely little fairytale, that is," she said and laughed viciously.

"You should know that even though I felt like it, they wouldn't let me have any!" I lied to her, "Because I'd told them that I got a job! So go ahead and laugh until you choke!"

I was already out the door when I heard her shouting, "Cheeky bastard! I hope he sacks you!"

I started running when I suddenly recalled Rico saying that the trips could take a good few days and that I needed to be ready with a change of clothes, so I ran straight back home. In my panic, I just stuffed a bag with my toothbrush and the clothes I'd slept in. Then I ran straight to the bus, which luckily stopped just in time for me to get on.

I was twenty minutes late when I got there, panting breathlessly. I said a quick hi to Don, the same security guard from my previous visit, and pushed the button for the lift.

"Where do you think you're going?" he stopped me.

"Don't you remember me? I'm part of the family now."

"Sorry," he replied, "Arms up please."

"You serious?" I asked, stunned, "How do you not remember me being here yesterday, with the note from my mum? Are you taking the piss? I'm twenty minutes late as it is, help me out mate, Rico told me to come by."

"I'm just doing my job," he said and felt me up and down.

I was stressed and pissed off, mainly at myself. I felt bad for being weak and messing everything up with the drugs, and I was worried Rico would realize I'd partied at night. I took a deep breath and waited for Don to finish checking me. Luckily, he wasn't too thorough, only checked over my clothes. I quickly got in the lift and headed to the third floor, where I got out and ran all the way to the office door. I took a few deep breaths and knocked. I was surprised when Rico opened it himself and said, "You're late."

"I'm sorry."

"I don't like people being late!"

"Of course," I nodded in agreement.

He pressed a button and said, "Two black coffees, make one of them strong, and get me some cookies," he ordered. "The sugar will wake you right up. Take a seat."

I did as he said and he continued. "You'll be away for a week or so, Iggy, are you ready for that?"

"Yeah... clothes... toothbrush, got it all right here," I said and lifted the bag to show him.

I was very excited. It felt like a real adventure, going on the road in a truck, stopping at roadside cafés, meeting random weirdos. It was my first time doing it, and I wanted to ask if it would be all right for me to bring a mate along, because I immediately thought about Tommy, but before I even managed to ask, the door opened and a massive fella came in. He was tall and ridiculously fat, with a very small head compared to the rest of his body. He had these tiny sunglasses on and sported a thin mustache, like Fidel Castro's. He wore a shocking brown plaid suit with oversized pockets, and looked straight out of the seventies. It was really ugly but made of some sort of expensive, high-end material.

"The Laurel and Hardy auditions are next door, mate," I jested, but the two maintained their serious expressions. I felt I'd lost some points for my sense of humor, and immediately erased any hint of jolliness from my face.

"Iggy, this is Russ, he'll be joining you this time. I always make sure to have a veteran chaperone on the first trip. It's not that complicated, but it'll save you from any worries. There are all sorts of things I want you to learn, and he's just the right man for the job."

His phone then rang, and he went over to answer the call.

"Nice to meet you," I said and reached my hand out to Russ, but he didn't budge, and my hand remained hovering in mid-air for at least thirty seconds, until I gave up and lowered it back down.

I felt embarrassed. I never did get the whole idea of being snobby, or why anyone would block someone they've only just met. It might have something to do with survival instincts, a kind of deep knowledge that this person can't serve any of my agendas, and therefore I have no interest in him. People always look for connections with anyone that can potentially be of use to them. But there are other reasons too, like jealousy or fear, that stem from a lack of self-confidence. I assumed that Russ had been insulted by people in the past, and my joke about Laurel and Hardy must have been precisely the kind of banter that made him block people out, which was why he didn't shake my hand and why I'd been marked as a bad guy.

"Listen mate, I was just joking, I hope you didn't take offence," I told him.

He didn't react, but I could see the threatening look in his eyes as he stared at me through his sunglasses. I was showing off confidence on the outside, but there was none of it inside. I didn't know what to do with myself, and I prayed for Rico to finish his call and come back to break the ice.

The door opened and Don, the security guy, came in. He was holding a tray with cups of coffee and cookies. I smiled at him, but he maintained his standoffish attitude as he came up to the desk to put the tray down. Rico, still on the phone, introduced us to each other. "Iggy – Don, Don – Iggy. Now it's official."

To my surprise, Don reached his hand out and shook my hand.

"Iggy, finish your coffee," Rico ordered, "We'll go downstairs for a short briefing before you two head out."

We went down to the parking lot, where a gorgeous, huge silver truck was awaiting us. Next to it were rows of crates lined up on the ground. Rico gave me a set of keys and I climbed up into the driver's seat. I inspected the spacious cabin and glanced back, where I saw a bed and even a little fridge. "Wow, wicked!" I said in awe.

"Come down here, there's a few more things I want to explain."

I hopped out and walked with Rico to the back of the truck. He took out a form and gave it to me. "Don't lose this. Once you reach your destination, give it to Russ – he knows the fella you're going to meet. This time, all I want from you is to watch him and do as he says – listen and learn. There's a map in the glove compartment with a mark showing where you need to get to. You good with maps, Iggy?"

"Oh yeah, of course," I replied.

"Good. I want you to come with me and count how many crates are going in."

I immediately started counting the crates on the ground, but Rico stopped me and told me he wanted me to count them as they were taken into the truck. He stressed that this was an important aspect of deliveries – counting what goes in and what comes out. He said I needed to count everything with the other party present, and both parties had to sign the form saying that everything's been loaded in or taken out.

"After you count all the crates," Rico continued, "Pay special attention to make sure the doors are closed shut and the keys are handed to you. This is a very crucial moment to maintain alertness, seeing as we're talking about expensive goods which are worth a fortune. Once everything's done, they'll give you the payment. You just watch what Russ does and back him up. And remember, if there's anything in this world that we have plenty of – it's crooks and thieves."

I counted precisely how many crates were loaded into the truck by the laborers, down to the very last one. "Seventy crates," I told him.

"Brilliant," he replied.

After that, I checked to make sure that the door was shut and that I had the keys. "That's it, we can start her up," I announced.

Rico looked at me with a serious gaze. "Everything's tidy and double-checked, yeah?"

"That's right," I told him.

"All right Iggy, then open the back doors," he said.

I followed his order and discovered two laborers sitting inside, waving at me. "See that?" he said, "If that happened after you left the place then we'd have a serious problem on our hands! After any and all loading and offloading, you don't take your eyes off the laborers for a second, all right? For all I care, you can count them too, or take a photo of anyone coming near the goods, as long as you keep your eyes on them and watch as they close the doors and hand you the keys, is that clear?"

"Crystal," I said.

"Once you reach your destination, you call me up to say everything's all right," he added, "And if a copper or a traffic warden stops you for any reason, just show them the form and don't say anything, you're just a deliveryman. If there's an issue, then Russ will deal with it, just go with whatever he says and learn from him. Clear?"

"Absolutely!" I replied.

"Good. This'll cover your expenses," he said and handed me an envelope stuffed with fifty-pound notes. "Any questions?"

"No," I replied and started walking towards the driver's cabin.

"And Iggy," he called out, "No unnecessary stops!"

Suddenly it dawned on me – I didn't bring anything to sort myself out. I went completely pale and felt hysterical as I deliberated whether to ask Rico for a quick stop at my place, or to pretend as though I'd suddenly remembered something on the way and just tell Russ it had to happen, or just drive straight over to my place without saying anything and act like it was no big deal. The pressure rose within me while Russ was already situated in his seat. I walked slowly, trying to bide my time, and eventually decided not to risk it and just ask Russ if it was all right to stop at my place for a moment. 'I mean, why would he say no?' I thought as I got into the truck and started the engine.

I turned to face Russ, but he kept his eyes straight ahead, maintaining his tough appearance. That was such a bummer. On the one hand, I was excited by the trip and the new vehicle. 'I'm genuinely working,' I thought, 'But on the other hand – what do I do with this miserable git?'

We started the drive. 'Here goes nothing,' I thought as I took a deep breath and turned to him again. "If you don't mind, I'd like to stop at home for a minute, just to grab something..."

"No unplanned stops from the moment we start driving till the moment we reach our destination," he replied, "If you've got any issues with that, then take it up with the boss."

"No problem, I just forgot something important at home, it'll be a thirty-second stop at the most."

"What did you forget?" he asked.

"It's personal, like a kind of good luck charm."

"Take it up with the boss," he said.

I felt like the whole thing was getting too complicated so I just gave up on the idea. I checked the map and continued driving.

We were completely silent for the first hour. I couldn't stop thinking about how I could get my hands on some gear, worried that I'd go mad without it. I wanted to connect with Russ and break the ice, and then maybe I could convince him to make a brief stop somewhere, just to get my head sorted before leaving the city.

"Long drive..." I said. He didn't reply. "So, what's Russ short for?" I tried to get him to talk, but he continued ignoring my questions, and that was doing my head in.

Eventually, I stopped trying and turned the radio on, hoping that some music would pacify my thoughts, but no matter what came up in my mind, everything led me back to how I could get some gear. I drove for hours, flooded by fear. I couldn't calm down and my body was aching all over, so I tried to imagine my happy future, just like Angie had taught me, when Russ suddenly addressed me.

"You should stop at a roadside caff or a petrol station."

"Are we getting some grub? A loo break? Freshen up?" I asked enthusiastically, but he fell silent. I took a deep breath, but my frustration grew stronger. We finally got to a petrol station with a café and I stopped the truck.

Russ got off first and disappeared inside the café. I quickly got out to look for a dealer or a junkie, but there was no one around to fit those descriptions. I had to go in so that Russ wouldn't notice what I was going through. I looked for him amongst the diners, but he was nowhere to be found. I went into the bogs and looked for flyers or phone numbers on the walls, but there was nothing except for some perv's number. I pissed and came back out, bummed as hell. I still couldn't see Russ anywhere, so I sat down at a table and waited. Suddenly, some random bloke came up to me and said that the table was already taken.

"Really?" I asked, baffled, "I didn't see anyone sitting here, but if you say so then fine." I got up to clear the table for him, but then Russ appeared behind me and motioned for me to sit back down.

The bloke looked at him dismissively and said, "This is my table, ask Charlotte, the waitress. My mates should be here any minute now, and it would be a shame for things to get messy, you feel me, bruv?"

Russ didn't pay him any attention and just sat down. I looked around and saw that most of the other tables were clear. I really didn't feel the need to start something with some local dickhead, and with who knows how many of his mates. 'We'll be outnumbered,' I thought and started rising from my seat, but Russ motioned for me to sit down again, and I had no choice but to comply.

The man started getting pissy, and then the waitress showed up with the menus. She noticed the tension in the air and looked a bit concerned. Russ grabbed one of the menus from her hand and asked, "Say, Charlotte, what would you recommend for a fat man like myself to order?"

The pissy fella quickly replied instead of her, "I'd recommend for a fat man like yourself to get up and vacate the table before I cut your gonads off and feed them to the dogs outside."

Russ immediately got up and grabbed the man by his bollocks, leading him outside. He came back nonchalantly after a few minutes, called the waitress over, and sat down in front of me.

"Now, where were we, Charlotte?"
"We've got some lovely steak with fried eggs and chips…"
"Sounds good," he said. She turned and looked at me.
"I'll have the same…" I mumbled.
"And get us some nice scones too, eh? And some ketchup," he added.

I actually wasn't hungry at all. I started feeling sick and I was worried I wouldn't be able to get through the entire drive, but I acted as though everything was fine, and made sure not to ask any unnecessary questions. I occasionally glanced out the window, hoping some dodgy-looking fella would come by and I could finally get myself sorted.

The waitress came by with the food. Russ devoured his dish and I hardly touched any of mine.

"You going to have that?" he asked.
"Nah, I'm not that hungry…" I replied.

Russ seemed pleased by that. He took my plate and ate the entire thing. Once he was done, we went into the shop next door and I bought some beers, a pack of fags, and a snack for the way. As we filled the truck with petrol, I noticed that there were three blokes tied up near the watercooler. They were bent down in a way that made them look like they were trying to eat their own bollocks. One of them was the fella who'd threatened Russ in the café. I suddenly realized who I was dealing with. Russ had given the guy a proper lesson in 'Watch what you say.'

We got back into the truck and continued the drive in silence. Time goes by slowly when you're quiet, and it literally crawls when you're driving and being quiet and you've got no drugs. I tried to concentrate on the drive, but the pain in my body was getting unbearable. It started getting dark, Russ fell asleep, and the road became blurry. I stopped on the side of the road. Russ was sleeping heavily and snoring his head off, and I quietly shifted to the back of the truck. I took out a fag, opened a couple of beer bottles, and downed them in no time. I felt this intense heaviness, and my body was trembling all over. I seriously needed a wee, but Russ was completely out, and I couldn't be bothered to step over him in order to get out of the truck, so I unzipped my trousers and situated my cock over the bottle's rim, managed to keep it all in, and it even filled the bottle perfectly. I shut it back tightly and then placed it aside and tried to fall asleep.

All of a sudden, the cabin filled with the most minging smell I'd ever come across, and I could feel everything in my stomach coming up. I quickly skipped over Russ, opened the door, and jumped out. The smell wasn't coming from outside, and I realized Russ had let one rip. That was the smelliest fart I'd ever experienced in my entire life – except for my own, perhaps, but when it's mine, then it doesn't really smell bad. There's a form of acceptance of your own farts. And generally speaking, there's something about us that makes us unaware of our own foul odors.

Naturally, I didn't even think about telling him off or anything like that. I just lit a fag and waited for him to wake up.

"Hey, do you fancy driving for a bit?" I asked once he got up and came out for a piss.

"No," he replied dryly. He closed his eyes again the moment he got back in the truck.

I felt agitated and helpless. I imagined grabbing him and pulling him by the nose, kneeing his face, tossing him onto the road, and repeatedly running him over with the truck. But instead, I started the engine and continued the drive.

I smoked like a chimney and sweated my ass off, but it wasn't from the heat. My muscles were cramping and my legs felt as heavy as cement. I couldn't wait to finish the long, exhausting drive and get back home already. I got incredibly agitated – I was clucking like mad and I had no idea how long it would take to pass and if it was noticeable. 'If I weren't with Russ, everything would have turned out so differently,' I thought.

I put my hand in my jacket's inner pocket, looking for the new pack of fags, when my fingers came across something. I pulled it out and couldn't believe my eyes – a baggie with a lone, sweet little ecstasy pill, just waiting for me. Guess I'd forgotten it there at some point. I was on cloud nine. *'At least I've got something!'* I thought.

"God must love really me!" I blurted out.

Russ woke up and looked at me as though I'd gone fully bonkers, but I didn't care – I was tickled pink.

I secured the baggie back in my pocket and pulled out the pack of fags. My mind focused on the first chance I'd get to down that bad boy and spend the rest of the drive feeling sweet. 'Just a bit more to go,' I thought, 'And I'll only take it when I get proper desperate, and even then, I'll halve it and keep some for when it gets unbearable again.'

We passed by a sign advertising a little hotel nearby and Russ piped up in a chilly tone, "We should spend the night there … get some kip before tomorrow."

"You got it," I replied.

We arrived there after a few minutes and I parked the truck. Russ got out first, and I couldn't wait any longer so I took the pill out of the baggie, bit half of it off, and quickly swallowed it. I popped the other half back in the baggie and put it in my pocket.

We went in and found a sleepy-looking receptionist. Russ asked him for two rooms for the night.

"Sorry, we're pretty full up, I've got a twin room if that's all right." We had no choice but to take it.

As we walked to the room, I noticed someone who looked like a dealer – I've got a knack for that sort of thing. I saw him talking to someone and going into a room, and took a mental photo of the room number. I planned to go back there when Russ wouldn't notice it.

Once we got into the room, Russ sat down on the bed, took out a little notepad, and dialed a number. I took the opportunity to get straight in the shower. I turned on the hot water and quickly undressed, fantasizing about how I'd come out, with Russ then going in for a shower, and then I'd sprint over to room 1302 to get a gram of coke and calm myself down a bit. I looked in the mirror and my heart stopped – Russ's face was staring right at me. He was standing behind me with this evil look, like that hefty bulldog in those Disney films.

"I need a shit," he said.

I felt the veins in my neck throbbing and swelling up, with my body simmering. I stared at him for a moment longer, and then realized that I was actually better off letting him in. 'By the time he comes back out, I'd have already returned from room 1302 with my gram of coke.'

I got dressed and ran out as fast as I could. I sprinted over to room 1302, pressed my ear against the door to hear if anyone was in, and then knocked. The man from earlier opened the door, and I told him that I'd noticed him and that he seemed like a man who knew what he was doing.

"Know anywhere good for skiing on some proper white snow?" I asked. Luckily for me, the bloke was savvy and immediately asked me how much I needed. Before I even managed to reply, he went in and came back with two grams. His price was pretty steep, but I couldn't haggle considering the state I was in, so I paid him and rushed back towards the room, opening the baggie as I ran and taking a hefty hit straight out of it. I was so pleased about managing to find some gear that I wasn't even careful when I got back into the room. All of a sudden, out of nowhere, this huge hand grabbed my throat from behind, as though I were a bloody chicken about to be slaughtered. I felt myself choking and tried to put up a fight, but I couldn't move.

CHAPTER 12

I was shocked and couldn't figure out what was happening. I felt the hand tightening its grip around my throat and my eyes felt like they were about to pop out of their sockets, and then, all of a sudden, he let go of me and threw me to the floor. I looked up to see my attacker and discovered it was Russ.

"You little cunt!" he whispered venomously, "You're lucky the boss didn't allow it, cuz I'd gladly bury you underneath the tiles right here and now!" I wanted to say something, but my voice wouldn't come out. I was confused and I still didn't understand what was going on. "That's the last time you go out without telling me!" he continued, "What is it, are you some sort of batty boy?"

"What? No! Not at all!" I replied.

"Then what were you doing in room 1302?" he asked.

"I … I thought I'd recognized someone from my neighborhood, I noticed him when we were on our way to the room, but it turns out he just looks like him."

Russ gave me a suspicious look and said, "I don't care if you see your best mate, your mum, or your bloody kindergarten teacher, this is the last time you endanger yourself and whoever's working with you. What didn't you get by 'no unnecessary stops?!'"

"I'm sorry, I didn't realize it was that serious."

"Well you do now, so is that finally clear?"

"Crystal," I said.

He went back into the bathroom. I stayed on the floor for a few more minutes, then got up and lay on the bed. Even though he'd hit me, the pain I'd endured from clucking was much worse, and I was pleased about managing to get some gear. After I sniffed a line, the penny suddenly dropped about Rico's business. 'Welcome to the family, security searches, no unplanned stops on the way, getting major dosh for deliveries, no information in advance about delivery days or destinations... Of course it's not a moving company, or a legit delivery service for classified material!' But I was already sorted with my gear and finally felt relaxed, so I didn't care all that much. I was just the deliveryman, and the main thing was making as much money as I possibly could.

Russ came out of the bathroom wrapped in a towel, steam rising from his pale skin and filling the whole room. I could see his entire build, which really was humungous, and covered in black hair. I couldn't help but wonder if he'd ever had a shag in his life – and if he did, then who was the crazy woman who'd agreed to get into bed with that.

I got back in the shower and reveled in the stream of hot water, it felt like paradise. When I came out, Russ was already sprawled across the entire bed, which clarified that I'd either be sleeping on the floor or on the chair – but I didn't care! I was as far from sleep as I could possibly be. The ecstasy and the coke had worked their magic and I paced back and forth through the room all night long, restless. I was itching to get out, but I knew better after what had happened. I spent the night thinking about the long journey I still had to get through with crazy Russ, and it really bummed me out. My head was exploding with thoughts about how I could get that hairy lump of flesh to loosen up, when suddenly I had a brilliant idea – a foolproof plan! I waited for morning to come with bated breath.

At six o'clock, while Russ was still snoring away, I called reception and ordered room service. "Two coffees with lots of sugar, and two chocolate croissants please."

Once they brought up our breakfast, I laid it out on the table, popped the lid off Russ's paper cup, sprinkled half an ecstasy inside his coffee, added sugar, and stirred the hell out of it, then popped the lid back on and woke him up.

"Hey, mate," I said, "Sorry but I didn't get a wink of sleep at night, I've got a terrible toothache and I have to find a pharmacy to get some painkillers."

Russ opened his eyes, looked at me suspiciously, and immediately sat up. "Toothache's the worst, innit," he muttered as he stretched his arms and yawned.

"Yeah... I ordered room service for us, just some coffee and a couple of croissants, that way we can leave quickly."

He went over to the table, devoured a croissant in two bites and downed his coffee as though it were a glass of water. "Bitter coffee, that," he said and then pointed at the other croissant.

"Help yourself mate, I can't," I said and pointed at my allegedly aching tooth.

Russ ravaged the second croissant and started getting dressed. I was as pleased as punch – the mission was complete and all I had to do was wait. We got ready and hit the road, and I waited patiently for the pill to take effect. I assumed it would take a while, considering Russ had just eaten and food usually delays the effect, but after about thirty minutes of silence, it began.

"Stop the truck," he said.

I stopped by the pavement and anxiously asked, "What's the matter?!"

He pointed at the other side of the street. "There's a pharmacy over there, you said you had a toothache, innit?"

"That ... that's right, yeah," I stuttered, frightened by the fact I'd almost forgotten my own lie.

I went into the pharmacy. Luckily, there were only two people ahead of me in the queue and I got to the counter pretty quickly. I bought some painkillers and a bottle of water and went back to the truck. Just as I got in, Russ was turning the air-conditioning on. "I don't know what's the matter with me, I've got currents all through my body, like heatwaves, it's bizarre, and everything looks weird."

"Maybe you should have a drink of water?" I suggested in an innocent tone and handed him the bottle.

"Thanks! That's spot on mate, that beer was warm as hell and it smelled like donkey piss," he said and pointed at the now-empty beer bottle I'd taken a wee in.

I quickly tossed it out the window and calmly said, "Oh, minging, it's probably off or something." I thanked my lucky stars that Russ was out of focus – he'd have murdered me if he found out he'd gulped my own piss down.

"Thank you so much," he said, "Listen, I know I've been tough on you, but don't take it personally, I just have to be like that with this type of work. Plus, your Laurel and Hardy joke was uncalled for."

"I really am sorry, that was messed up, I didn't mean it," I said.

"Never mind that, you're a good lad, I just don't have the patience for tactless people. Let me teach you something about life and about people – a man has to trust his instincts. Some people feel wrong to you the moment you meet them, so don't try to change the way you feel. You messed up straight off the bat, so you gotta let time do its thing, innit. We'll either connect eventually, or we won't. Don't be scared of long silences, just learn to go with the flow, just be. In your case, you really didn't mean to mess up, but some people are asses and you'll let them slide at first, but then they'll mess up again and you'll let that slide too, and you'll end up spending loads of time with them while accumulating more and more frustration, and with time, your stomach will get bloated from all the baggage and it'll end up exploding all over the place. I'm sure you know a few dickheads that you bear a grudge against. Just have a good long think about how good it would feel to let it out and tell them what you really think about them. After that, they'll either fuck off out of your life, or they'll sort themselves out and get with the program."

I nodded my head absentmindedly. I found his philosophical musings a bit intense at that point in time.

"In any case," he continued his words of wisdom, "You always feel a lot better once everything's out in the open. You might end up with less mates, or even completely alone. But people come and go, and the most important thing is for you to feel good about yourself, with or without them. There are millions of people and places, and you'll end up exactly where you're supposed to be, with whoever's supposed to be there with you. You feel me?"

"Of course," I replied. He had no idea how much I truly felt him. Truth be told, I was a bit jealous. I'd have loved to get inside his head. It's moments like these that make me think that drugs like MDMA and ecstasy should be legal, moments where a measly half a pill can open up an entire communication channel. If the leaders of the world took some ecstasy before their negotiations, everything would get resolved in no time and there'd be world peace. On the other hand, wars bring in lots of dosh, and lack of communication helps leaders create fear so that they can control their subjects more easily. "You're a very wise man!" I flattered Russ.

"It doesn't matter does it, everyone still takes me for a joker," he replied. "I don't give a toss about what other people think of me. At the end of the day, anyone who tries to judge me always ends up crawling back on their knees to beg for their lives."

"I don't get it," I said.

"Better off that way. You ain't got nothing to worry about, you're a good lad. Pull over for a minute," he said, and I veered to the side and stopped the truck. "Give us a squeeze, mate!" he said as he pulled me in for a bear hug, "I swear, you remind me of my little nephew, Arnold."

I was ready to burst out laughing at that very moment, but I managed to restrain myself. I'd have paid anything to have my mates watch this spectacle – especially Tommy.

"The best thing is to be real. I don't understand what's happening to me!" he suddenly sat up straight and stared at me in a strange way, "Did you slip something in my coffee?!"

"Two sugars," I replied timidly.

"I don't know what's come over me, it's inexplicable, I guess my stomach's full to the brim with baggage. Don't judge a book by its cover, eh? Beneath all this size and toughness is a sensitive heart that just wants to let loose every now and again, and I constantly have to restrain it, you know?"

"Yeah, yeah," I said while starting the engine and getting back on the road. "It's all good, let it all out, mate," I added.

"It's not easy," he went on, "With birds, for example – I'm not attractive and I ain't got a normal job. And the birds who fancy me aren't the kind of birds I'd want raising my kids, you know? What about you, you got a love of your own?"

"I do," I said, "I have a love of my own, but we're not together right now. She's all I ever wanted in this life, that's why I'm working this job."

"Oh, all right, so you're not a poof, then," he laughed.

"No, I'm not a poof!" I replied.

"Iggy, I want us to start with a clean slate. Just to be clear, no matter how close we get, work always comes before anything else, so don't mess it up, yeah?"

"How would I mess it up?" I asked, genuinely intrigued.

"Anything that would make a royal mess of things, all right? That's all I can tell you; you feel me?"

I thought I did, but what sort of mess was he talking about? I really wanted to understand, but I was scared of getting information out of him that he'd regret later on, so I just nodded my head and turned the radio on to get some good vibes going. They were playing these old love songs, and he closed his eyes and surrendered to the sounds and the emotions. I occasionally glanced over to make sure he was all right. He seemed deep in thought, and at some point, he opened his eyes and asked me to stop the truck so that he could walk for a bit. Guess the speed was rushing through his body and he needed to let it out somehow.

Russ walked alongside the truck for about an hour, looking like an oversized twelve-year-old. Once he got tired, he motioned for me to let him back on. "I'm thirsty!" he moaned in a childish tone.

I stifled my urge to laugh and told him we'd stop at the next café, which was about an hour away according to the map. Russ closed his eyes, and only opened them again once I'd stopped the truck by the roadside caff.

He was blatantly coming down by the time we got a table. The ecstasy was wearing off and he was incredibly hungry, judging by the amount of burgers, pasta, salads, and garlic bread he'd ordered and then proceeded to guzzle down within seconds. Once he was full, he turned to me and said in an overly soft tone, "Iggy, look me in the eye and tell me you didn't put anything in my coffee or in the croissants. I'm giving you my word – I won't do nothing to you, just tell me the truth."

I thought I was a dead man. I stayed silent for a long while and felt his eyes piercing straight through me. "I asked you something, so answer me!" he growled.

The blood froze through my veins, but I managed to mumble in a trembling voice, "Russ, I didn't put anything in your coffee or in the croissants."

"In that case, listen," he said, the suspicion immediately evaporating from his eyes, luckily for me, "I don't know how to explain this, But I've never experienced anything like I did today. Like some sort of spiritual awakening. I enjoyed every second of it. I don't know – and I don't want to know – if you put anything in my coffee, but let's be clear about one thing: no matter what happens and what sort of status we'll end up reaching in this life, nothing about what happened here today is leaving your mouth, is that clear?"

"Crystal," I replied.

'I really am a lucky fucker,' I thought. 'First of all, considering how well he took it, otherwise I'd have ended up in the hospital and then they'd have run some blood tests and figured it out straight away. In fact, I took a real chance without even knowing whether he'd ever taken drugs before. If he did, then he'd have realized it very quickly and would have probably killed me, then chopped me up into little pieces, and had me for lunch. But, luckily for me, everything went smoothly, which just goes to show that risks are worth taking every now and then.'

From that moment on, the rest of the ride was brilliant. The ice had thoroughly melted between us and we continued talking about life, he even told me about how Rico had saved him back when he was a kid. I told him about Angie, and he gave me some proper surprising tips about romantic relationships. I occasionally sniffed a line without him noticing, and we eventually reached our destination. We called up our client – Thurman was his name – and marked the map according to the directions he gave us.

We arrived at the location and after a few minutes, a few more cars showed up and led us to a huge hangar nearby. There were no signs around, nothing but a vast, spacious, empty hangar. We all turned our engines off, I handed Russ the form Rico had given me, and we got out of the truck. Another truck arrived and a massive bloke got out of it. Russ whispered to me that it was Thurman. He came over, they shook hands and Russ introduced us. Thurman shook my hand and motioned for Russ to come with him. Russ motioned for me to stay put, and I complied. They spoke amongst themselves and I kept an eye on the truck. I even counted the people present, just like Rico had instructed me – there were five men standing behind Thurman, and then he motioned for them to go to the truck. Russ waved at me to go with them, and I opened the back doors as three of them got on and started unloading the crates. The other two stood next to me and counted along with me, just like Rico had said they would. I kept my patience and counted the seventy crates that were unloaded, same as what was stated on the delivery form. Thurman's men shut the doors, locked them, and handed me the keys. Their truck was parked right in front of ours, and they started loading everything into it. Once they were finished, they shut their own truck's doors and locked them, while Thurman and Russ approached us. Thurman's men nodded to him that everything was fine, and he gestured for two of them to go to his car. In the meantime, Russ stood next to me and waited for them to come back. They returned with four suitcases which they placed next to us, and two envelopes which they handed to Thurman.

Thurman came up and thanked us. Russ thanked him and whispered for me to do the same, so I did. The two of us remained there until Thurman and his men went back to their vehicles and left.

After that, Russ loosened back up and grinned at me. "That's it! All good, we can make a move!"

We grabbed the suitcases, got in the truck, and started our journey back. Russ looked at me, a sense of relief in his eyes, and tossed an envelope onto my lap. I ripped it open with one hand, and when I saw the amount of notes stuffed inside it, my hand slipped off the steering wheel and I hit the brakes.

"Seriously? Does this seem like the right timing to almost kill us, mate?" he chuckled.

We counted the envelopes – there was four thousand quid there, two thousand for each of us.

"Two thousand quid!" I screamed, "Is it for me?!"

"Of course!" he replied, and I was on cloud nine. "You best get used to it and all, you'll be seeing a lot more where that came from," he promised me. "I just hope you'll be smart enough not to waste it all on rubbish, because you never know what tomorrow brings, son, and you should always put something aside for a rainy day."

"I'm stunned, I don't know what to say. What have I been doing all this time?!"

"Listen mate, you've got a real place in my heart now, and I don't want to sound like I'm preaching to you or nothing, but my suggestion is that maybe now that you have a proper job, then you can wise up and stop messing around, you feel me?" he said and tapped his finger on his nose, raising his eyebrows.

"How did you know?" I asked.

"We know everything, and if you hang in there and get deeper into the business, you'll get to know a lot of things too. And now – we're going to celebrate!"

"Celebrate… what?" I asked.

"Life! Every day is a gift, son. Celebrate a job done well, celebrate … our manhood!" he said and pointed at his groin.

"And what about love?" I asked.

"Love's the world's greatest illusion, but we'll celebrate that too, if you insist."

The way back home was the absolute best – the cherry on top, if you will. We stopped at nightclubs and Russ turned out to be a proper party animal. Every place we went to, they literally pulled out all the stops for him. All the birds working the bars knew him and threw themselves at him. He danced like a maniac and scattered fifty-quid notes all around like there was no tomorrow – which wasn't quite in line with what he'd told me only hours earlier about saving up for a rainy day. 'Guess he's got his rainy days covered by now,' I thought.

In one of the clubs, he got a stripper to sit on his face for fifteen minutes straight, spending around three hundred quid on her alone. Every time she wanted to get up, he pulled out another twenty note. I'd had a few shots by then, as well as some lovely lines, so I felt comfortable enough to tell him he was wasting both his money and his time on her. I came up to him as another bird was hanging over his neck and shouted into his ear, "Hey, aren't you better off taking her back to the hotel for a shag rather than waste all that dosh just to keep her round your neck?"

The bird heard me too and immediately backed off from Russ. She looked me straight in the eye, surprised me with a rattling slap to the face, and walked away. Russ burst out laughing. "That's no way to behave, Iggy," he said as he wiped his sweaty face. "Listen, shagging ain't the main thing, I enjoy the foreplay much more, and I like making them feel good about themselves, just like they do for me. They don't judge me and I don't judge them, we're just having fun. To be fair, I'm kind of like their whore too."

"But you're the man with the millions," I said.

"Each with their own advantage in life. She's got something I like, and I've got something she likes."

To be honest, he was right. I could really connect with his way of thinking, and I felt bad for having judged her. I suddenly thought about Manu and realized how humiliating it was to get slapped by a bird.

Russ was drunk and staggered on his way to the stage, motioning for one of the birds to come closer. He whispered something in her ear, stuffed a fifty-quid note down her knickers, and she turned her head and looked straight at me. 'What could he have told her about me?' I wondered as she started approaching me. She looked fit as hell, wearing this tiny, see-through, black lingerie top, a slim G-string, and a pair of heels that could kill a man. She marched up to me with conviction and pressed herself against me, staring into my eyes with a look that could make steel melt. That got me mad horny! She neared her lips to mine and stuck her tongue in my mouth, and I loved the way she tasted.

We kissed for ages, and then she led me to a quiet corner with armchairs. She shoved me onto one, sat on top of me, ripped open a condom with her teeth, and within seconds I was already inside her.

I remember my cock remaining as hard as a rock even after I came. I just wanted more and more until there was nothing left in me and I felt completely emptied. When it was all over and the high started coming down, my conscience started bothering me and I thought about Angie. I felt horrible and empty.

I stumbled around awkwardly looking for Russ, and found him sprawled over one of the armchairs like a bloody ostrich, face down under the cushion. I woke him up and said, "We better make a move."

"So you shagged her and now you feel all empty inside, eh?" he asked, stretching his arms out.

"Yeah," I replied.

"That's because you're in a rush. Sometimes you just have to enjoy being in the company of a woman – and that goes for all people, actually. Don't waste all your energy in one go, keep your force inside you, trust me – next time just try it like that and you'll feel like you own the world. Just like I do."

"So … everything that happened here stays between us, yeah?" I asked. Russ nodded his head.

After that, we were so hungover that we spent the whole day in our hotel room. Room service came in and out with trays of food and coffee, and we kept downing the painkillers I'd gotten at the pharmacy. We mainly slept, and once we felt sufficiently refreshed, we continued our journey home. The ride was relaxed, and we continued talking about life. Russ kept surprising me with his wisdom and street smarts. He was intrigued by my life, and asked why I wasn't at uni or learning some sort of vocation to get me somewhere in life. I explained that I'd hardly managed to get through school as it was, and even that was only thanks to Andy and his fake report cards.

"I can't be bothered with studying," I said, "And to be honest, nothing seems interesting enough for me to dedicate myself to it, except my love for Angie."

He laughed. "But you're still young, what else do you want to achieve in life?"

"I want to be rich, but not just generically rich – I want to be a millionaire!" I exclaimed.

"Yeah, all right, money's a good thing, but it's a means – if you don't know what to do with it, then it just crumbles between your fingers. Try to figure out what you'd do with it, what you like doing, and maybe you'll find out that you don't need to be a millionaire in order to lead a satisfying life. Being a millionaire is wicked, but it comes with a heavy price, and the question is – how far are you willing to go in order to get there?"

"As far as it takes!" I declared, and then added, "And you, are you doing what you love?"

"Son, I'm doing what I was born to do. I was young and no one bothered to stop and ask me, I was told what to do. I entered this job's world head first, and trust me, there's no going back for me. But you, you've only just dipped your toes in the water, you're young and you still have a chance to do something with your life, maybe learn a trade to make a career out of. I'm telling you, from personal experience, if you don't do it, then you might regret it when you're older."

"All right, thanks for that, but I don't really believe in learning from other people's experience," I replied. "I don't mind listening, but I believe that everyone has their own uniqueness. If you give ten different people the same utensils, ingredients, and quantities, and ask them all to make you an omelet, it'll still come out different for each of them, because everyone does it with their own unique energy. So if you've failed at something, go ahead and tell me about it, I'd love to hear it, but it won't turn me off doing the exact same thing myself, because our end results will always differ. I like trying to do things the way I feel is right for me, and if I get it wrong or fail, then at least I tried. I think it's better to encourage someone rather than to fill them with doubts. What's the worst that could happen? Worst case scenario – I'll fall, get up, and move on."

"You're smart, but you're still young and innocent, and one day you'll realize that some things are irreversible, and that there's no going back from them."

"Yeah, I know," I said, "Tommy, my best mate, always says that there are three things you can never go back from – the day you're born, the day you bring a child into the world, and the day you die."

"I like that one, but let me embellish that a bit," he said. "The day you're born – yeah, no control over that one. But having babies is a choice to be made, there are stages to the pregnancy where you can still decide to change your mind! And death – well, if you don't take good care of yourself, then it might happen faster than you'd like it to!"

"I'm not sure I want to bring children into this world," I replied, "I know it might be too early on for me to say that. And as for death – each to their own fate, I'm not scared of dying, I'm scared of living a shitty life! And the way I see it, fifty-quid notes are a foolproof ticket into the good life!"

Russ took a deep breath and smiled. "The way you talk makes me think that this job may very well be a good start for you in getting all those fifties you're after. I really wish you all the best, son."

I now understand everything Russ had said that day much better than I did at the time. But I was so intoxicated by the amount of money in my pocket and by how easy it was to get it that I actually thought he was being a bit arrogant. In hindsight, turns out that I was the arrogant one, believing I'd be the one percent who'd manage to make it big time.

By the time we reached London, it had already gone dark. Russ told me we were going to meet Rico at the Patricia Club – one of the city's most elegant venues and the one with the most meticulous selection at the door – only the certified elite were allowed to enter. Our wettest dream as youngsters was to get in there one day, and when that name came out of Russ's mouth, I swear I felt shivers running down my spine. I was itching to call up my mates and tell them to meet me at the entrance, but I didn't dare ask him about it. I felt like I was making a dream come true, and I couldn't believe that I was wearing jeans and a dirty top and reeking after hours of driving.

"Any chance we could pop around my place for a quick change of clothes?"

"No bloody way! Get it in your thick head already – the job only ends after you meet Rico … only then are you free to go back to your life. And don't worry, you'll get plenty more chances to make an appearance and impress everyone. Just remember – it doesn't matter how well you dress, it's all about your confidence. That's the real deal right there," he said as he poured some water from the bottle into his palm and smoothed it into his hair.

"Then why do you wear all those expensive suits, and why are you fixing your hair?" I asked.

"I can afford to do that now. But back when we were young and had only just started making a name for ourselves, we went through all the clubs wearing jeans and white vests, and we'd still go home with the fittest birds. Never mind, you'll see once we get there."

We reached the Patricia Club and Russ told me to park the truck on the pavement, right outside the entrance to the club. "Security will keep an eye on it," he explained.

We grabbed the suitcases and walked towards the entrance, which was packed full of gorgeous people trying to get in. Russ walked in front of me and made sure they cleared a path for us to get in. All eyes were on us and I felt like some sort of film star. Within seconds, we reached the selector, who immediately gave Russ a little squeeze. When he said hi to me, I suddenly realized what Russ had talked about – I looked like a laborer, but I felt like a bloody king.

We walked in and I discovered the most beautiful place I'd ever seen. The DJ booth was suspended in mid-air, and the entire place was filled with lush furniture, even the peeling walls were part of the décor. Everything looked rich, and I'd never seen such a huge amount of fit women before. It was as though someone had driven a truck through the city streets, loading all of London's most gorgeous women onto it and bringing them straight there.

"They should change the club's name to Paradise!" I shouted excitedly to Russ.

He looked at me and chuckled, "You'll get used to it after a while."

I didn't mind getting used to that sort of thing at all. *I've spent my whole life being used to seeing the ugly bits, so I'm more than willing to get used to the fit bits now,'* I thought.

Russ led the way and I followed him around the bar and behind it. We went down a few stairs which led to a narrow, tunnel-like corridor with little rooms on both sides, and we reached a heavy wooden door. Russ knocked, and the bloke who opened it recognized him straight away, but gave me a funny look.

"This is Iggy," Russ told him.

"I'm Jean," he said in a thick French accent, "Rico is waiting for you in there," he added and motioned with his hand at a door on the other end of the room.

We walked into another room; it looked like a massive, upscale office. Rico was sitting behind a desk and got up to give us a warm welcome. I have to say that nighttime Rico looked even better than daytime Rico – he was wearing a lush black suit with a buttoned black shirt underneath, and sported a gold watch on his wrist that seemed well expensive. He hugged us and led us to his desk. There was a table in the corner of the room with three men sitting around it and playing cards. They nodded at us and one of them got up and took the suitcases off our hands, placing them on Rico's desk.

Rico opened the suitcases and gave a huge smile. When he was done inspecting them, he nodded to the bloke, who then closed them and resumed his card game. We sat down in front of Rico as he opened a box of cigars and handed them to us. "Cuban originals," he said.

I was so impressed by how powerful he was that I thought – *'That's precisely how I want to be when I'm older. He looks like the happiest man in the world.'*

"You two look bloody knackered," he said.

"Knackered, yeah, but mainly chuffed," Russ replied.

Rico chuckled and turned to me. "So, Iggy, how was it?"

"It was ... interesting," I said.

"Interesting? Interesting is good. We should celebrate 'interesting,' shouldn't we," he said and pressed a button on the phone set on his desk. "Come in," he said and released the button.

Within a minute, one of the most beautiful women in the world walked into the room. She had the face of an angel, long black hair and tanned skin, red lipstick, and a body that looked like God's greatest masterpiece. She wore these tiny shorts and a plain white vest, and she looked like the hottest, fittest woman that had ever lived – and I'd seen my fair share of fit birds by that point, but she was something else. She was holding a tray in one hand and a pen in the other, ready to take down our drinks order, and the moment she looked at me, I literally stopped breathing. There was something about her eyes that was so intense that I was genuinely hypnotized.

"Bring us a bottle of Macallan Pinerolo and some glasses," he told her and she rushed back out. "It's a rare scotch from 1939," Rico explained, "Do you drink, Iggy?"

"Every now and again, just a touch," I said.

"And what do you think of this place?" he continued.

"It's paradise!" I replied, "If I had a place like this, I'd just be sitting there wiping my ass with fifty-quid notes!"

Rico chuckled. "It ain't so nice, that, trust me, I've tried – the note's edges scraped my asshole and it burned for a bloody week!" Everyone burst out laughing at the King's banter.

I was so jealous of him. It must feel crazy for someone to know that they can do whatever the hell they want, and it only takes a whistle for them to make everyone around stand to attention. That's what it's like when you've got the dosh – the power's in your hands. At that moment, I realized Angie was right when she'd said we had to get off the drugs and the purging if we wanted to make it in this life – Rico reminded me of Tony Montana from *Scarface*, only he was clean. I felt like I was in the right place, and I had to get clean as soon as possible in order to make my dreams come true.

The gorgeous bird came back into the room carrying a tray with a bottle of scotch and glasses. She put everything on the desk and started pouring, and I couldn't take my eyes off her. I also couldn't help but wonder why she was working as a waitress. '*How can it be that no one's discovered her yet and made her a star?*' In any case, she intrigued the hell out of me. When she handed me a glass, I couldn't help myself and said, "Sorry if I'm overstepping, but you're the most beautiful girl I've ever seen."

She smiled at me politely and muttered a brief, "Thanks," then immediately shifted her gaze towards Rico.

"Is that all right, me saying that?" I asked.

Rico smiled and said, "Of course it is, if you didn't, then we'd think there was something wrong with you!" Everyone laughed again and he motioned for her to leave, which she promptly did.

"You've got good taste in women, Iggy. Now we just need to work on your taste in clothes and you'll be right as rain."

"Yeah," I said and waved my envelope, "I'm on it."

"By the way," he added, "When your mum was that bird's age, she was much more beautiful." He then turned to Russ and explained, "His mum had all the blokes wrapped around her little finger, that naughty gal."

I don't know why, but that embarrassed me. I felt like I was a volcano about to erupt. Still, I managed to restrain myself and gave a goofy smile. "Sorry, I can't think about my mum in those terms," I said sheepishly.

"Of course not," he went on, "What sort of sicko would think about his mum like that? I surely wouldn't! Would you?" he asked Russ, who immediately shook his head and contorted his face in disgust. "And you?" he then turned to the fellas playing cards in the corner, who shook their heads too. It felt like he was putting on a show at my expense. "Your mum's still fit, to this day…" he kept going, but I couldn't listen to it anymore and interrupted him.

"I'd really rather not talk about my mum, if that's all right with you."

"Of course it is, no problem, Iggy. One day, you and I will have a proper chat about it all," he said with a wink.

I was stressing, and Russ motioned for me to calm down. It seemed like Rico was trying to piss me off on purpose. I grabbed my glass and downed it in one gulp. Rico refilled it and I downed the second one too. I felt the urge to go to the loo and sniff a couple of lines to calm myself, but then that beautiful waitress came back in, and I fixed my eyes on her – blatantly, this time, since I was looser after the scotch shots, and also because I'd noticed that my staring at her was getting on Rico's nerves, and I was buzzing about having found that man's weakness. Russ noticed the atmosphere becoming tense and patted me on the back. "He's a bit tipsy, our lad, just mucking about, ain't he."

Rico laughed and announced, "No one's leaving till we empty this bottle, and that includes you," he told the waitress, who remained where she stood, stiff and motionless.

I had about six glasses and felt super loose and buzzing. I tried to chat her up, but she wasn't having it. "And what's her name?" I asked Rico and Russ as I pointed at her.

"I'm not a mannequin, I can talk for myself."

Rico burst out laughing and exclaimed, "A talking mannequin!" and we all joined and laughed. He went on to say that I have something magical about me that always works on the ladies, something about my innocence and simplicity that just turns them on. I thought that the beautiful girl actually fancied me, and that if Rico wasn't around, she'd have tried to pull me and all. Rico seemed to have noticed that too, and he said, "The bottle's finished, and so is my time. I need to get back to work. Oh, and this is for you two," he added and pulled out two parcels from a drawer, placing them in front of me and Russ. "Consider it a bonus, Iggy, and a good start – here's to new beginnings!"

"I love beginnings!" I called out.

Russ and I grabbed a parcel each, and I quickly put mine in my jacket pocket. I was proper wasted, and Russ helped me get up and walk towards the door, where he leaned in and whispered in my ear, "You're messing up, son!"

Before I'd even managed to retort, Rico asked me to hang back for a minute. Russ gave me a strange look and left the office, and I stayed standing there on my own. Rico lifted the receiver and said, "Tell Milly to come to the office," then hung up. After a brief moment, a girl came into the room. "Milly, this is Iggy," Rico introduced us, "I want you to treat him as though he were me!"

Milly nodded her head and held onto my hand. She led me out the door before I could even thank Rico. We went into a room that looked like a dressing room, and she just started undressing and kissing me and taking my clothes off, but then I remembered everything I'd felt back at that other club with Russ and everything he'd told me about energy and that, so I stopped her and said, "You're gorgeous, but I really can't right now."

"Don't worry, you'll be up for it in a minute," she said and continued stroking me. It felt wrong and I gently pushed her off me, "What's the deal, are you a prossy?"

Milly looked bummed out. "What's the deal, are you a poof?"

"No! Of course not!" I replied.

"Are you a copper, then?"

"Listen, I'm not a copper or a poof, I work for Rico in deliveries. And you're stunning, but I'm fine right now and I'm not up for it. I'm not a bloody machine, and you're not either, but don't worry, we'll act like we did it and it was wicked," I said and pulled out a couple of fifty notes from the envelope. "Will that do?" I asked.

She grabbed the dosh and put her clothes back on. "And you won't say nothing to Rico?"

"I'll tell him you were one of the best I've ever had," I promised.

She stuffed the notes in her bra, when suddenly a bloke appeared behind her – one of the three playing cards in Rico's office.

"Milly, what's happening?" he asked.

She went all tense and looked frightened. "Everything's fine."

"Are you just blabbering away or are you gonna fuck him?"

"It's all good, mate, you're interrupting our foreplay," I intervened. He glared at us and left the room.

"Don't worry, I promise you, everything will be all right," I calmed her.

Milly smiled and said, "I need to get back before I get into trouble." I asked her if she fancied a line, but she said no, gave me a hug, and left the room. I quickly went out to the hallway and called her name. She stopped and turned around.

"What's that beautiful waitress's name, the black-haired one with the red lippy?" I asked.

"There's a few of them round here, dunno which one you mean, just ask her when you see her."

She disappeared and I went back into the room to calm down. The scotch did my head in and I was feeling loopy. I sat down and smoked a fag, and then pulled out all the money Rico had given me and slowly counted it. I had 3900 quid, after having given Milly a hundred, and I was in seventh heaven. I'd never had that much money in my hands. It gave me the confidence and drive to devour the whole world! I put the parcel of dosh back in my pocket and checked to make sure I still had the envelope from Thurman. I took the coke out to cut a couple of lines, but I was so wasted and full of conviction about not doing drugs anymore that I decided against it, and tossed the baggie on the table in front of me. I looked around and saw a telephone on the other end of the table. I thought it would be wicked if Tommy could come to the club, so I lifted the receiver and dialed Angie's number by mistake.

"Hello?" she picked up the phone.

I was stunned. That wasn't the voice I was expecting, and I had no idea how I'd managed to dial her number instead of Tommy's. My heart was racing and I tried to get myself together so that she wouldn't realize I was stoned.

"What's up?" I asked.

"I'm fine, where are you? You all right?"

"Yeah, I'm all good. Listen, Angie, I started working at this job – a proper one – and I'm getting clean, I swear, and I made loads of dosh... Can you hear me?"

"Is that right? Wow, well done, where are you working then?"

"That's just it, I took your advice and got my mum to sort me out..." Before I managed to finish the sentence, two birds came into the room and started giggling when they saw me. I didn't want Angie to think they were with me, so I turned my back to them and continued the phone call. "Can you hear me?"

"Yeah, what is that, where are you?"

"That's what I'm telling you," I started explaining when one of the girls came up behind me and asked, "Is that coke? Can we have some?"

"What the fuck?!" I screamed at her, but it was too late. Angie had heard it all and immediately hung up. The girls freaked out and ran out of the room, and I wanted to die right there and then. I dialed Angie's number again but she wouldn't pick up the phone, so I called Tommy, who luckily answered straight away. I told him where I was and asked him to get dressed and come by ASAP. I also told him not to worry and that I had money for a cab and all.

"There in twenty!" he said excitedly and hung up.

But I was as bummed as could be. "This is the worst luck ever! How did this shitty timing come about?" I mumbled to myself as I stepped out to wait for Tommy by the bar near the entrance, but I wanted to stop by Rico's office first so I could thank him for everything. Jean, the security guy, wasn't there, so I kept walking till I reached the door to his office, which was slightly open. I raised my hand in order to knock, but then I looked through the crack and saw the beautiful waitress and Rico standing close to each other near his desk and talking. Instead of turning around and walking away, I got so curious that I stayed there and silently watched them, just like I used to do to my parents when I was a kid.

"You're doing it out of spite, because of her," he said.

"That's not true," she replied defensively.

"Of course you are, you were eyeing him up. You fancy him, don't you?"

"Of course not, why would I fancy him? He's a kid, he's nowhere near you."

"Why are you lying?"

"I swear, he's not even my taste."

'They're talking about me,' I thought.

"Then who is?"

"You!"

"No, except for me. Go on, girl, speak your mind, who's your taste? I'm just curious, is all."

"Rico, you're the only one! I swear!" she said and started sobbing.

"Then how come you're crying? Are you scared of me?"

She shook her head in fright, and he put his hand on her head and stroked her hair. "Then what is it?"

"I love you, and I'm scared you don't believe me."

"Then you are scared of me!" he said and grabbed her by the hair, causing her to shriek in pain. "People who are scared are usually lying!" he exclaimed.

"I ain't lying, I swear, please, you're hurting me!"

"That's nothing compared to the pain you're causing me, making eyes at other fellas right under my nose."

"Rico, that's not true…" she whispered in pain as he pressed her face against the desk.

"Then show me, show me how much you love me, go on then," he said as he pulled her shorts down, "You don't give me enough credit, do you?! I can't leave her, she's been with me for yonks, but I still give you everything, don't I?!"

I was horrified and felt completely torn up inside. On the one hand, I wanted to go in there and protect her, but on the other hand, I really wanted to get away. Either way, I found myself frozen in place and couldn't budge. She was obviously suffering and he was proper abusing her. Once he got her knickers off, he turned her around and had his way with her, viciously.

"Is that what you want, girl?" he whispered in her ear.

She groaned with pain, and I felt like I was going to be sick. I was so confused by what I was seeing. I felt bad for being so high at that moment. I'd have clearly acted differently if I were sober, but everything just whirled inside my mind. I was genuinely appalled, but also a bit turned on. I felt disgusted by the thoughts and feelings going through my body and my mind.

Rico picked up the pace, becoming even more brutal as he pressed her face down against the desk's glass top, until it wasn't clear if she was groaning because of being shagged that hard or because of her head chafing over the glass.

And then, all at once, he just stopped and leaned down onto her for a few seconds. Then he stood back up and calmly lifted his trousers. "Did you come?" he asked her. She nodded her head and forced a smile. Rico walked away from her as she got up and put her knickers and shorts on, looking humiliated and in pain. "Come here," he said.

She walked up to him, he looked her right in the eye and asked, "What do you love about me?"

"Everything," she replied.

He gave a huge, satisfied grin, pulled a few notes out of his pocket, and stuffed them in her shorts. "I'm crazy about you, you psycho!" he said and she smiled at him.

At that point, I really wanted to get the hell away, but I still couldn't get myself to move. That whole experience had thrown me back to my childhood, and the high wasn't exactly helping me get my energy back. Even when I saw her walking up to the door, I still remained planted in my spot, and she opened the door and screamed in fright. We looked at each other with surprised gazes, and then she just ran off and disappeared down the corridor. The door stayed open and I just stood there, like a thief caught red-handed.

Rico looked at me chillingly. "You one of those who come fast?" he asked.

"What?" I asked weakly.

"With Milly – that was pretty quick, wasn't it?"

The words jumbled in my mind. "No... I mean, yeah, she was ace! And I just came by to thank you, but you two were... and... so I couldn't, so I'm waiting for a mate... he should be here any minute. And I just want you to know that there's someone I really love and we're planning on getting married, gonna have kids and a family and all that, so that whole thing with that bird, I didn't know you two were... when you were talking about my mum..." Everything came out jumbled and confused, and all I wanted was to step onto a landmine and be wiped off the face of the planet!

"What's her name?" he asked.

"I don't know," I replied.

"The woman you love."

"Oh, Angie."

"Angie, Angel, nice name. You know, I had this German bird once called Angel. She was gorgeous and we had a wicked time together, but she barely spoke any English so we had a hard time communicating, and how much fucking can a man do, eh? At the end of the day, you want a proper relationship, don't you? I had an American Angie, a Belgian Angelique, a Russian bombshell called Angelina. I've had a whole alphabet of women, a whole bloody flock of birds, and you?"

"Me, what?" I asked.

"How many women have you been with?"

I was embarrassed by his question, and even more so by the truth, since I hadn't really been with that many women. "Oh… not that many, me," I stuttered, "Umm… you know… I never really counted, eh? But probably … dunno … twenty, maybe," I lied.

"Virgin!" he cried out and laughed, "Just say you're a virgin! Twenty women's still a virgin! When I was your age, I'd already passed the hundred mark. Let me tell you something about women… Women, the minute you start being kind to them, they lose interest in you and start playing you like a toy. A real man should always keep his cool and show them who's in charge. Never be scared of losing them! That goes for all the people and everything in your life – never be scared of losing anything – even your own life, if it goes against your principles. Now, shut the door behind you, good night."

"Good night," I said and got out, heading straight over to the bar near the entrance. I was shaken up by that last experience and continued thinking about Rico. 'How many contradictions can one man possess? If a man lives his life feeling like he's never scared of losing anything, then he probably doesn't genuinely care about anything either, which means he's not in touch with his feelings. So what on earth is he doing using the word 'family?' And what the hell is his deal with my mum?!'

CHAPTER 13

I snorted a bit straight out of the baggie, just to calm myself. I took comfort in the thought that even with all the damaged scum I'd met that week, I still had Angie, who was the purest thing in the world. Deep down, I knew that she still loved me, and that if I showed her that I was fighting for us, she'd never give up on me. That motivated me to keep doing whatever I could until I got enough dosh to make our dreams come true.

More than twenty minutes passed, or maybe even a few hours; I'd lost track of time. People started leaving the venue and there was no sign of Tommy. I went outside. The sun was out and I was wasted, so I stopped a cab and went home. I got into bed, and only then did I start processing everything that had happened between Rico and that waitress, and between me and Milly. How could it be that I stayed silent about those things? Why wasn't I shaken up like a normal person? There was rape there, and from what I could tell, there was sex trafficking too.

We were just raised in an environment where it was normal for a man to abuse a woman. Almost every other woman in our neighborhood had been abused. And it wasn't just the men who found it acceptable, it was the women too – that's how the world worked in their minds. I remember this one night, after one of my parents' wild fights, I saw my mum in the kitchen with bruises on her face and hands, and it was a routine thing. She was crying and drinking, and I came up to hug her, but she pushed me away.

"Stop it, leave me alone, Iggy."

"I don't want to leave you alone!"

She ignored me and kept on crying and drinking, and I just sat there and watched her, so she looked at me and said something I'd never forget – "I hate him because he doesn't love me, and I hate myself because I love him. And that's why I don't deserve for him to love me, but I need his love so badly! Do you get it? No, you don't, you're a child, and you don't know anything about life and love!"

She then got up and went to her room, crying her eyes out, and that sentence continued echoing in my mind. "You're a child, and you don't know anything about life and love."

So on the one hand, it was clear to me that what had happened there was bad, but on the other hand, she accepted it, and I didn't know anything about life and love.

Maybe Tommy was right and we really do live in purgatory, because all of the good things harm us, and all of the bad things make us feel good. Tasty food's bad for us, bland food's healthy, drugs are good for our soul and bad for our body, alcohol does the same thing, and love – there's not a single person in the world who's never been burned by it. Friendship is a good thing, yet everyone gets hurt by their friends at some point. And money blinds even the smartest of people. In short, everyone's damaged in one way or another. Everybody hurts, physically or emotionally. I was exhausted, but my longing for Angie was too intense for me to rest. I wanted to hear her voice so badly, to explain what had happened back there at the club, and with that thought, I finally fell asleep.

I don't know how much time had passed, but I was woken up by the phone ringing. It was Tommy, and he sounded high. "Where are you, bruv? You have no idea what happened!"

"What's the matter, where are you?" I asked.

"Seriously mate, it's bigger than any drug I've ever taken," he said.

"What's the matter?" I asked again.

"Bruv, I'm in love, crazy in love, you have no idea!"

"What are you on? What did you take? And why didn't you show up at the club?"

"I did show up! I mentioned your name at the entrance and they let me in straight away, and I looked everywhere but I couldn't find you. And suddenly she walked by and our eyes met, and it was more powerful than anything I'd ever felt! As though God had orchestrated it himself! We magnetized straight away, can't explain it in words. We spent the whole night together; it was love at first sight!"

"So she's with you now?"

"No, she couldn't come over, said her dad's coming to pick her up and he's very conservative, but she gave me her number and I swear – it was love at first sight!"

"Bruv, I'm really chuffed for you, but let's have this convo after you shag her, yeah? I've got a lot to tell you, why don't you come over?" I suggested.

"On my way, mate."

He showed up, and luckily my mum hadn't slept at home. We went into the kitchen to make breakfast and I told him about Russ, the birds, and all the money, and promised I'd get him a job at Rico's during the coming week. Then I told him about how Rico had abused that waitress. He was even more nonchalant about that story than I was, and it pissed me off to realize that we were like that.

"Love comes in many forms," he put on his philosophical tone, "Everyone loves in their own way, and everyone's ready to give up a lot for the sake of love. Maybe they're so in love that she's willing to accept his behavior, as long as he's happy. That might seem crazy to us, but it's her choice. Maybe if she saw your relationship with Angie, she'd say that it wasn't love."

"You're full of rubbish," I said angrily, "No one could say that about me and Angie."

"Listen, bruv, you're both addicts – not quite the sober types. It could very well be that without your addictions' filters, you'd have split up a long time ago. I reckon that if that waitress was genuinely suffering, she'd have run away or at least made a complaint about him, but it sounds to me like she's at peace with it."

"What about you and me? Are you saying that maybe our friendship isn't real, because we're not exactly the sober types either?"

"That's not the same thing, Iggy. You and I grew up together, and we bonded long before we'd ever touched drugs, but that wasn't the case with Angie, was it?"

"Yeah, but we were proper kids, and that was back when we still thought girls were minging!" I replied and attacked, "And do I look like a bellend to you? She was blatantly scared of him! You'd get that if you saw them! My mum lived with my dad for years and never ran away either, even though he used to beat her up, because she was scared of him!"

"I don't know what the crack was between your parents indoors, but out there, everyone thought that she was the one wearing the trousers."

"But he was the one beating her up! So how could she be wearing the trousers?" I raged.

"Well, then, that just reinforces my point, doesn't it?"

"Leave it out mate, you're too dazed today, you're not feeling me at all and I don't get how we're even talking about my parents' relationship," I shouted, "And what do you even know about them? What do you know about love? You live in a self-made bubble and keep all of your emotions out. To be honest, you and Rico are pretty much alike, you're both great at working from your head, but your emotions are fucked up. You've never longed for someone so badly that your entire body hurts. You've never gone out of your way to please someone for more than a few days, and you've never been in love, so how dare you preach to me about love?!"

"Wow, wow, Iggy, mate, that's far enough now, calm down," he patted my shoulder, "I'm on your side, and let me explain my theory to you – you don't need to be in love with a bird to know what love is. Every child is the product of love! Shagging's a product of lust, but if the couple that's doing the shagging decides to keep the baby, then it becomes the product of love. We're love seeds, and that's what we evolve from. Love's in our DNA. We have pure love within our core and that fertilizes us, and we live off it for nine months and then we're born, each to their own parents and their own ideals. So I've seen and absorbed that love, the same love that ruined my parents' marriage, the same love that shattered my mum's life. She loved my dad and she loved me too, and she was torn between her two loves because she didn't want to give either of us up. My dad wouldn't share her love, it was either him or me, and she was broken up about it. I'd hear him crying at night and telling her how sorry he was, but it was stronger than him, he just couldn't stand someone else getting her love. 'I love you,' he'd tell her, and then say, 'Let's give him up for adoption,' can you imagine that?! She couldn't give me up, and she promised he wouldn't even notice me around, and that was the only thing to calm him down. So, in the name of love, she'd devote herself entirely to me between eight in the morning and four in the afternoon, and from the moment he came back from work, she'd only love him, until morning. So her love for me always had a time limit. Like I said, love comes in many forms, bruv. Can't argue with the fact that she loved us both."

"I don't know, sounds to me like she loved you and was scared of him!"

"Yeah, I know it's hard to accept, I thought the same for years, and I was even grateful that she didn't give me up despite the fear. But then they found out about his disease, and I was sure that the moment he'd die, she'd be free and then she'd make it up to me for all the years she'd spent in his shadow. But after he passed away, none of that happened... She met Amos after two months, and he was even worse than my dad. And then the penny finally dropped – that's what she knows, that's what she loves."

"Sorry, bruv, but sounds to me like Stockholm Syndrome," I insisted. "Your mum's used to living under constant threat and that's what she knows, so she looked for it until she found it. That's why you grew up with wrong ideas about love, and I don't think you even understand what that really feels like."

"You're getting confused, bruv, I agree with what you're saying, but that still doesn't contradict what I'm saying, because everyone experiences love in their own way, even if it's through a damaged part of themselves – the feeling's the same. My mum felt that she was in love, and that's the whole point. The reasons behind it are a whole different story, but do you get what I'm saying? Do you know a single couple in the neighborhood with a healthy relationship? If you ask David the greengrocer, who beats up his wife all day long, whether he loves her, he'll swear that he does! And that goes for everyone we know. Doesn't matter what their syndrome is, that's how they love! I won't lie, I'd love to feel what you feel with Angie, it really does look like the kind of love that everyone aspires to, and I want to try that with Nicole! I'm willing to give it everything I've got. She won't leave my head, and I'm having all sorts of thoughts … about the future … never felt like this before. But do you get what I'm trying to explain?"

"Yeah, I do, you do have a point there, and I'm glad that's what you want and that's what you think of me and Angie. Just so you know, sometimes I get jealous of how easily you surrender to birds and then run away without a shred of guilt. I'm full of it. Anyway, love is complicated and family's complicated, and fuck whoever invented them to begin with. I think we should change the entire concept and go for nature's way – once the baby can stand on two feet and can get along on its own, that's it, leave him to it. We have to get it in humanity's mind that love is amazing as long as it has a beginning, middle, and end, and that it's only ever temporary."

"So you and Angie – that's temporary?"

"It's too late for us, I'm talking about the next generation. Just like you said on the way to Blacktown, even though we know it doesn't make any sense and it's wrong, we still live according to those concepts, because they've been embedded so deep into our system that we can't shake them off. So we have to start educating the new generation with lighter concepts."

"But I love you, Iggy."

"Bugger off!" I replied and we burst out laughing.

The front door slammed, startling us. "Anyone home?" we heard Andy's voice and realized the lads were all coming. They burst in excitedly, and Smiley was wearing a top with a huge Star of David he'd drawn on it. Within a minute, they'd ravaged everything we'd set on the table, and we all moved to my room, which then resembled an ER on a weekend. Pills flew in the air, the bong was constantly lit, and the table hosted beautiful, neat little lines of cocaine. We had way more gear there than we usually did.

"What's up, and what are we celebrating? And why are you wearing that?" I asked Smiley.

Manu pounded his fist on the table. "Tonight's all about celebrating! Tonight, we're celebrating the exciting meeting between Smiley and his mum and the Glick family!"

Tommy and I looked at Smiley, stunned, and he nodded joyfully, "I got a call yesterday from a social worker with the Israeli Jewish Agency – they've found my mum! Or rather, she'd contacted them and asked them to help her get in touch with me cuz she didn't know how to go about it, and she was scared I'd reject her. The social worker said my mum lives in a kibbutz in Israel with her two daughters – so I've got two sisters!"

"Way-hay!" we all cheered.

"Turns out my dad passed away two years ago, and there was good reason for us not communicating; it was for my own good," he said in a tone of self-persuasion, "And she wants to tell me all about it if I agree to meet them. My mum misses me and not a day goes by without her thinking of me, so she's sending me a ticket to fly out and ... I'm getting on a plane to Israel in three days, to meet my family."

We were shocked but also very excited for him, leaping up and hugging him as though he'd just gotten married. To be honest, I was a tad jealous of Smiley that his life was about to change and that his mum was going to compensate him for all the years she'd been away. 'I wish my mum was like that,' I thought.

That was one of the best nights I'd ever had with the lads. We were immaculately united and felt an optimistic, positive vibe. We spoke for hours on end and listened to wicked music until we finally crashed.

CHAPTER 14

I was the first to wake up. I opened my eyes, saw that everyone was still out and didn't want to disturb them, so I went to the kitchen and made some strong coffee. I lit a fag and peered out to see if my mum was back, but her room was empty, so I went to the lounge and sat down, took out the envelope filled with dosh, and started counting.

"Wow!" I heard a voice and jumped in fright. I was sure everyone was still asleep, but Smiley was wide awake, and he counted each and every note along with me.

"Am I dreaming, or did you just count three thousand nine hundred and thirty quid?! Who did you rob?"

"That's my wages, you ass," I said.

"Swear on your mother's life! All of that from deliveries?!"

"Deliveries, you know," I winked at him.

"No way, bruv! Sort me out too and I'll postpone the flight by a few months!"

"Well, it ain't that simple, mate," I explained, "But I'm on it, so get yourself on that flight, and by the time you get back, I'll hopefully have some good news for you. In the meantime, take this, so you'll have some spending money on the flight," I said and handed him three hundred quid.

Smiley took the money and grinned. "I have to go! Got a lot to sort out before the flight," he said.

Andy and Tommy woke up and suggested we walk Smiley home together, so we got dressed and tried to wake Manu up, but he was totally out, so we left him there, shut the door to my room, and went out. The streets were bustling with people. We walked around cheerfully, not a care in the world, no rush. I allowed myself to enjoy the atmosphere and glance at the shop windows.

I couldn't recall the last time I'd strolled through the streets just looking around. I'd walked along that street my entire life, and I'd never before strolled through it, I'd always just rush through it on my way somewhere. I felt like the dosh in my pocket was providing a sense of security I'd never experienced before. I was calm, walking around with my head held high, and the more I stared at the shop windows, the more I felt the urge to spend the money – but not on myself.

I wanted to buy presents. Up until that day, the most I'd ever spent in one go was a hundred quid that we'd all collected for gear. In fact, most of our spending money usually came from Andy's jobs.

"Lads, let's do some shopping," I declared, and everyone was up for it. We bought Tommy a killer bong. We went into a shoe shop, tried a few on, and left with matching pairs of shoes – including a pair for Manu. We bought wicked T-shirts, sunglasses, and awesome hats that Smiley picked out for us. We even sat at a café and ordered two plates of pasta alfredo, a green salad, and some chocolate soufflé – which is a hot cake that once you stick your fork in it, this burst of chocolate cream streams right out. We walked around, delighted and carrying a ton of shopping bags, when a shop door suddenly opened and a cloud of pleasant scents filled the street, so I stopped and looked inside. It was a perfume shop, and I immediately thought about Angie and decided to buy her some perfume.

I had no idea how to go about it, I'd never bought her anything on my own, surely not of that caliber. I'd only ever gotten her small, casual things, or specific things she needed, and I always went for the cheapest since we never had the money for proper shopping – that was on our lottery wish list.

I tried to recall the shape or the name of the perfume she always dreamed of, and felt bad about not managing it. I guess it only highlighted the fact that she was right – I really didn't pay as much attention to her as I should have. So, I decided that this was my chance to make it up to her.

We went in and stared at everything like a bunch of little kids. It was a huge shop, the décor was magnificent, and I'm not exaggerating when I say they must have had around two thousand types of perfumes there, all neatly filed on shelves in exquisite-looking bottles.

Tommy examined them and said, "Iggy, look, each one has an open bottle you can smell, it says 'tester' on it."

We immediately started spraying all the bottles on ourselves and on one another. Once we calmed down, I decided not to let the packaging confuse me, so I closed my eyes and tried to choose the scent that reminded me most of Angie. For me, that was a deep thought, but from the side, we must have looked like a bunch of kids playing pin the tail on the donkey. I smelled and sniffed and got a different brand of perfume stuck up my nose every second, but at some point, my sense of smell went haywire and everything just seemed to smell the same.

"Here, try this, it'll sort out your sense of smell," we heard a voice behind us. We turned and saw a saleswoman, who was blatantly a salesman. He was black and sported a blonde afro, full-on makeup, and the whole shebang. He handed me some coffee granules as he devoured Tommy with his eyes. Tommy freaked out, and the salesman shifted his eyes away and tried to focus on me.

"What do you mean, should I smell the coffee?" I asked.

"Yes, it helps neutralize smells," he explained.

"That's cool, I like sniffing," I joked, and we all sniffed the granules.

"What are you looking for?" he asked with a forced smile.

"I'm looking for a good perfume for my girlfriend, but something proper good, you know what I mean, mate?"

"Miss," she corrected me, then asked me to follow her as she marched towards a shelf. "Let's start with this," she said and grabbed a bottle, "It's Chanel no.5, classy and very present. No matter what she uses, this one's a must for any respectable woman."

We smelled it and weren't too keen. "Smells like old hags!" I exclaimed, "I'm not looking for something for my mum, this is for my girlfriend, so get me something younger, please."

"How about this one? I highly recommend it, and it's very young and fresh... Amarige by Givenchy."

"That's better," I replied, "But still not the one."

Smiley asked to try it and he didn't like it either. We tried a few more that almost hit the spot, but still weren't quite it, and then she suggested I try Giorgio Armani, and from the second that scent entered my nose, I knew that it was perfect for Angie!

"This is Gio, the scent of ocean and love – that's how I call it," she said.

"Done deal, I'm taking it," I said excitedly.

Smiley, Andy, and Tommy approved of it too, so we followed her to the tills, she wrapped it up nicely and I paid for it. She put it in a little bag and handed it to me, and I thought that it was more than enough, but then Smiley gave me a funny look and said, "Is that it? Kind of small, innit? I'd add something else to it."

"Patience, mate," Andy piped up, "Next stop's the Mercedes dealership to pick up the new car he's getting her." For a moment, it seemed that Smiley believed him, but then we all burst out laughing.

"It's not the quantity mate, it's the quality – this is well expensive!" I added.

"True, but why not go all the way... Add a little something to it, like maybe a cream that smells the same, my nan got a present like that once."

"He's right," the saleswoman intervened, "People usually buy the body cream to match, it harmonizes the bodily scent..."

"Harmonizes, eh? All right, let's have it," I gave in.

"Go all the way," Smiley said.

When we left the shop, the entire sales staff thanked us and said goodbye, and that really amazed me – we'd never been treated like that before. You wouldn't believe how everything changes once you've got the dosh. You get treated like royalty! It's a proper addictive feeling.

"I want to be treated like that for the rest of my life," I announced to my mates as we reached the entrance to Smiley's place. Tommy told me he'd never had that much fun before, and said it really made him feel like starting work already. "What's the crack with your boss?" he asked, "Did you get a chance to tell him about me?"

"Not yet, but I will as soon as I can. I want all of us to work together," I replied.

Andy said he felt like we were maturing. He told us that he had a few new jobs, and he wanted to concentrate on making money and getting somewhere in life. Smiley piped up and said that once he came back from Israel, we'd all step up our game and get on it. We felt that the time we'd spent together that day had opened up a new sort of channel, and it was hard to say goodbye to Smiley.

"Come on, lads, it's just for a couple of weeks," he said, "Not for life! I'll be back."

"Yeah, well, if you don't come back, I'm getting tickets for all of us and we're coming to squat your mum's place in Israel," I said.

"And don't forget to send us photos," Tommy added with a wink.

"I will!"

"Of your sisters, yeah?"

"Fuck you!" he exclaimed.

We said goodbye and everyone went their separate ways. I calmly walked along the streets and thought about how to bring Angie the perfume without her slamming the door in my face.

I got home and checked for any messages from Rico – I was pretty disappointed to learn there weren't any. I was completely up for working that day, any day, every day, all day.

I went into my room and put the shopping bag on the bed, lay beside it, and started fantasizing about knocking on Angie's door with the presents I'd gotten her. In my fantasy, she opened the door and looked at me, stunned. Then she leaped onto me and we hugged tightly for at least an hour, without letting go. Then I gave her the perfume, and as she unwrapped it, I mentioned that it was real. "The perfume?" she asked.

"My love for you," I replied wittily, and then she gently neared her lips to mine. My cock went hard just thinking about her lips, and I put my hand down my pants, but then I heard the front door slamming and my mum's high heels clicking closer and closer to my room. I managed to get my hand out and cover myself with the duvet before the door to my room swung open. She stood in the doorway, partly leaning against it, and even though her face was covered by a massive pair of black sunglasses, you could tell she'd just been through something serious.

"What happened?" I asked.

"Nothing, what do you mean?" she replied, not budging from the doorway.

"You charged in here, you're standing at the entrance to my room, hardly managing to stand, to be fair… So, is there anything you want to tell me? Or could you take your sunglasses off at least?"

"Don't feel like it!"

"Okay, then tell me what happened."

"Can't be bothered, I'm tired of this life! Nothing ever works, I'm a failure, no one loves me, I always bring out the worst in people, I'm a hag…" she said in a weak tone.

Wow! I was not expecting that! Chills went down my spine and I tried to understand if I was dreaming, so I sat up in bed. Mum suddenly looked like a little schoolgirl. She'd never shared anything about how she felt. It was the most unexpected thing, hearing her talk like that, and I didn't know how to react or what to say.

"Maybe I'm not the brightest bulb, but I do have a brain," she said, "And maybe I'm not young, but neither is he!"

"Who?" I asked, but she ignored me and went on.

"So I drink too much, I know, but at the end of the day, I'm devoted and loyal, and loyalty's the most important thing in the world."

I immediately thought that she was talking about Rico because he'd said the same thing about loyalty, but then I got even more confused when she said in tears, "Do you hate me?"

I was shocked! I'd never seen my mum that fragile, and she'd never spoken to me like that before. I didn't even know how to console her. If this were our usual banter, I'd have said yes to her question, but I was scared of hurting her in her current state, so I said, "No, I don't hate you!"

"You do, I'm not an idiot, I wanna die!"

"Stop it, what's gotten into you? What happened? What did he do to you?"

"You're changing the subject cuz you hate me and you wish I was dead."

"What's the matter with you? I don't hate you."

"You don't love me either! No one in this world loves me!"

I didn't know what to tell her and I started stuttering, "I... I dunno how I feel, but... I want to love you!"

"See? You don't look at what is, only at what isn't. You live in my home and you don't pay a penny for it, I let your girlfriend live here too and never asked for anything in return! And don't you dare think I don't notice you grabbing money out of my bag every so often. You eat and drink out of my pocket, but people are selfish and they don't see anyone but themselves, and I'll always be judged for everything that I ain't! I can't be bothered anymore; I'm not made for this life."

I felt bad. I'd never looked at things the way she'd just presented them, and it really shook me up. 'She's right!' I thought, '*I was being a shithead, and I still think Angie loves me. Maybe everyone really is hard on her, it's crazy for someone to think that no one in the world loves them, I didn't think she was even aware of those sorts of things.'*

"You're right," I told her with a trembling voice, "You've never said any of this to me before, we've never had this kind of conversation. I'm sorry, and you do matter to me, I do love you! I was just disappointed, and I guess I wanted you to see me all these years, and I was sure you didn't love me."

Mum was upset and wasn't listening to what I was saying, she just kept crying and told me, "I want someone to love me, I want someone to tell me he can't live without me, I want someone to think of me!"

I could genuinely relate to everything she was saying – it was precisely the way I felt, and it was the first time I ever felt that I actually resembled my mum! That was a turning point for me, and I wanted to amplify it so badly that I immediately said, "I actually did think of you, and I bought you something." I showed her the bag with the perfume. She lifted her head and wobbled over to the bed, sat down next to me, and took the bag hesitantly. "See that, Mum? That's for you," I said, "I went by a shop today and got an urge to go in and get you a little something."

"Iggy, I'm stunned! Really? What is it?" she asked.

"Open it and see for yourself," I said.

She tried to unwrap the packaging, but she was so drunk that her hands just sort of slapped the box over and over again, so I helped her open it.

"Wow, Iggy... dunno what to say..." she said in an impressed tone, and I was pleased. "This is for me?" she asked.

"Of course it is, who else would it be for?"

"Angie," she mumbled.

"But we're broken up, why would I buy her anything?"

"You got your wages eh? He pays good money, doesn't he...? You should have listened to me ages ago!"

"Yeah. Open it up and smell it."
"Gio! Cor blimey, you've got good taste, son."
"Of course I do," I said proudly.
"Dunno what to say."
"I don't either, to be honest," I said and meant it.

This wouldn't have happened in my wildest dreams, which only goes to show that life really is full of surprises.

"But how come you thought of me all of a sudden?" she said as her face contorted. She opened her mouth and I thought she was about to say something or cry, but then a burst of vom sprayed all over me and across the bed. I leaped back and she collapsed face down, sunglasses deep in a puddle of vom, and mumbled some vague sentences. I lifted her up, carried her to her bedroom, and laid her on the bed. I got a wet towel to clean her face and took her sunglasses off. She had a swollen black eye. Someone had beaten her up. "What the hell? Who did this to you?" I asked in a panic.

But she didn't reply and just waved her hand in dismissal, so I covered her in a duvet and left the room. I promised myself that the moment she woke up, I'd find out who did it and go out there and break his neck.

I went into my room and cleaned everything up, changed the sheets, and popped the dirty ones in the washing machine – I'd usually just chuck them over it and not even bother, but I was filled with motivation about being a good son to my mum.

I looked at the perfume and smiled to myself. She loved the perfume I'd gotten Angie. If I really did think about my mum, I'd have probably gotten her that Chanel no.5, and then she'd get pissed at me for buying her some old-smelling perfume. I went back into her room quietly, placed it on her dresser, and went back to my room.

'Now I don't have a present for Angie...' I thought. 'But I can always get more perfume, and moments like what I'd just had with my mum – now that's bloody priceless.'

I lay in bed and fell into a deep sleep. I only woke up because I was desperate for a wee, and it was already dark outside. As I headed to the loo, I saw my mum sitting in the kitchen, so I came up to her from behind and hugged her. "How are you feeling?" I asked.

She moved my hand off her. "Fine, better, I was knackered! Say, did you bring me some perfume, or was that a dream?"

"I did, yeah."

"Wow, I can hardly remember anything, I'm well hungover."

"We had an amazing talk, Mum, you told me how you felt, you were open about it all, and you just wanted to be loved. Now, can you tell me who hurt you?"

"Oh, it's nothing, I tripped at the entrance to the bevvy shop, I was off my face," she said dismissively, but she was clearly lying. If she really did trip then she wouldn't have tried to hide it behind her glasses.

"Go on, tell me, I promise not to do anything you don't want me to."

"Stop it, Iggy! I won't tell, and I don't fancy all this stickiness."

"What do you mean?" I asked, baffled.

"I mean that you seem to think we'll be like some sort of Hollywood mum and son duo, and that ain't gonna happen! I've never been a good mum and I'm not planning on starting it now!"

"Why would you say that?"

"Oh, come on, don't be so naïve, Iggy. I was as high as a kite, had a rough day, and you were here – but it could just as well have been the cat and I'd still talk to it. Think about it, it would never work and we'd just bicker all the time. I'm not going to suddenly change in the middle of my life, and neither are you! It's a bit too late for all that, and I just can't."

Her words felt like nails piercing into my stomach. I felt so exposed and vulnerable, and it threw me back to age six behavior as I shouted, "Great! Because I felt bad about lying to you with all those kind words, but you're not just any evil woman – you're the bloody devil! People like you don't deserve to live! You're a shit mum, and I hate you!"

"Well, at least we're back to our usual routine," she said coldly, touching her face with self-pity.

I grabbed her head and tried to force her to look at me. "Look at me!" I screamed at her.

She freaked out and jumped off the chair. "Leave me alone, are you crazy?!"

I was completely broken. Within a mere few minutes, she'd managed to burst through years' worth of defense walls, so what are those walls even worth? I'd never experienced such an intense emotional rollercoaster, and I really did feel like I was losing it. I was flooded by hatred and revulsion towards her, a million times stronger than usual.

"It's a shame that whoever beat you up didn't kill you!" I shouted at her, "I hope you'll die, and I'm sure I won't be the only one to dance on your grave, just die already!"

She was frightened and ran to her room, locked the door, and screamed, "Leave me alone and go live your own bloody life!"

CHAPTER 15

I went into my room, poured out the baggie's contents onto the table, and cut two huge lines out of it all. I sniffed them and felt the adrenaline rushing through my body like a wild river.

The phone rang and I went over to pick it up. It was Andy, he was calling from the police station and said he'd been detained for questioning. This wasn't new – he was arrested quite frequently.

He talked to me in codes: "Do me a favor mate, my sister's got an important exhibition and I can't make it. Go down to the gallery and sort out the paintings so they don't scatter about, and take them round to her place. Tell her I can't make it and take her something nice for me. Buy her something at Randell's shop. But do it soon, don't want her getting angry with me."

By exhibition he meant documents. The gallery was the shed where they were, and Randell's shop was right behind it so the two spaces shared a wall, and that wall was where we would hide the goods. Andy wanted me to do it quickly so that the coppers wouldn't get there before me.

I was usually bummed out whenever Andy got arrested, even though they never really found anything and always ended up letting him go, but at that point, I was buzzing and full of adrenaline, so I was really glad to have a reason to get out of the house.

I rushed out and ran over to the shed, which was a rancid, 9-square-foot space belonging to some gangster who'd let Andy have it in return for a few odd jobs. We'd tidied it up so that Andy would have everything he needed to work. We duplicated a set of keys for each of us, and no one knew that it was ours. That way, every time the coppers looked for Andy or searched for evidence to prove he was doing something illegal, they'd always go to his parents' place, and they'd obviously never find anything there. Nevertheless, one night, we all went over there, popped two bricks out of the back wall, and hid all the documents and equipment inside, in case they'd ever find out about the shed somehow. That's how it became our meeting point whenever we got into trouble. When Andy got a job, he'd get the equipment out of the wall, do the work, and then put it all back in again.

It was strange that out of all of us, Andy was the one who'd turned out to be a criminal. It's pretty ironic considering that his parents, Jacob and Ida, worked for social services their whole lives. They were so busy with other families' hardships all the time that they neglected to notice how their own family was the most dysfunctional one in the neighborhood. Andy was a brilliant forger, and his older sister had a high-profile job for the council and fell in love with one of her dad's patients. Her lover was a married criminal, and I reckon he'd only had an affair with her so that she could help him out using her dad's connections. Alfie, Andy's younger brother, had started doing drug deliveries at the age of seven – he worked for Mossa, an Arab dealer from Chelsea, and his parents were convinced that he was just an innocent pizza delivery boy. If they ever found out about what their kids were really up to, they'd surely kill themselves.

I quickly grabbed all the documents I saw, as well as the stamps, plastic laminates, ink, and the cutting machine. I was so stressed that I couldn't find a bag anywhere, so I took off my shirt and bunked everything inside it. I put my coat back on, ran to the hiding spot, making sure no one was around, and then I popped the bricks out and shoved everything inside. I put the bricks back in place so perfectly that no one would ever think to check there.

Once I was done, I went by Cuba's place – my dealer. I bought some gear and went back home. The door to my mum's room was open but she wasn't in. I went into my room and sniffed a couple of lines, just to calm down a bit, but I was so hyped and filled with adrenaline that it was of no use, so I went to my mum's medicine cabinet, grabbed a couple of sleeping pills, and downed them.

I woke up later on, went straight into a heavy comedown and felt completely disoriented. The sense of emptiness was eating away at me, and the room was filled with a putrid smell of smoke. There were cigarette butts strewn all over and I could hardly breathe. I felt a strong urge to get up and go out, so I quickly got dressed and left the house.

I walked around aimlessly, filled with guilt about everything that had happened the previous day. The wind was intense and my throat went dry from inhaling all that cold air. After about an hour, my breathing became heavy, and I felt like I was having some sort of panic attack. I ran home, took the key out with trembling hands, but the door wouldn't open! My heart was pounding and I didn't understand what was happening to me. I couldn't swallow and I was sweating like mad – I was sure I was going to die. I tried to jiggle the key around, but nothing worked. I felt like I was in a nightmare when suddenly I heard Agatha, our neighbor, shouting to me, "Iggy, what's the matter? Do you need my help?"

"No thanks, Agatha, I just can't get the bloody door to open," I shouted back.

"You do know that's my door you're trying to open, yeah?" she asked from the other side.

I quickly pulled the key out of her lock and stood there for a moment, stunned. I was so stressed that I hadn't even noticed which door I was trying to unlock – and just to be clear, our door and Agatha's door looked nothing alike. I was spinning and I couldn't figure out what was wrong with me, so I headed over to my door and went inside. I headed straight to my room, cut a few lines, and then got in the shower to try and calm down under the hot water.

I prayed and pleaded for a miracle to save me, and then the phone rang. I quickly picked it up and it was Rico, asking me to come over as soon as possible. "Little job, big pay," those were his words.

That was precisely what I needed! I thanked God for sending me that miracle and then thanked my granddad – maybe it was his doing.

Within no time, I was already at Rico's office, but he wasn't alone. There was another man sitting there, an old man. He was short and tough-looking, dapperly dressed, his thin gray hair was oiled back, and he was holding onto a black walking stick. I stared at his mean-looking face, and the first thought that came to mind was, *'There's no way I'm going on a ride with that fella!'*

Rico motioned for me to sit down while he escorted the old man outside, and I breathed a sigh of relief. Then it was just the two of us, and I thought that this would be the perfect opportunity to suggest bringing Tommy along for the ride.

"How have you been, Iggy?" he asked.

"I'm all right," I replied.

"That day, when you and Russ came back, you told me you were waiting for a mate of yours at the club…"

"That's right! I swear, that's exactly what I wanted to talk to you about! His name's Tommy and he's a top bloke, guaranteed. He's looking for work and he's trustworthy and hard-working, kind of like me…"

"Excellent!" he interrupted me, "Do you know Shirley Sanders?"

"Shirley Sanders… the actress?" I asked.

"That's the one!"

Shirley Sanders was one of the most successful actresses in England. She was every bloke's wet dream – especially Tommy's. "Of course I do, everyone knows her," I replied.

"What do you think of her?"

This time I chose my words carefully, trying to learn from past experience and all that. I didn't want to fall for the same trap I'd almost tripped into with that waitress from the club. "She's a brilliant actress, incredibly talented," I replied with a film critic's sort of tone.

"That's right," he said.

"She's the best!" I added.

"Yeah, well, Shirley and I have been friends for years now," he explained, "In fact, we were mates long before she became famous. She's moving home and she's asked for my help. I promised I'd send her someone experienced, someone I trust, and I want to send you. You can take your mate along so he can give you a hand. Think you two can manage that? Can I count on you?"

Could he count on me? That was like cracking open the cheese pack and asking the mouse if he could be trusted to deliver it. Even though I didn't entirely trust Rico by that point, and I was pretty sure he was the one who'd beat up my mum, I didn't care about anything at that moment except making money, getting back together with Angie, and helping my mate out.

"Of course you can count on me!" I said confidently, "And of course I can manage it, and Tommy's just the right man for the job. You won't regret it; we'll do a wicked job of it!"

"I want you to take personal care of her," he emphasized.

"Personal care, you got it," I replied.

"But not too personal, eh?"

"No, of course not, you've got nothing to worry about," I said and we both laughed.

Rico wrote the details down on a note and handed it to me. "Go downstairs, Don's got the keys to the van, it's already got boxes and tape inside, and there's money in the glove compartment in case you need anything. Any questions?"

"It's all crystal, I'm off," I said and sprinted to the lift.

My mood had gone from shitty to ecstatic. My boss trusted me, I managed to get Tommy in, and we were about to meet the ridiculously fit Shirley Sanders, and even get paid for it! What on earth could ever be better than that?! I glided into the lift and pressed the button for the ground floor, counted thirty seconds until the doors opened, and there it was! Don's face staring right at me.

"Keys to the van, please," I sang and held my hand out.

He didn't say a word and just got into the lift, pressed the button for the parking floor, and looked straight ahead. The smile immediately vanished from my face. I couldn't figure out what his deal was, but I decided not to pay attention to him. I assumed that once we reached the van, he'd hand over the keys.

The lift's doors opened and we went out to the parking lot, heading towards the van. We stood next to it, facing each other, and I patiently waited and kept my mouth shut. He looked at me and took out a set of keys from his pocket, but the moment I reached my hand out to take it, he dropped it on the ground, right between his legs. My instinct was to lean down and pick it up, but I held back and waited for him to do it. He didn't budge, just stood there and waited. Unfortunately, he had the upper hand, considering he had all the time in the world, whereas I was supposed to get a move on.

"You dropped it," I said.

"You need it," he retorted.

I didn't understand what was wrong with him and why we needed to play those ego games. "What's this about?" I asked.

"You think you're the dog's bollocks, barely here for two days and you hold your hand out at me and demand the keys as though I fucking work for you? You better get off your high horse and learn how to show some respect."

I was shocked. Who would ever think of that? How did he even come up with it? This was purely his own interpretation, but he looked so angry that I didn't dare challenge or taunt him. I also didn't want him to think that he was right by what he'd said, but I finally decided to just bend down and pick up the keys myself without saying a word. I didn't mean to, but I blurted out, "Fuck this," as I grabbed the keys.

It wasn't aimed at him, I was just agitated, but before I even managed to straighten back up, his leg flung through the air and he kneed me in the face. I lost my balance and landed on the ground, and he towered over me and got me into a stranglehold. "I don't work for you, is that clear?!" he said venomously, "And next time you address me, show some bloody respect, you muggy little loser. Now get up and get in the van. You're lucky there's CCTV here, otherwise I'd see to it that you wouldn't get back on your feet for a good long while!"

After that speech, he let go of me and I slowly stood back up. My nose was gushing with blood and my shirt was stained. I got into the van, stunned and humiliated. I took a few moments to shake the whole thing off, and then I revved the engine and drove away.

My nose was aching really badly, but I managed to get over it. My battered ego was the most painful aspect of it all. Just the thought of Don running around and telling everyone about how he'd played me like I was some sort of keyring – it made me feel impotent, and evoked a sense of revenge that I'd never experienced before.

But I had to focus on the job, so I stopped the van near a phone box and called Tommy, told him the good news, and told him to wait downstairs for me. As I drove over there, I cleaned the blood off my face with some tissue and pressed my nose for it to stop bleeding.

Tommy waited for me outside. He looked terrible – his clothes were all wrinkly and he was unshaven. "What's the matter with you?" I gave him a bollocking, "Didn't think a shower was appropriate before you go to work for the first time? I could live with how you look, but you stink, mate! At least put some bloody deodorant on!"

"Go on, drive," he muttered, "We're going to do a lot of carrying so we'll stink either way. And look who's talking – you look fucking awful! Your shirt's full of blood. What's the matter, sniffed one too many?"

"It's not what you think, and it's not that kind of job either," I said and turned the engine off. "Do me a favor, go back in, put some clean clothes on, and some deodorant too, and get me a shirt will you?"

He looked at me, surprised. "Why? Where are we going?"

"Never mind that! Jog on, do what I said and be quick about it, we ain't got much time," I insisted. He shrugged his shoulders, got out of the van, and went back upstairs.

I took the baggie out of my pocket and cut a few lines over the dashboard, but immediately regretted it. My nose was bleeding like crazy and I was scared it would make it worse, or maybe sting more than it usually does. I got the gear back in the baggie and waited patiently. Tommy came back down after about ten minutes, and the moment he got in and shut the door, I stepped on the gas and sped the car over to Shirley's address.

He looked me up and down and said, "What's going on?"

"It's all shit!" I replied and told him about the incident with Don. Tommy fumed and suggested we all go beat the shit out of that asshole. "No mate," I said, "I don't want to mess things up with Rico. If we're going for vengeance, then we need to be clever about it, make sure no one knows it was us. Let's focus on the job right now – once we're done, we can have a proper think about how to fuck him up."

"Fine. Where are we going?"

"Oh, we're just going to help the boss's mate move house."

We arrived at Shirley Sanders' neighborhood – a posh area filled with the kind of lush homes you only get to see in films. Tommy and I were psyched up about it. "You see, Tommy? One day, we'll live in a house like that too."

"What, you mean here? Would you really want to live here?" he asked.

"Dunno, but I'd like to have the money to live here."

"Oh, I see, yeah, I'd like that too. But if you could, would you move here?"

"If I could…" I hesitated, "Then I'd want to live in the Caribbean. I'd probably fancy some golden sand, sunshine, palm trees by the sea, Angie, happy people, good vibes…"

"You prick, what about me?" he exclaimed, "I could do with all of that romance on a paradise island too you know!"

I decided to see how serious he was. "Let's say you could choose any neighbor you wanted, out of all the fit birds in the world, who would you pick?" I asked.

"Mate, I'm in love with Nicole!"

"Who's Nicole?"

"Come on bruv, the waitress from the club, the one I told you about," he said. "Her name's Nicole. We've grown real close, and I spend all day thinking about her… But, if you insist, I wouldn't mind having Claudia Schiffer or Cindy Crawford as our neighbors, just in case."

"And what about Shirley Sanders?"

"No way mate, are you mad? Shirley Sanders is an existential threat, the kind of neighbor who could make a real mess of any romantic relationship. You see, Claudia and Cindy are all about attraction; I just look at them and all I want is the good life – parties, shagging, beach, booze, and drugs. But Shirley Sanders, now that's about character right there – she's the kind of sweetheart you'd want to come home to after a holiday, the kind you could fall in love with. See the difference?"

"Not really," I said. "When it comes to Angie, she makes me want all of that – the sex, the beach, booze, and drugs, but then I also want to go home with her. What I don't get is why wouldn't you want to do all of that with the woman you love?"

"And what I don't get is how anyone could give all of that up for just one person. After all, if God wanted us to spend our whole lives with one woman, He would have surely made the world that way to begin with. But He created diversity, and we're all born with urges. So why do you think He did it – just to play mind games with us? Education is what limits us, mate, and when you look at it from the outside with some perspective, then this whole thing of being committed to one person for your entire life is actually one of the biggest reasons for beef between people. Women hate other women and they're scared of one another, men constantly compete, and that's why people get divorced, and why they cheat and lie to each other. You know what? Forget about all that, let me give you an example. Am I your best mate?"

"Yeah!" I replied.

"But I've got other mates too – Andy, Manu, Smiley, and I'm crazy about them. Are you jealous?"

"No!" I said and chuckled.

"And if I happen to make some new friends during my lifetime, will you be jealous then?"

"No!"

"See? That's why we'll be friends forever, I'd never lie to you or worry about losing you just because I've met new people. I'd also never hide it from you – on the contrary, I'd share it with you and you'd get to know them too and have loads of shared experiences with us. Today's romantic relationships are based first and foremost on fear. Say you meet someone incredible and now you two are busy trying to impress each other, and then busy being scared of losing each other – you create two sides, or two camps, if you will. She'll talk to her mates about all the things she can't talk about with you cuz you'd get offended and leave her. And you'll talk to your mates differently than how you talk to her, because you'll be scared of hurting her and losing her. That in itself creates a distance. What I'm saying is that the world needs to stop stuffing our heads full of fear – we gotta get Hollywood to start making romantic movies showing genuine harmony and peace among people, and maybe that way, we'll be exposed to other ways of thinking, start working towards true love and companionship, and allow ourselves to enjoy people's endless closeness."

"Sound cool in theory," I said, "But if everyone goes with everyone, then we won't know who's fathered which kid … pregnancies, love, money, it'll all get chaotic."

"It is chaotic! Everything's already happening exactly the way I've described it, only discreetly. Ninety-nine percent of the world's population keeps things under wraps, and they're all bloody miserable."

"You've almost convinced me there, but you know what? If I saw Angie fancying another man and pulling him, there's no way I wouldn't kick both their heads in!"

"Let's start by getting sex out of the equation, okay? But isn't it only natural for you two to admit that you fancy other people besides one another? Or that you'd connect with other people too because you find them interesting? We do it behind each other's backs as it is, so might as well keep it real and get some genuine trust going, innit?"

"But there's a higher chance of her cheating on me if I agree for her to go out with a nice bloke that she happens to meet," I explained my reservations. "As it stands, she doesn't let any other men in, which makes playing the field that much harder."

"That's not true! First of all, it's a matter of character – if she's naturally loyal, then it doesn't matter what happens, she'll always be a one-man kind of woman. But if she's horny and feisty, then even if she's in love, she'll still be tempted to get some on the sly. Second, forbidden fruit, mate … we always want the things we're not allowed to have. Third – and don't get pissed – it may very well be that she does let other fellas in and you just don't know about it. Everyone's got their own world outside their relationship, and we all live a kind of lie!"

"I dunno, I agree that something's not working properly and that we're a bunch of stupid, overcomplicated creatures, but I still can't think of a way to make the world better," I sighed.

"It's all a matter of education and conceptualization of right and wrong – that's what they get into our heads. If you were educated along with the old-world generations who viewed sex as a casual thing, then you'd surely see everything differently. Right now, you're still wired to be jealous about other blokes, and it's so deeply rooted within you that you can't see it any other way."

To be honest, he had a point – why are we raised to believe that this is the way things are supposed to be? Granddad Elijah used to tell us that King Solomon had a thousand wives, and no one ever had an issue with that, but over the years they got it in our heads that monogamy's the natural choice – and that's got to be wrong considering it doesn't work! "Hey, should we include Madonna in the friendly-next-door-neighbor category?" I asked.

"Fuck yeah!"

"Done deal," I replied as we finally arrived at Shirley Sanders' place. I parked the car outside, changed my shirt, and we got out of the van. I pressed the doorbell, and even though I was jittery, I kept my cool and tried to look standoffish, hoping Tommy wouldn't notice how excited I was.

She opened the door after a few seconds – that's precisely how I want them to open heaven's doors for me! A beautiful woman with a striking presence, an ultra-fit bird who knows it and flaunts it – perfect! We were both stunned. Even though I knew that I was going to meet her and even though I'd felt prepared, I just stood there in front of her, completely speechless.

"Hi," she said and smiled at us, but we didn't react, just kept standing there like two silent twats. "Can I help you?" she added.

I looked at Tommy, hoping he'd save us by saying something – which was his expertise, talking was his greatest gift – but to no avail. This was the first time he'd ever gone into shock because of a bird, and he wasn't functioning at all.

Suddenly, without warning, Shirley slammed the door in our faces. We both jumped with fright, which gave us a little wake-up call.

"Iggy, you dickhead!" he pounced on me, "Tell me you didn't know!"

"I did!"

"What kind of asshole are you? Why didn't you tell me?! What were you thinking?! And what is that woman about? How could anyone ever create something like that? What kind of a once-in-a-lifetime-shag does a person need in order to get a kid like that?! It's mental, mate, she's a stunner on screen but she's bloody phenomenal in real life!"

"Yeah," I concurred, "I wanted to surprise you, but I was surprised myself by what she's really like. What do we do now, though? She's slammed the door in our face and she's probably calling the coppers, Rico's going to kill me. Let's just get our shit together and cool down. I'll knock, you talk, sweet?"

"Sweet," he replied as I knocked again.

After a few seconds, we heard her voice through the door. "I've called the police so you should leave now. I appreciate all my fans but I won't accept any invasion of my privacy."

I was so stressed by the thought of Rico finding out about all this. "Sorry, Miss Sanders," I spoke politely, "My name's Iggy and I'm here with Tommy, Rico's sent us to help you with the move. Sorry about the awkwardness, we were just excited, that's all."

She opened the door immediately. "Well that's a relief, I was genuinely scared – thought you two were a couple of crazy fans. Come in," she said.

We went inside. I glanced at Tommy and saw he wasn't all there yet, and that pissed me off.

"Do excuse the mess in here," she went on, "Did you bring any boxes? There's still a lot of packing to do."

"We did!" I replied, "Just show us around, tell us what needs packing, and we'll take care of it all."

I suddenly noticed that Shirley couldn't take her eyes off Tommy. "Wow, you're gorgeous," she said and smiled at him, "You look like a film star."

That line was the ultimate key to free Tommy. From that moment on, he literally came back to life. He smiled back at her, "And you're even more beautiful off-screen."

"Thank you," she said and ran her hand over her hair – the final bit of proof that she fancied him. He'd taught me that there are a few moves a bird does when she talks to a man she fancies, and one of them is touching her hair.

Shirley gave us a little tour of the house, showed us what was important to pack, and we got straight into it and worked quickly. She and Tommy couldn't stop flirting, and I was proud of him. The way I saw it, if he managed to shag Shirley bloody Sanders, then he'd be the ultimate, unbeatable king.

"You boys want something to drink?" she asked.

"Yes please, some water would be great," I replied politely.

"I'll have a glass of white!" Tommy winked at her.

"Oh well, why don't you two take a break and I'll fix us some drinks?" she suggested.

"I… I think I'll keep at it…" I mumbled. "I don't drink on the job, knocks me right out. But Tommy's the opposite, it just makes him go harder," I added, hoping the pun wasn't too obvious.

"In that case, I really should get a drink in him – I just have one request. See that white wooden table?" she said and pointed at the table behind me, "That's my most treasured possession. It's a family heirloom that we've had for generations, and it's the only thing that reminds me of home, so don't move it on your own, okay? We'll leave it to the very end, it's heavy and the glass top might break. I don't want to take any chances with it, if anything happens to it… even the smallest dent… it'll be the end of me."

"No problem," I said.

"Great, then I'll take the hard worker for a drink in the kitchen, he seems thirsty to me," she said and winked at Tommy. He chuckled and the two walked down the corridor, went into a room, and shut the door behind them.

I took the opportunity to go to the loo. The nosebleed and the pain had ceased, so I did a couple of lines and that got me going. From that moment on, I worked fast and didn't stop for a second. I finished loading most of the things on my own, left the table for last just like Shirley had asked, and waited. I started getting bored, so I went in the loo for a few more lines and came back out feeling great. I strolled around the house, and every little move of mine made an echo. There was nothing left but the white wooden table, standing there on its lonesome. I looked at it for a while – it really was beautiful and seemed well-kept. 'It's not that big,' I thought, figuring I'd be able to move it on my own. I decided to surprise her.

I examined the table, gently touched it, and thought to myself that it wouldn't be a big deal to move it. I deliberated for a bit and decided to lift it all the way to the entrance, just to see how heavy it was. I stood where I had a good grip on it, then picked it up and started walking towards the front door, when I suddenly heard a scream that made my bollocks shrink. "Look out!!!"

I have no idea how it happened, but I must have gotten so frightened that I slammed the table into a wall, and then Shirley screamed again – "What are you doing?!" That really stressed me out, and then I lost my grip on the table. It slipped out of my hands, and the glass shattered all over the floor. I was in utter shock. This never would have happened if she hadn't screamed so hysterically.

"You idiot!" she shouted at me and started crying.

"Shirley, if you hadn't scared me with your screaming, then this never would have happened..." I said.

"No, you cheeky fuck, if you'd listened to me then this never would have happened!"

I tried to apologize and explain what had happened, but she didn't want to hear any of it. She went over to the table and leaned down to pick up the pieces, sobbing loudly.

Tommy came up to her and tried to calm her down. "It wasn't on purpose, really, we'll pay for it."

"Is that right?" she turned to him and shouted, "Do you have any idea how much this table's worth?! Its last appraisal was a hundred and eighty-seven thousand pounds! Even if you both spend the rest of your lives working non-stop, you'll never have that kind of money! And I don't give a shit about the money, its sentimental value is priceless… Do you even get what I'm saying? Or do values mean nothing where you come from?!"

And there it was. Within that split second, she lost all of the credit we'd given her, and ended up sounding just like that mean old hag from the ferry. But we had a lot at stake, and the whole thing couldn't get out of hand – Rico could never find out, or we'd be in real trouble! I realized that Tommy was about to lose his shit so I leaped onto him to stop him from making a mistake, but he shoved me away and I flew backwards.

"Fuck your cunting table and fuck all of your bogus values!" I heard him say coldly. "Go ahead and take all of your family's precious generations and shove them up your ass! Who do you think you are, passing judgment on us? You were sucking my cock a minute ago, and now you're taking the piss out of us for a fucking wooden table? It's thanks to people like us that you're a bloody celeb to begin with! We're the ones who buy tickets to see your shitty films. You're not even worth a hand job. Come on Iggy, let's go."

CHAPTER 16

I felt all the blood leaving my face. The whole situation was stressing me out. I started thinking about the trouble I'd be in with Rico – he'd definitely sack me, and he'd never want to hear about Tommy ever again. And that's the best-case scenario.

Shirley looked at Tommy with her eyes wide open, then turned to me and whispered, "Iggy, do me a favor and get the phone from the kitchen, will you?"

"Sure," I said and rushed over to get it for her. She grabbed it off me and walked away from us.

Tommy pleaded with me for us to get out of there. I tried to calm him down and explain that we had a lot to lose by doing that, but then we heard Shirley crying over the phone. "I'll never forgive you for this! What did I bloody ask for? You sent me two unprofessional brats! They broke my table, and one of them even assaulted me!"

Tommy and I were stunned. He was fuming and barged in on her. "You lying cunt!"

"Can you hear how he's talking to me in my own home?" she spoke louder and cried.

I felt like I was suffocating. I wanted to snatch the phone out of her hand and tell Rico she was lying, but I was scared she'd get even more hysterical, so I walked up behind her and shouted towards the phone, "Rico, she's lying, that's not true…"

But then she started screaming, "Get away from me!"

I panicked and took a few steps back. We realized that things were getting worse by the minute, so I grabbed the car keys and my pack of cigarettes and we ran to the van and got the hell away from there. After a few minutes of driving, we remembered that some of her furniture was still in the back of the van, which could actually give Shirley cause to charge us with theft. We were stressing like mad. Tommy was holding his head in his hands, and I was driving like a maniac. We knew that we were going to pay for that whole ordeal – big time.

"Where are you going, Iggy?"

"Rico's office," I replied, "We have to get there as quickly as possible and tell him our side of the story. And we'll have to get all the furniture back to her somehow."

"No fucking way!" he shuddered, "This ain't the right time to go see him! She's probably filling his head with stories as we speak, and it's her word against ours – who do you reckon he'll believe? How long has he known you for, a week? And he doesn't know me for shit. Let him calm down while we go sit somewhere and figure out how to deal with all of this before we get nicked and put away for life. I'm definitely going to do time! Do you know how much you get for rape and theft – of a celebrity, no less?! I'm fucked, Iggy, royally."

"Oi! Mate, you've gone too far," I shook him, "It wasn't that bad, we just broke her table, it could have happened to professional movers too. Trust me, it's more important for us to figure out how to deal with Rico, I don't think he'll get the coppers involved, but where are we going to come up with a hundred and eighty fucking quid for her?! And she didn't say rape, she said assault. And either way, so fucking what? If I happen to walk by a bird on the street and she decided to point a finger at me and say I raped her, is that it? I automatically go to prison?"

"If they find your cum inside her then yeah, you do," he said.

"You shagged her?" I asked, stunned.

"Left right and center," he replied.

"Fuck! We're in serious trouble!" I pulled the van over and we did a few lines to calm ourselves.

"Mate, we're in trouble because you decided to move that table on your own, she told you not to touch it, what did you do that for?"

"Because I could! And if she hadn't screamed like that and freaked me out then none of this would have happened!"

"Leave it, bruv, let's just figure something out before we find ourselves hanging from the ceiling by our cocks in some abandoned fucking warehouse."

"Right ... let's think..."

We both went quiet and tried to figure things out. I suggested we call Rico, at least to assess his level of hostility over the phone, and try to explain what had happened, but Tommy refused and claimed we needed to give him a few more hours to calm down.

"But he won't calm down, he must be fuming by this point," I said worriedly, "And if we don't show up, then he'll get even angrier. And her stuff's in the van, so right now it looks like we stole her shit and disappeared with the van. We're so screwed, bruv."

We decided to drive over to Andy's house. We stopped by a phone box to make sure he was home. Tommy got out to make the call, and I stayed in the van and locked the doors, just to be on the safe side.

Suddenly I heard a loud car horn from the side of the road. I turned to look and saw a car stopping next to me – with none other than Blood, the cowboy from my dream. He smiled at me and waved his hand. "Howdy, Iggy, what's the crack?"

"You following me?" I asked.

"Always!" he replied, "I see you didn't take my advice."

"Go fuck yourself!" I replied angrily, but he didn't seem to mind. He waved his hand again and drove away until he disappeared from sight. I turned my head the other way and saw Tommy banging on the window, so I opened the door for him.

"I've been knocking on the window for a full minute now, mate!"

"I don't know what came over me," I said.

"You were in a wormhole, mate!"

I didn't tell Tommy about the dream, we were stressed enough as it was, and it didn't seem like the right time to tell him the whole story about Blood.

"Drive over to Andy's," he said, "He's waiting for us."

We finally reached Andy's house, and the three of us sat down for some brainstorming.

"I reckon you two should drive back over to Shirley's," he suggested, "Bring all of her stuff back and try to calm her down, apologize, and see how you can pay for the damage. Maybe the table's insured, so you could promise to pay the difference from your wages. Ask her if you could just finish up the packing and the loading, and get her to call Rico and tell him it was all one big misunderstanding and it's all sorted now."

"No fucking way, bruv, she's bonkers!" I exclaimed, "You should have seen her, she was a proper psycho, she might even call the coppers. And who knows, Rico and his lot might already be there! No way!"

"Then you need to send a woman there," Andy said, "Someone who'll play a saleswoman or something. That way, she can check if there's anyone else there, and if there is, she can try to get her to buy a product or something and just leave, but if no one else is there, then she can try to persuade her to listen and say you two want to make it up to her and just bring her stuff back."

"Great, so all we need now is a bird who'd be willing to do that for us," I said sarcastically.

"Angie!" Tommy jumped up.

"How about Nicole," I retorted angrily.

"All right, all right, I get it, never mind," he said.

"Listen, mate," Andy said, "But don't get angry now, just hear me out…"

"Well? What is it?" I asked impatiently.

"Your mum was the one who'd introduced you to Rico…"

"No way mate!" I interrupted him.

"Listen, Iggy, there's no other choice! She's the only mutual contact you have with him, and she could talk to him and help you out."

I gave in and called my mum. I could tell straight away that she was in the loop. "Iggy, where the hell are you?!"

"Mum, you have to listen to me…"

"No, you listen to me!" she interrupted me, "I don't care how any of this happened, you call Rico right now and then go over there to sort this mess out!"

"Mum, just hear me out for a sec, it's not what it looks like!" I tried to explain what had happened, "It just got messy really quickly, and I don't know what you've been told but that bird's lying, I'm just asking you to listen to me."

"Iggy, I'm not the one you need to talk to! And even if you're right, it's no use! Call him up right now and calm him down, you can't just run off and disappear like that. Be a man and sort out the mess you've made, is that clear?" she said and hung up immediately.

"That's it, I have to call Rico," I told the lads.

We were all very stressed. I lifted the receiver and my hand was trembling. I dialed his number and he picked up straight away. "Hi, Rico," I said.

"Where are you?" He was fuming. "Now you listen to me, you get yourself over here right now! This is the last time you leave the office for a job and don't come straight back here afterwards, I don't care what happened, even if someone cut off your fucking bollocks and you need to get to a hospital, you stop at the office first. Is that clear?!"

"Yes," I said quietly.

"And where the fuck are Shirley's things?" he screamed through the phone.

"Everything's still with us in the van, but it wasn't like she said…" I tried to explain, but he interrupted me.

"Get your muggy little asses back to her place right now and finish what you started. Once you're done, get back to the office – you and your little mate," he said and hung up.

"He said we must go back to Shirley's," I told the lads, "So he probably doesn't believe that we did something to her, otherwise he wouldn't tell us to finish what we started. And he also said that once we're done, we both need to go to the office … so maybe it's not that bad after all."

"Off we go then," Tommy said.

"Let's go!" I said, recalling my ride with Russ, when he'd told me that the boss always knew about everything.

"He must know what really went down there, despite what she said. We messed up and got stressed for no reason, and I think we didn't give Rico the credit he deserves," I added, trying to calm us both down.

We got in the van and headed to Shirley's place, but she wasn't home. There was a young man waiting for us there instead. He told us that Rico had sent him to help us out, and the three of us cleaned up the broken glass and loaded the rest of the furniture and boxes into the van. Then we drove over to her new place and unloaded everything as quickly as we could, with the young fella telling us where to put everything. Once we were done, we thanked him and drove over to Rico's office. On the way there, I told Tommy that I was worried about what was coming next, and I said that even though Rico had asked us to come together, I thought it best for me to go there on my own.

"He doesn't know you," I explained, "And he seems to be real close with Shirley, romantically that is, and from what I've gathered so far, he's pretty possessive and vengeful, so I think I better go there alone and tell him everything I saw – meaning I'd leave out the bit about the shag and concentrate on the whole table business. If you're not there, and considering I never saw the two of you when you were alone, it might actually sound believable."

"But she said I assaulted her!" he seemed stressed again, "And where was I while you were lifting the table all on your own? You really think he's that stupid?!"

"No bruv, but she lied through her fucking teeth, and so will we!" I explained my plan to him. "It'll be her word against ours, and our version says that we lifted the table together and that's when it slipped and fell, shit happens! And then she got pissed off and made up a load of bollocks. Think about it, why would she tell him that you assaulted her?"

"I see what you mean. That bitch can't tell him that it was consensual if she's having an affair with him cuz that would get her in trouble. So she lied."

"That's right! So we'll lie too – her word against ours."

Tommy agreed. I pulled the van over near a bus stop for him to get home, and he looked at me and smiled before he got out.

"What are you grinning about, bruv?" I asked.

"Think about it mate, at the end of the day, putting aside whatever happened, I just shagged Shirley Sanders…"

"Yeah mate, you're the dog's bollocks! Now go home and tell Nicole all about it," I said and laughed.

Tommy slammed the door shut and I continued driving, thinking about everything that had just happened, and how there's never a dull moment in this life. In fact, life is just a sequence of memories, and let them say what they will, one thing is clear – in this life, we're the players on the field, not the spectators.

I reached the parking lot and stopped the van. I kept imagining the coming conversation with Rico in my mind. I couldn't wait to put the whole thing behind me, and I just prayed for everything to go smoothly.

I grabbed the bloodied tissues and the pack of fags full of cigarette butts, put it all in an empty shopping bag, got out and locked the door, and headed towards the bin to toss it before going upstairs, but then I heard a strange noise. I looked around, but the parking lot was empty, with no one in sight. I kept walking, and then, all of a sudden, the lights went out and it turned pitch black. I felt like I was in some sort of horror movie.

CHAPTER 17

I stood motionless for a few minutes, trying to calm my heavy breathing. I convinced myself that it was just a coincidence and that everything was fine, and continued feeling my way through the darkness towards the building's entrance. I heard noises again, but this time they sounded like footsteps, so I froze in place. My heart was racing and I felt like something bad was about to happen. I stood there silently, trying to figure out if I'd really heard something or whether I was imagining things. The footsteps grew louder and came from a few different directions, and before I even managed to try and run away from whatever it was, I felt a huge thud to the back of my head, which knocked me to the ground. I vaguely remember someone approaching me with his face covered, but I recognized his voice – it was Don. He towered over me and whispered, "You're in a world of trouble."

It wasn't just him there. I have no idea how many people were with him, but they started beating me mercilessly. I closed my eyes and tried to protect my head with my hands as much as I could. It hurt for a few seconds, and then it didn't anymore. I stopped feeling or even hearing anything. The sound of the thuds went mute and my body felt loose, as though my soul had left it and was now just floating through the air, freely and tranquilly.

"Hey, your heart," a familiar voice rose through the darkness.
"What about it?" I asked.
"Reach your hand out and grab it."

"But I have no hands now," I replied.

The voice burst out laughing. "Trust me, you do, reach them out, your heart has to go back!"

"Go back where?"

"Back to life."

"I don't want to go back," I insisted.

"Don't worry, just go back, and at some point, you'll come back here again, and then again."

I suddenly had a hand again and it grabbed my heart. I felt it pulsing for a few moments, and then it climbed onto my hand, and sensation started flowing in my body again – through every muscle and every bone. The pain was excruciating. I tried to open my eyes, which hurt too, and I didn't give up until I finally managed it. Everything looked blurry and I couldn't move. My body felt like a dozen cannibals were standing over me and biting my flesh. I wanted to scream but I couldn't get my voice to work, nothing came out but a strange gurgling sound. I was sorry that I'd come back. I closed my eyes, hoping my soul would come out of my body again, but it didn't.

I suddenly felt someone breathing on my face. I opened my eyes and saw my mum leaning over me. She looked into my eyes.

"He's awake. Iggy, can you talk?" she asked me. I tried, but an odd mumble came out instead. "He can grunt," she said mockingly.

A nurse came up to me. "Hi Iggy, glad to see you've woken up. How are you feeling?"

"Hurts…" I managed to say in a weak voice.

"Yes, I'll get some painkillers in your IV right away." She injected something into the IV and said, "You need to rest, you've sustained a lot of injuries and you've had some internal bleeding from the bruises. I'm sure it hurts a lot, but you're very lucky that you didn't need any surgery and that nothing's broken. The police officers will be coming around later on, they've asked me to let them know once you've woken up, they want to ask you a few questions, but I'll let you rest first. Good thing your parents are here."

"It hurts so bad," I moaned.

"Just a few minutes and the painkillers will kick in. I'll be back in a bit," she said and left the room.

I looked at my mum, who seemed incredibly glamorous. She had makeup on and her hair seemed smooth and neat. I even smelled that perfume on her, the one I'd bought for Angie.

"You should be thankful it's only come to this," she said, "I'm lucky they didn't get your spine, otherwise you'd be a cripple."

I wanted to tell her what I remembered, but then my eyes closed shut. I tried really hard to open them again, but then I freaked out when her face suddenly swapped with Rico's.

"You look like shit," he said and turned to my mum, "Go grab us a coffee, gorgeous."

From the corner of my eye, I saw her leaving the room. She was wearing a dress I'd never seen before, and high heels – she looked different. Even her walk was different and exaggerated, as though she were a bloody catwalk model.

At that moment, my brain was suddenly flooded by a million thoughts. I suddenly realized why Rico thought that my mum was a beautiful woman. She didn't usually look like that. 'And he called her gorgeous... She's definitely one of his lovers... Then could it be that he was the one who'd beaten her up?' I wondered.

Rico looked at me. "Shame we didn't get to sit and talk. You'd have understood that your mum's the only woman I love."

I was furious. My mum's the only woman he loved? That waitress from the club was the only one he loved to shag, and Shirley Sanders was his close mate. There were obviously a lot of other women with whom he loved doing God knows what, and I was sure that he was the ultimate motive for my dad walking out on us and disappearing.

But nothing could have prepared me for what he said next. "Iggy, some police officers will be coming around soon, so let's make this short and sweet. You went for a night out with a mate and you were assaulted. You don't know who assaulted you, and you actually don't remember anything about what happened. And that'll be the end of it. Is that clear?"

I immediately understood what he was saying and nodded my head. My heart was pounding wildly and the monitor started beeping. The nurse rushed into the room and came up to me. "What's the matter?" she asked worriedly.

"He says he's in pain, the poor dear," he told her.

"I've given you plenty of painkillers, we'll wait fifteen minutes and if it still hurts, then I'll give you some more. Try to keep yourself calm," she said and rushed back out.

"You know, there are two types of people I can't stand," Rico began his manic monologue, "People who are stupid, and people who don't appreciate things. Why, you ask? Because it doesn't matter how much you do for them, they'll always take it for granted. And what pisses me off the most is that sometimes – well, seldomly in my case – I don't even notice them when they're right under my nose. My dad, rest his soul, he was a very smart man. He taught me that everything in life has value, doesn't matter whether it seems good or bad to us. We have to understand that there are lessons that we love and lessons that we hate, but we learn from them both, and we have to appreciate them both. I learned that the hard way. I didn't know how to appreciate what I'd thought of as bad – and trust me, my dad was cruel. I was angry whenever he punished me, I couldn't stand him, and I felt humiliated. How could a man treat his child that viciously? His own flesh. Whenever I ran to my mum and told her he was being bad, she'd tell me that there's no such thing as 'bad.' She took me out to the garden one day and said, 'Look around you, is the garden pretty? Is it good?' It was a beautiful day out and I nodded my head. And then she told me, 'Everything seems calm, at peace, the plants and the kind trees, but what you don't know is that underneath the ground there's a war of life and death. See how the tree branches cast their shade over the flowers beneath them? To you, it might look like just another part of nature, something good, magical even. But what's really going on is that the tree's fighting the flowers and blocking the sunshine from them, so that the flowers die and the tree's roots can get more water. So the tree roots drink up all the rain that trickles into the ground, and the poor flowers wither and die. The flowers fight to get even just a few measly drops so they can survive, but the tree's stronger, they don't stand a chance against it. So, in order for the flowers to live, I water them, and I occasionally trim the tree branches so that the flowers get some sunshine.' I told her that she was doing something good, but she replied that it might be good for the flowers, but the tree wouldn't feel the same. When my father passed away, my mum cried and I was happy – just like the tree and the flowers. I think that was when I understood that everything has a good side and a bad side. So I get it, you believe something bad happened to you, but trust me, I went easy on you. I can see your potential... something about you reminds me of myself when I was a young lad, and I'm telling you, no matter how you look at it, I deserve a thank you!"

The nurse and my mum came into the room. The nurse injected something into the IV again, even though I tried to signal for her not to. Within seconds, my body went loose and my eyes closed. There was a cyclone whirling within my mind, and I fell asleep immediately.

I was woken up by the sound of talking. I opened my eyes and saw my mum talking to a couple of uniformed coppers. She explained to them that I must have been high, and that a gang of thugs had attacked me in an attempted robbery. She claimed that it had happened to me before and that she'd just nursed me at home back then.

'Where did she come up with that bollocks?' I thought. I was confused and couldn't figure out whether she knew the truth and was covering up for Rico, or whether he'd fed her that story and she was just embellishing it to make herself look like a good mum.

"Hi Iggy, how are you?" one of the coppers asked me.

"Can't you tell?" I replied.

"Yes, I'm sorry. Think you could manage to answer some questions?"

I felt paralyzed by Rico's monologue, and I still wasn't entirely sure about the answers. I looked at my mum and tried to figure out whose side she was on. I considered talking to her, but then she piped up before I even managed to say a word. "Officer, you can tell he's knackered. I think you should let him get through the night and come back tomorrow. He'll be better by that point, and then you can do your holy work properly."

"I understand, but it's only a few brief questions, we'll get it done as quickly as possible and then we won't disturb you anymore," he said.

My mum turned to face me. "Iggy, Aunty Rebecca asked for you to call her once you're awake."

"Who?" I asked, baffled.

She ignored me and turned to the officer. "That's his favorite aunt."

"I see," he said and motioned to his colleague for them to leave, "We'll drop by again tomorrow."

It was just the two of us left in the room.

"Who's Aunty Rebecca?" I asked her.

"I just made her up, I didn't want them bothering you, you look completely out and I didn't want you saying something silly by mistake. We're better off going through everything together, so that when they come back tomorrow, you'll be ready, all right?"

"But you know what really happened, don't you?" I asked, "You know that Rico sent his men to beat the crap out of me, and he's just admitted it to my face? He warned me not to talk, do you know that?!"

She looked at me with a wide, cold stare. "Now do you see how good it was of me to send that copper away? Otherwise you'd have blurted out all that rubbish and gotten yourself into even more trouble!"

"No, no, you don't get it! You told me to tell the truth and that's the truth, Mum, you know that, right? At least tell me you know…" I pleaded with her.

"The truth is that you left the club with a mate and you got jumped," she recited in a chilly tone, "You couldn't make out their faces and everything happened so fast that you don't remember anything."

"Okay, I don't mind saying that," I mumbled gloomily, "But please, just tell me that you know the real truth."

"The truth is that you left the club with a mate and you got jumped by a few blokes and…"

"And I don't remember anything," I interrupted her, "And who was I with at the club, eh? Which mate are we talking about?"

"Good question, tell them that it was just a random bloke you met at the club and you two left together, and you were so high that you don't even remember what he looked like. Explain that you two were going in different directions, and that the attack happened when you were on your own – that way they won't ask any more questions!" she ruled.

I was stunned. Her reply made it crystal clear that she knew what had really happened – and worse, she proved yet again how she didn't give a toss about me, her son, her own flesh and blood.

"Cool, that's what I'll tell them…" I said in a trembling voice.

"Great, so I can be calm now. And you need to show Rico more respect, he's always supported me and stayed loyal, and he loves me and looks after me."

"He loves you?! He's loyal to you?! I saw him shagging one of the waitresses at his club with my own eyes, and he even told her he loved her!" I exclaimed.

Her face went bright red. "Great, I'm so glad to know that I have a snitch for a son and a cunt for a boyfriend!" She quickly grabbed her purse. "I'm leaving, Iggy, and I just hope you'll do the right thing."

I suddenly realized that what I'd just told her was going to get me in trouble with Rico. 'She's probably going to give him a bollocking because of me, and I'm going to pay for it!' I thought.

"Mum!" I tried to stop her, but she was already out the door, slamming it behind her.

I was hysterical! I tried to figure out how much time I had left before she made it to Rico's place with this whole thing. 'After he hears what she has to say, he'll definitely pay me a visit I'll never forget – if I even get to keep my brain in one piece, that is.'

My heart was pounding, it was as though it were frantically knocking on some door and pleading to leave my body. It stung and cramped, trying its hardest to find a way out of me. My body started burning up and I got a rush of adrenaline. I felt completely helpless and I was aching all over, but I decided to make an escape nevertheless, so first of all I ripped the IV out of my hand so that the monitor wouldn't start beeping.

It was hard for me to get up, but I refused to give in. I overcame the pain and sat up in bed. I tried to calm down my pulse with slow, deep breaths, and looked around to figure out what my options were. I could have really done with some gear, just a few lines to help me forget about the pain. I knew I had to find a phone, call Tommy and check up on him. I wanted to warn him too, and ask him to come and get me out of the hospital before Rico or the coppers come back.

I managed to get off the bed and onto my feet. I grabbed the IV pole and made it look like it was still hooked into me. I grabbed my stuff and walked towards the door, and then I leaned on a wall that led me straight to the reception desk. The nurse sitting there immediately got up and approached me. She tried to help me and said I had to go back to my room to rest, but I insisted that she let me make a call first and said I'd only go back to the room after that. She agreed and I called Tommy. I breathed a sigh of relief when he picked up.

"Bruv, I'm at St Thomas' Hospital," I told him and asked him to get there as fast as he could, and also to bring me some clothes and some washing powder – our codename for cocaine.

After that, I went back to the room and counted the minutes – my head wouldn't stop working. I kept imagining scenarios where my mum gets to Rico's place and tells him everything and then he comes to the hospital with his people and they skin me alive. I decided it would be best for me to leave the room, just in case Rico surprised me and showed up before Tommy. I opened a crack in the door to peer out and make sure it was safe to come out, but there were a few doctors standing right outside, so I shut the door and waited until the coast was clear. As luck would have it, when I opened the door again, a woman with a tray in her hands was standing right before me, and she almost collided into me. "What are you doing? I've brought your lunch, get back into bed, you need to be resting!"

"I have to stand up for a bit, I've got bedsores on my bum, just put the tray down and I'll get back in bed in a bit," I promised her. She put the tray by the bed and left. I felt really hungry all of a sudden, so I grabbed the tray and ate everything on it, still standing. Then I limped back to the door, filled with pain. When I opened it, Tommy was standing in front of me. I got such a fright that I let out a scream just like ET did in that Spielberg film. Tommy calmed me down and quickly went in and shut the door behind him. He was holding packs of pills in his hand.

"What are those?" I asked.

"I accidentally went into room number 80 instead of 108," he explained with a wink, "And there were loads of medication there, so I loaded up on painkillers and antibiotics. It's expensive gear, so I thought – what the hell, why not?"

He pulled some clothes out of a bag he'd brought and helped me get dressed. While we cut a few lines, I filled him in on everything that had happened, from the moment I'd let him off at the bus stop until the moment my mum left the hospital room. Within a few minutes, we were already making our way out of there, carefully and as quickly as possible, with Tommy supporting my limp the whole time. We stopped a cab outside and I asked to make a pitstop at my place. I told Tommy to get in through my bedroom window and find my hiding place with all the cash in it. He came back after a few minutes and the cab took us to Andy's shed – that way no one would ever find us.

I lay down on the mattress that was set on the floor. My body was barely handling all the pain. That was the moment I realized how lucky I was that Tommy had lifted all those painkillers, and I popped a couple in my mouth immediately. After that, he sorted me right out – full mind and body treatment, as it were.

"When you came to see me, did you say your name at reception?" I asked.

"No, I just asked the nurse which room you were in," he replied. "After she said you were in 108, I accidentally went into room 80, and then I came straight to you."

"That's good, that way no one knows you were there! This is scary, bruv! We're in serious trouble!"

"It'll be fine, Iggy, fate will lead us to the right place."

"Is that right? Fate? Well, let me tell you something that I think might be connected to that," I said. "Ever since I started working for Rico, I've been having these strange dreams about the same man. His name's Blood and he's a genuine cowboy out of some Western. He told me that I'm destined to stay an addict, and that the more I try to get away from that shit and make something of myself, the more I'll get into trouble because that's my fate! What do you think about that?"

"Dreams are all about our subconscious," he immediately said, "And that Blood fella's just a manifestation of your fears. Everything that you and I went through was a series of unfortunate coincidences. And at the end of the day, no matter how you look at it, the people you work with and the woman who sorted you out with that job – they're all shits! And when you have that much shit floating around you, there's no way you'll be able to keep yourself squeaky clean. Forget about all of that rubbish, making a change is a good thing, but maybe we should do it right, find a job that pays less but keeps everything calm and in order… Don't you think?"

To be fair, he was right. Nothing good ever comes out of dodgy business. Money makes us blind, but if we take into account all the trouble we get into in order to get it, all the uncertainty, the unexpected people, the weird characters, the night-time hours, and the kind of fears that the devil himself couldn't think up, then no – it isn't worth it. That was my gut feeling, anyway. But then my sick mind suddenly perked up – the one which always has the worst timing when trying to get a life of its own. So, instead of agreeing with Tommy and changing direction in life, I said, "No! We're already way too deep in it all! Trust me, all we need is some guts and creative thinking, and we have both. We can do this, we're smart! There's a goldmine here, mate! We have to figure out a way to calm things down, buy some time, and then catch Rico and his gang by surprise!" I was excited by my sudden courage. "They ain't got nothing on us, bruv, and look at him – he's swimming in dosh. There's no reason for us not to make it, trust me! Soon enough, we'll be sailing on our yacht, completely carefree, no stress, with a ton of cash, and with our loves."

"And lovers!" he added and we laughed. Then we sat there for hours coming up with ideas, but just as fast as they came, we immediately decided against them. At some point, I recalled Rico's speech about his dad, about good and bad, and about how you need to accept the bad just like you do the good. As I told Tommy about it, I suddenly came up with a brilliant idea.

"Listen, I should go over there and surprise him, tell him that I came over to accept the bad in a respectful manner, that I accept whatever he deems right to say or do to me. So he'll break one of my ribs – that's a lot less scary than living with the uncertainty and constantly being on the run. After we get through that, I'll ask him for another chance to get back to work. He'll most likely appreciate that and believe that I'd genuinely learned my lesson, so I'll suggest that you and I work for him pro bono until we settle the debt with Shit-Show-Shirley. You see, we might not get our wages, but the fat service charge alone is worth any CEO's three-month salary. In the meantime, Andy will sort us out with some passports, we'll book a flight, and when the moment's right, we'll plan a delivery and instead of going back to Rico with the money, we'll head straight to the airport and fly as far away as possible. You, me, and Angie – free and filthy rich! What do you say?" Tommy listened to me, but his mind seemed to be elsewhere. "Tommy? What do you say?" I repeated impatiently.

"Sounds sweet, but only if we get Nicole in on it too."

"Done," I replied.

"And what if we fuck up and the plan goes to shit?" he suddenly said, all stressed out, "Or what if Rico suddenly realizes what we're up to? We're not only endangering ourselves but the girls too, right?"

"No one will be able to figure it out," I quickly calmed him down, "You and I will be the only ones who'll know the full plan, the destination, and the flight date. The girls only need to agree to go with us and be ready to drop everything and head to the airport when the moment's right. Everything will be sorted and we'll be travelling with fake passports, so no one in the world will ever know! We'll even change our hair color and our wardrobe."

"And what about my mum? What about our mates? You might be fine leaving everything behind cuz you'll have me and Angie with you, but I love my mum."

"Yeah, I get that," I mumbled hesitantly, "To be honest, I didn't think about that. But let's at least make a start, bruv, work for him together and make some money, and then we'll think about how to take it from there. Maybe we'll even earn enough to pay for the flights and just hang out on some lush island for a few years."

The door suddenly burst open and Andy rushed inside, panting. "Are you two fucking mental or something? The whole world's asking about you! Iggy, your mum's fuming! Richie even pulled his car over on the street and asked if I knew where you two are, I had a feeling you were here, but I told him I didn't know... What did you get yourselves into this time?"

Richie was one of the neighborhood's oldest hooligans, from my parents' generation. He wasn't as major as Rico's caliber, but rumors had it that back in the day, he was considered one of the toughest. It was only after he'd served five years that he lowered his game. He was also one of the first to discover Andy's talent at document forgery, and he worked with him even when he was doing time.

CHAPTER 18

We brought Andy up to speed, and he suggested bringing Richie to the shed and personally asking for his help. And indeed, fifteen minutes after he called him, Richie showed up.

We told him the whole story. He laughed at the Shirley Sanders bit, but then went dead serious and corroborated our biggest fears. "You messed with the wrong man, you're in serious trouble! If it weren't for Andy, I wouldn't be sitting here with you right now, you're damaged goods! Being here with you is considered treason in our books, but I trust Andy and I've known you lot since the day you were born… And truth be told, I've been waiting for years for Rico's downfall!"

He then lowered his voice and continued with a dramatic tone. "What I'm about to tell you can't leave this room. Twenty-odd years ago, Rico was considered one of London's toughest criminals. He controlled the smuggling market, and I have no idea how it happened, but he somehow connected with Ethan Reznik – your dad, Iggy. Ethan was a major hooligan but not a heavyweight criminal – more of a charismatic, clever swindler. We called him 'The Fox.' He always managed to get involved in all sorts of shady deals, making a few bob and building trust with the biggest mobsters, and everyone had his back. He had his charm, even though he was a con man. Even I loved him. But he had two weaknesses – getting high, and your mum, Sarah. Everyone knew that. Anyway, from the moment Rico and Ethan connected, they saw each other's potential and became mates as well as partners, and within no time, everyone in the crime world knew them, and they always had each other's backs. Rico helped Ethan get off the gear and get on the straight and narrow, and that really upped his stocks around our lot. They were so strong that even the Met Police had them marked and tailed them all the time. One day, they came to me and said they had a serious plan and wanted to get me in on it. I was psyched to begin with – who wouldn't want to work with those two? They were planning a sting operation around the whole of Europe, researching all these million-dollar companies."

Richie sounded like he was reliving the story and started detailing their plan excitedly. "You take a junkie, pay him a few quid to break into the company offices, find their checkbooks and rip out two from the center, and you also get him to turn on the Follow Me service on their phones, directing the calls to our number. Then you forge the company signatures, and at the same time, you forge IDs to match and send someone over to the bank with a cheque and a suitcase. He shows up there and hands the cheque over to the clerk, who sees the huge sum on it and goes over to the manager to get the withdrawal approved. The bank manager calls up the company but reaches our guy because of the Follow Me service. Our man impersonates the company accountant and approves the withdrawal. The manager approves the clerk's request, the clerk loads the suitcase with cash, and Bob's your uncle! Of course, this gets done after the companies' working hours, just as a precaution. By the time they realize that their phone's on the Follow Me service, we're already long gone. Every day – different company, different bank. Finish up in one country and move on to the next. They had almost everything set up by the time they told me about it. They had junkie burglars, and contacts who'd speak to the bank managers on the phone. They decided that the people who were going to cash the cheques at the banks would be Rico, Ethan, and Sarah. They wanted me to be in charge of the forgery. Twelve companies in each European country, each cheque for six hundred thousand dollars. Switzerland was supposed to be the pilot run, and if everything went smoothly, they planned to continue with the rest of the countries and become multi-billionaires. Do the math – there are fifty countries in Europe!" I tried to calculate it all, but I got something wrong along the way and decided to just keep listening.

"We were a big team," Richie went on, "And the whole thing was costly – the forgery, the contacts in every country providing intel about the businesses, where they kept their checkbooks and what sort of security measures they had. Team leaders were in place in every country, a proper crazy operation. Meanwhile, something happened between Rico, Ethan, and Sarah. Iggy, your mum was one of the hottest women around, but if your dad's nickname was The Fox, then hers should have been Lilith."

Richie's voice suddenly went cloudy and I saw a black screen in front of my face. I wanted to tell him to stop – there's a limit to how much a person can hear about his own parents! But I decided to act like a man and keep quiet, even though the curiosity was eating me up.

"Those three had spent so much time together that I guess something started there, it was like a lethal Bermuda Triangle," Richie said, using the kind of phrase that almost made me burst out laughing, which actually calmed me down. "I reckon that there was jealousy there. Between Ethan and Sarah, Ethan and Rico, Sarah and Rico… It got proper messy, and we tried to keep our focus on the plan but it was getting tricky. They kept arguing and fighting like toddlers, and the stress of it all made Ethan start using again, which put us all under a lot of pressure. We started rethinking whether we should even get into this operation and risk everything we'd had going for us up until that point. And, if that wasn't enough, Sarah found out that she was pregnant. By that point, everything was already prepared and ready to go! We were itching to make it work, but they didn't want to risk Sarah and the pregnancy, so they asked me to fill in for her, and I said yes. She erupted like a bloody volcano at first and tried flexing and all that, but she eventually calmed down. We set a date, and a week before the flight, we decided to get Ethan off the gear. We ambushed him and got him in a basement we'd prepped with all the necessary things that could help. We left two guards with him, who were also team leaders for the operation and were meant to fly out with us."

Richie took a dramatic pause and then resumed his tale. "What can I say, Iggy? Your dad lost it… And then … well, no one knows how he'd managed to persuade one of the guards to drive him home for an hour so he could see Sarah, but in any case, the second they reached his place, Rico opened the door. They had a proper fight and knocked the shit out of each other. Meanwhile, the guard freaked out and started running around looking for me, but he got run over on the way, so the plan was short another person, and we were in a real pickle. Ethan disappeared but we assumed he'd come back, Rico was all bruised and swollen from the fight, and one partner got hit by a car – can you believe that? What a bloody mess! Anyway, we needed to find someone trustworthy to take on the guard's role as well as find Ethan, otherwise the whole thing would go down the drain and everyone's pockets would take a serious hit. It was all incredibly complicated. Two days before go-time, Ethan came back and connected us with a bloke he knew and trusted, but something seemed fishy to me. Call it intuition, or sharpened senses, but it was as though I knew that something bad was going down, and I decided to pull out of the operation abroad at the last minute. I didn't care about my losses, I knew I'd make it back within a few months, and the main thing was that I'd get some peace and quiet again. Ethan and Rico tried to convince me to stay on board, but I was determined to get myself out of it. I promised I'd sort out their documents, but I insisted that I wouldn't fly out with them. I tried to talk some sense into them, I said that after all that bloody mess they shouldn't be forcing it and that they'd be better off waiting for a while, but those two couldn't see straight, and what happened after that was a proper catastrophe."

Richie stopped to take a breath and immediately continued. "It turned out that Interpol was already on to them back when they'd planned everything – someone had snitched, we don't know who to this day. Interpol notified the Swiss companies and they were ready for us, they had everything – photos as well as recordings. We were clearly screwed. They gave them a proper welcoming at the airport, with evidence from here to Timbuktu. Ethan and Rico were given twenty-five years each, in separate prisons. I was nicked and sentenced to five years in the same prison as Ethan – who, like I said, had connections with all the biggest mobsters. They helped him from the outside, and he took care of me and Rico. Up until that point, everything pretty much sorted itself out. But that wasn't really the case, because within two months, four of the biggest mobsters who'd helped Ethan were arrested. Someone had obviously opened their big mouth about some operation that the four were a part of and which no one had known about, and since Ethan was the only person who was in the know about their operation, everyone suspected him. Remember I told you how everyone always trusted him? Well, at that point, it was the other way around, everyone thought that he was the snitch. And if that wasn't enough, there was a whole media frenzy around the story and it was published in all the papers. Somehow they knew about Ethan's connection with those mobsters and wrote about it, which increased everyone's suspicions about him. And, if that wasn't dodgy enough, the police made sure that the four wouldn't get transferred to Ethan's prison because they were worried about his safety. Instead, they were taken to Rico's prison. Now, you'd think they'd try to kill Rico considering he was Ethan's partner and closest mate, right? But that didn't happen, and Ethan took that as a clear sign that Rico must have sold him out – one word of theirs to any prison, and he – and anyone connected to him – would be dead within seconds. Ethan got the hint, he realized that it no longer mattered if he really was the snitch or not – he was about to get his ultimate sentencing. As a precaution, and since he felt like he had nothing to lose anymore, he requested an urgent meeting with the prison warden, and after that, he turned state witness and got into a witness protection program. Now, putting aside the fact that he'd abandoned me and had only taken care of himself, the worst bit was that he didn't include Sarah, the love of his life, who was pregnant with his child – with you, Iggy! Your dad was both a snitch and a loser who'd abandoned his pregnant wife, and that was the final proof that he really was the one who'd snitched about the mobsters, as well as about our own operation. He screwed everyone! Rico took advantage of the situation and got chummy with all the major criminals. He also got closer with your mum and kept her safe. He got parole after a few years, and within no time, he used all of his contacts from prison to become a criminal meteor."

"I can't believe it…" I heard myself mumbling with a heavy heart.

"And rightfully so," Richie said and looked me in the eye, "I had a lot of time to think about that whole story, and at this point, I reckon that Rico was the one behind it all. I think he was jealous of your dad, and he was also having an affair with your mum. I think that's what they were always fighting about. On the other hand, even though Ethan maintained a cool façade, he was a very innocent, gullible person and trusted Rico, and had probably told him all of the crime world's biggest secrets. I reckon he was the one who'd made sure everyone suspected Ethan and tried to take him out, and that way he could take his place amongst the criminal world's elite, as well as in Sarah's heart. But he didn't expect Ethan to beat him to it and disappear before they managed to off him. Anyway, that's the short version, yeah? There are a lot of things that no one will ever know except for your parents and Rico – it's worth writing a book about it one day. But you lot should get it in your head – Rico's a psycho, he likes to mess around with his prey, he enjoys tormenting people, he likes to plan and play with his victims much more than he does killing them. If it weren't for your dad, I'd have never gotten close to someone like him! Can't trust Rico, and I can't stand that treacherous man!"

We were completely engrossed in Richie's story and listened to it in utter shock, it was as though he were talking about other people, unrelated to us. But the moment he finished, my heart felt like a heavy dumbbell – I suddenly realized that I didn't know anything about my dad. According to Richie's story, he had no choice but to disappear, even though he wasn't a shitty person – not like Rico was, anyway. I felt the ground beneath me trembling, I was so baffled that I thought I could never trust anything in this world anymore. I can't explain the madness and the range of emotions I experienced during that moment, but all I managed to say was, "Wait, something doesn't add up. If my dad disappeared while my mum was still pregnant, then who's the man that I thought was my dad all these years?"

"Rico," Richie corroborated my worst fear, "You mean to say you didn't know it was him? Didn't you recognize him? Don't you remember him?"

"No, but now that I'm connecting the dots, I suddenly understand why he'd only ever come around at night, and why I wasn't allowed to leave the room whenever he came, and why she tore up all of the photos and keepsakes she'd had of my dad. I understand a lot more now."

"When your dad was with your mum, he loved her so much that she always had whatever she wanted. He was completely smitten with her," Richie said softly. I guess he was trying his best to make me break down.

"See? I didn't tell you that for nothing!" Tommy piped up, joining my heartbreaking chorus, but all I could think about was that I had to get back at that dickhead Rico who'd ruined my family, even if it cost me my life!

"I swear, Rico's going to die while looking me right in the eye," I muttered quietly, as befitting of the man I wanted to be, "And my mum will pay for what she did and for all the choices she's made."

"That won't be easy, Iggy," Richie tried to cool me down, "Don't underestimate his power, you have to be patient! For years now, I've been trying to come up with a way to get back at him. I did serious time, five years, and from the moment your dad took off, Rico didn't take care of any of us, even though he could have. Not all of us came out of this story alive, I personally have looked death in the eye on more than one occasion, and I had to survive on my own."

"Easy or not," I fumed as I turned to leave the shed, "Rico's a dead man!"

CHAPTER 19

"Iggy, don't do anything stupid!" Tommy shouted and grabbed me.

Richie looked pensive and distant for a few moments and then said, "Now that you lot are in the picture, this might be a good opportunity to plan something together that would bring that fucker down once and for all – but we have to be careful and plan things out. Listen, I have this mate, Marvin, I trust him… He comes up with the kind of things none of us would ever think about! I ain't promising nothing, but I'll call him up and consult with him. If anyone can come up with a good idea it's him, and with him on our side, we might actually get something done. Give me an hour and I'll come back here, but in the meantime, make sure to stay out of trouble." Richie got up and gave me a weird look.

"What is it now?" I said in an angry tone.

"Nothing," he said, "Just had a crazy thought for a second there."

"Tell me, what is it?"

"Look, isn't it strange that your dad abandoned your mum when she was pregnant? It was unlike him, and he loved her more than life itself."

"What the hell? Don't fuck about with me," I swear it was as though I was hearing myself from the outside. "I'd wondered whether Rico and my mum had had an affair and I thought that maybe he was the reason for her and my dad splitting up, but there's no way I'm Rico's son! If I was, then my mum would have treated me differently, and I think he would too. What are the odds that he knew he had a kid – with the woman that he loved, no less – and still alienated me? Especially when Ethan was no longer around."

"Dunno mate. Anyways, I'll make a move, see you lot later," he said and left the shed.

We called up Manu and asked him to get there straight away and bring some food for Tommy. I wanted a few lines because I felt sick to my stomach, and I didn't believe I'd ever feel hungry again. We told him that no matter who asked, he couldn't tell anyone where we were.

We were on edge. We couldn't believe the trouble we were in. My mind was racing with all these confused, contradicting thoughts... If the whole Shirley thing had never happened, maybe I'd have continued living the lie I'd been fed my whole life. How could it be that I had no recollection of Rico from my childhood days? Could it be that I'd noticed something special about him because something in my body or my subconscious remembered him? Most of all, I felt frustrated about never having had the chance to know my dad.

According to Richie's story, he sounded like a proper good man, and I reckon we would have gotten along. He probably would have loved me, if he ever got to know me. That actually made me feel better – as though there was still a chance for things to turn out all right. I suddenly thought about Smiley and about how great it is to have a parent who loves you and wants to reconnect with you. But, at the same time, I loathed my mum and everything she represented as a human being, as a woman, and as a mother. I genuinely hoped that one day, she'd pay for the choices she'd made.

Tommy was upset too. He missed Nicole and was certain that she was angry with him for not getting in touch with her all that time. He wanted to find a phone box and call her, and even though I knew exactly what he was feeling, I explained to him that it was way too risky and that he had to wait.

We tried to close our eyes and rest for a bit, but even though we were knackered, it proved difficult. The second we got close to properly falling asleep, Manu showed up with some food and supplies. He told us that no one had said or asked him anything about us.

We devoured the food and did a few lines. Andy warned us not to use drugs in front of Richie because he hated junkies, so we quickly hid the gear before he came back. We anxiously waited for him to return and prayed that he'd found his mate and was just held back because he couldn't choose between all of Marvin's brilliant ideas. When an hour had passed and he still wasn't back, we started realizing that prayers are worthless when you only say them in emergency situations. I guess we should have maintained at least a partial religious lifestyle for them to work.

Andy tried to calm us down and said that Richie was a busy man and that he must have had other things to sort out. "If he doesn't get here within the hour, I'll personally go out and check in on him," he promised.

"You, personally?!" Tommy shouted at him, looking like he'd lost his mind, "Why should we trust you? Why did you bring Richie along and force us to tell him everything? You've only gotten us into a deeper pile of shit, don't you get it?!"

"Chill, Tommy!" I said, frightened. I'd never seen him lose it like that before. "He'll come back eventually … and it would be a shame…"

"I don't care about anything!" he roared, "I have to go call Nicole, no matter the cost! Iggy, don't you get it? This life is bullshit! An illusion! Everyone's complicated and everyone keeps messing things up, and by the time we finally find something this pure, we have to walk away from it?! When will there ever be a good time for you to talk to Angie, eh? When we're hiding out and we're not allowed to contact anyone? Or when we have bags over our heads, a moment before our bodies get thrown down the Thames? What's the matter with us? What are we waiting for? Maybe Richie got cold feet and decided not to intervene, or maybe his mate never even showed up. It's been two hours, and we're sitting here waiting for salvation like a bunch of knob-ends. Let's think of something that only we could come up with. We've always managed to get ourselves out of trouble – without anyone else's help. I'm gonna call Nicole, and when I get back, we'll think up a solution. If Richie and Marvin show up by then – brilliant! But if not, we have each other, and that's good enough in my books."

"You're right," I was easily persuaded, mainly because I was itching to hear Angie's voice. "Let's call them up… What could go … wrong?" I stuttered at the end of that sentence.

Tommy picked up on my reservations and said, "Iggy, dying only takes a few seconds, and then you don't feel anything anymore. We believe in fate, don't we?"

"Yes," I said.

"Well, if our fate is to die today then nothing will help us either way! How would you rather die, scared shitless in this stinking shed, or while talking to Angie?"

That's all it took – I was thoroughly persuaded. Tommy managed to fill me up with a heroic spirit with just a few sentences. As I'd mentioned before, this was his expertise, and he proved it each and every time. Even if a firing squad were waiting for me outside, I'd tell them to fuck off and die like a king.

There were two phone boxes about thirty feet away from each other. Tommy and I split up while Andy and Manu kept an eye out, just in case. I got in one of the phone boxes and picked up the receiver with a trembling hand. I missed Angie so badly, and I had so much to tell her that I didn't even know where to begin. I had no idea what to tell her if she asked where I was, or what I'd do in case my mum had beat me to it and managed to fill her with lies. Moreover, if I told her the plan, then she'd be in danger. My mind was racing and my mouth was dry as I dialed her number.

"Hello?" she answered. The second I heard her voice, shivers went down my spine, my tongue was stuck to the roof of my mouth and I couldn't get a word out. "Hello?" she repeated. All I wanted was to tell her how much I loved her and missed her, how much I needed her, but nothing came out. "Hello… Iggy…?" she said my name. I was so shocked by having been exposed that I hung up straight away. I was panting and it took me a couple of moments to catch my breath. I couldn't figure out how she knew it was me.

I looked at Tommy in the other phone box. I couldn't hear his conversation, but it seemed like his entire body was talking. I was so frustrated that I felt out of breath. I was angry with myself and with the world. I guess that's why I got the urge to call my mum, cuss her out, and tell her that I knew everything. I planned to threaten to go to the coppers and tell them the whole story, scare the shit out of her.

"Hello?" I suddenly heard her voice, and only then did I realize that I really did call her – an incredibly stupid idea no doubt, and one I'd never even dream of doing had I spoken to Angie.

"What's up?" I asked unwillingly.

"Where are you?" she asked dryly. It's not like I'd expected her to ask how I was, but my anger was fueled, nevertheless.

"I'm at a mate's place, has anyone been looking for me?"

"Your dad!" she replied sarcastically.

"Rico or Ethan?" That managed to shut her up for a few seconds.

"It's … it's complicated." She suddenly sounded calmer than ever, which wasn't like her.

"It's complicated? Why? Because of the affair you had with Rico when you betrayed my dad and got pregnant? Or because of the lies you've been selling me all these years, letting me think that Ethan was my dad, when the truth was that you couldn't stand me because I was a constant reminder of just how rotten your soul is?"

"The asshole who sold you that story's going to pay for it!" she exclaimed, "And it would be foolish of you to believe any old nonsense that comes out of some wanker's mouth. If you want us to talk about it then fine, but I'm not doing this over the phone."

"Why did you never even bother telling me about it?"

"Iggy, everything in life has its own time. You're well within your right to know all of it, so let's just meet up and have a talk."

"Oh yeah, I'd love that!" I shouted, "But what can I do, I'm not entirely sure I'll make it out of that meeting alive! Some mum, right?"

"Don't be a knob! No one's going to do anything to you, I promise! Just come over and we'll talk about everything."

"Yeah, only thing is that right now I'm a knob with a battered body, so don't tell me no one's gonna do anything to me!"

"You should be thankful it only came to that," she continued pissing me off, "You lot could have rotted away in prison for what happened at Shirley's! Tommy raped her while you were breaking her furniture, you bloody junkie!"

"That bitch is lying!"

"Oh yeah? Then why did you do a runner?" she insisted, "You left a mess, took her furniture, and you actually expect anyone to believe you?! I'm telling you, you better get here and tell me everything… If Shirley's lying then trust me, we'll expose her, but in the meantime, all the evidence is against you! And if that's not bad enough, you're now rummaging through a past that everyone prefers to forget! I'm telling you, Iggy, this isn't something to talk about over the phone, and you'll be sorry for opening the whole thing up, because now you're not the only one in trouble, you're endangering your mates too! I'll say it again, hang up the bloody phone and get over here to sort out the mess you've made! And bear in mind that if you lot stay where you are, they'll find you soon enough, and then it won't just get worse for you – it'll be irreversible!" And with that final threat, she hung up on me.

I felt so upset. Even though I knew that I couldn't trust a word that came out of her mouth, everything she'd said seemed to make sense. I looked to the side and saw that Tommy wasn't in the phone box anymore. Andy was still there and motioned for me to come over. I walked up to him and we headed back to the shed.

"That was a long talk you had with Angie," he said.

"Yeah," I lied. I was scared to tell the lads – and especially Tommy – that I'd spoken to my mum. When she said I was endangering my mates, I felt like I had been punched in the stomach. I couldn't handle the thought that something would happen to them because of me. '*I would rather die alone,*' I thought. And what she'd said about the person who'd told me the truth made me think that she knew who it was, and that really troubled me. It made me realize that Richie wasn't coming back, and that the responsibility for my best mates' lives was on me and me alone. I felt it was my personal duty to get them out of this mess as quickly as possible.

"Did you tell her what happened?" Andy's voice sawed away through my mind.

"Not quite, we talked about the future." I was shocked at how quickly I was able to come up with these lies. "I didn't want to worry her with what's happening, and I didn't want her to know too much and get into trouble because of me, know what I mean?"

We went into the shed and found Manu and Tommy there. Tommy looked beat and was mumbling all sorts of unclear rubbish. I managed to gather that Nicole had told him she wanted out because she'd gotten back with her ex, and that she'd asked him never to call her again.

"See that?" he mumbled in pain, "The only girl I genuinely fell in love with is also the only one who's ever left me. How did that happen to me? Can you explain that?"

"Sod's law," I said. My mind was busy figuring out how to explain that we had to get the hell out of there without revealing the fact I'd spoken to my mum.

"Mate, I think you're just finding it hard to accept that someone doesn't want you," Manu tried to say in a sensitive tone, "But it happens to everyone, and anyway, who knows how long you two would have lasted. Knowing you, I reckon you'd have made her fall in love with you and then you'd do a runner. Maybe it felt different to you with her because you hadn't yet fully swept her off her feet?"

"Could be ... dunno," Tommy said, his voice finally sounding more stable, even though he still had a tormented look on his face, "And maybe I'll never know. Besides, at the end of the day, what could I have possibly added to the relationship in my current state? I reckon it was too much for me as it is! I've got no money, no place of my own, and she's the kind of bird that needs a successful man who pampers her and buys her things, gives her a sense of security. Love alone couldn't be enough for someone like her... But Iggy ... we're still going to get filthy rich ... and when we do, I'll fight for her. Right, Iggy?"

I nodded my head as excitedly as I could. I couldn't bear to see him that gloomy. His face finally started looking normal again, and he even managed to ask, "How did it go with Angie?"

"Never mind that, bruv," I quickly dismissed him, "I can't be bothered right now, and I have a feeling that Rico's found Richie and squeezed everything out of him, including our hideout! Basically, we need to make a run for it, and I have an idea! Manu needs to run over to the car lot and buy us the cheapest car he can find so that we can stay mobile. Tommy and I will drive as far up north as we can and try to get to the Scottish border. We'll find an isolated place where Rico won't be able to locate us. In the meantime, Andy will work on some passports, and once they're ready, we'll find a way to send them over to us and we'll get the fuck out of England for a good few years!"

"Why don't we get Andy to make passports for all of us," Manu suggested excitedly, "And then we can all fly over to Smiley in Israel!"

"And what if Andy and Manu get caught and tortured so Rico can find out where we are?" Tommy asked the most crushing question possible.

"Then tell them everything I just said," I sighed, "I was lying anyway. I'm not really going to tell you the full plan. Don't say anything about the passports cuz they'd never think of it on their own, they'll just want to know where we are, that's all. So, where are we going, Manu?" I asked him.

"Up north, as close as possible to Scotland," he replied hesitantly.

"Exactly!" I gathered up all my strength, trying to put out a sense of confidence in my plan's chances of success, but even I didn't believe myself. It was only after we did a few lines and I took some more painkillers that I started feeling more confident.

We gave Manu some money and he went out to get us a car. In the meantime, we sorted out our stuff and thought up the worst-case scenarios, when the phone suddenly rang and Andy quickly answered it. He'd hoped it was Richie, but it was a reverse-charge call from abroad – Smiley was calling from Israel, and Andy accepted the call immediately.

We all huddled around the receiver to hear him, but the line was shit and we couldn't understand anything Smiley was saying except for a few mumbles and the word 'mum,' and then the call got disconnected.

We were so bummed out. We thought Smiley would call back, but he never did. We cussed him – in the best sense of the word – for having the time of his life while we were literally fighting for our own lives.

Andy quickly ran home and came back after a few minutes with a bag containing a change of clothes, just in case. We grabbed the drugs and the medication, put everything in the bag and waited for Manu, who was supposed to come back with a car.

Suddenly, we heard noises and voices outside. Andy went out to see what was happening and he rushed back in hysterically. "Listen lads, get out right now and run as fast as you can towards the petrol station on the way out of the city and hide there! And stay off the main roads, the bloody Interpol's here!"

CHAPTER 20

Tommy and I got the hell out of there. I held the bag and the shoes in my hand that was less painful but it was difficult, and Tommy took the jackets. We ran through the side streets and headed towards the petrol station. I leaned against Tommy for a considerable amount of time because I was still in pain, despite the painkillers. We arrived almost completely out of breath, and the moment we got to the petrol station, a car approached us, its lights blinding our eyes. We couldn't see a thing, so we turned around and ran in the opposite direction. Frighteningly enough, the car continued driving after us, but then we suddenly heard a familiar voice. "Oi! It's me, Manu!"

We calmed down. Manu had shown up in an old blue Morris Marina. Tommy and I quickly got in and we all drove towards the city exit.

"Where's Andy?" we asked him.

"You have no idea how many people are looking for you!" he said. "Besides Interpol, there were two other random fellas who came by and snooped around. Andy was standing with them outside just as I arrived. I heard them asking him questions… He gave them a load of bollocks and motioned to me with his eyes and hands to get in the shed. When I went inside, I saw a note he'd left me, telling me to drive as quickly as possible to the petrol station to meet you, so I ran off and he stayed there."

"I don't understand, why's Interpol after us? That's not like Rico," I said.

"Maybe it has nothing to do with Rico," Tommy said, "Maybe they want you to testify. You escaped from the hospital, and that must have seemed suspicious to them. I reckon they're looking for you in order to finish up with their investigation, and the two random fellas must be Rico's men."

We quickly got in the car and sped towards the north, but at some point, we stopped at a shop and bought a map. We decided to head north through the villages and not the main roads, at least until we felt safe, but before that, we dropped Manu off at a train station. We said goodbye and promised to call the lads with an update the moment we could. We waited until he was out of sight and then turned and headed towards Ireland, making sure that he had no idea which direction we were heading – that way he couldn't expose our location if anyone were to try and question him.

During the entire ride, I deliberated whether to tell Tommy about the conversation with my mum, but I was scared that he'd be upset with me, that he'd tell me I was a fuck-up and that he couldn't trust me anymore, and I was already filled with so much guilt – if it weren't for me, we wouldn't have gotten into this mess to begin with.

In the meantime, he told me about Nicole. Turned out she had a tough dad – a kind of mobster – and she was adamant that he wouldn't find out they were together.

"She said that he was very controlling, know what I mean? She was constantly scared he'd find out about our relationship," he explained, "But she swore that she was protecting me more than she was protecting herself. What kind of dad does that to his own daughter? And then, all of a sudden, she told me she'd gotten back together with her ex. And what about her dad, eh? Suddenly it's all right for her to be with her ex, of all people?"

"Maybe she's hiding something," I suggested.

"Yeah, that's more likely. Maybe it's because I'm skint, Iggy. She's a classy bird, you can tell that she's swimming in dosh, all prim and proper."

"How can a waitress be that rich, bruv?"

"What do you mean? Rich women have jobs too."

"Waiting tables at a nightclub? And her controlling dad's all right with that? I don't know, mate, sounds dodgy to me."

"True," he agreed. "On the one hand, after just a short amount of time she was already talking to me about a future together, kids, feelings she'd never had before until she met me, and on the other hand, she was scared shitless that someone would see us together, and then she flipped and promptly threw me out of her life. It was really strange, bruv."

I have no idea what it was he'd said that made me suddenly realize who Nicole was, but it just suddenly hit me. "Say, does she have black hair? Was she the one with the shorts and red lippy that day when you came by the club?"

"That's her, yeah! That's Nicole!" he said excitedly.

The penny finally dropped. I realized that Nicole was Rico's lover – the waitress from the club! I told Tommy about how I'd met her. I reminded him the story about Rico raping the waitress and helped him connect the dots. Tommy was proper shocked! He finally understood that something seriously dodgy was going on there, and that the girls were probably forced to stay there.

"So, maybe he was actually next to her when I called, and that's how he found us?"

'Could very well be,' I thought, *'Guess I'm not the only idiot here, and maybe it wasn't because of the conversation with my mum but because of Nicole.'*

"I hope he didn't do anything to her," Tommy added. "I'm worried, Iggy. I have to call her and make sure she's all right."

"No fucking way! That's not going to happen, mate," I ruled, "We're not making the same mistake again. You do realize that if you call her now, she's a goner. He's definitely next to her, so what would you tell her? Anything you say would be used against her, don't you understand? And you can't trust her either, because he'll try to use her to get to us. We have to find a way to get to him and confront him without putting ourselves at risk!"

"But how are we going to do that?" he asked.

"Let's just keep driving until we're far enough to use a phone box," I said. "That way, even if he tracks our location, we'll be long gone by the time his men get there. We'll try to feel out his vibe during the call, figure out what he's after. Then we'll be all the wiser… Maybe we'll come up with an idea… But we have to figure out what the crack is first of all, and understand what we're up against."

Tommy agreed. After a five-hour drive, a few lines and a lot of painkillers, we stopped at a petrol station, and I called Rico.

"Yeah?" he answered immediately.

"Hi, Rico, it's Iggy."

"Where are you?!"

"Rico, we don't want any trouble."

He ignored me and repeated his question, "Where are you?"

I evaded a reply again. Tommy wasn't really helpful when he pleaded with me quietly, "Don't tell him! Ask him what he's planning on doing, ask about Nicole."

"Rico, I know you must be pissed," I said gloomily, "But seriously, things have gotten way out of proportion, and I have no idea how we've gotten to this situation. I … we … we're asking for a chance to sit down and explain our side of things. We're even prepared to find a way to reimburse Shirley for the table, we want to take responsibility … and … after what happened at the parking lot, I'm not coming back until you give me your word that nothing will happen to us."

"Are you seriously telling me your conditions?!"

Tommy covered the receiver with his hand and whispered, "No, no conditions – a promise … tell him to give you his word."

Rico heard us whispering and said in an authoritative tone, "Tell that little shit next to you to step aside, I want to speak with you alone."

"Tommy, go over there for a minute," I said and winked at him, then motioned for him to keep quiet. We waited for a few more seconds, and then I told Rico, "I'm alone."

"Now you listen here," he said, "I'm going to give you two options, whatever you choose is fine by me, I'm prepared for both. The first one's based on the assumption that you already got what was coming to you. I won't lie, considering the circumstances, anyone else wouldn't be talking to me right now – they wouldn't be able to talk ever again, that is. And I won't hide the fact that I'm angry about you running away like a coward from the hospital, and that you told your mother all those lies. And the whole thing with Richie – what was that good for?! And still, despite all that, I'm willing to forgive you. Ask me why."

"Why?" I asked.

"Because that's what I feel like doing," he replied, "So with option number one, you and your mate show up at my office at eight in the morning tomorrow! You make sure he's with you, and you stay out of anything that happens. For all you care, it's business as usual – our score is settled, and we'll be starting a new leaf. Option number two – you lot continue running to wherever it is you're going, and I'll eventually find you, and then it'll be open season on you, son! I'll deal with both of you the same way! So, which will it be?"

Tommy and I exchanged looks – we understood what he meant. I could see the fear in Tommy's eyes, even though I knew that I'd never give him up, even if my life depended on it.

"Wait, let me see if I understand," I tried to control my voice and keep it from trembling. "You told me once that the most important thing to you is loyalty, right? But if I take you up on your first offer then I'd basically be betraying my best mate, and then you'd never trust me again. And, if I go with the second option, then you'll definitely never trust me... Did I get that right?"

"Fuck's sake, Iggy, you're such a waste of talent," he said in an amused tone, "Look, a man needs to pick sides during his life, put all of his bollocks in one basket. The way I see it, the day you were hired is the day you should have realized that your loyalty was first and foremost to Rico King. You have no idea what happened in Shirley's room because you went on working while your mate snuck in there! That piece of scum raped my best mate and..."

"He didn't rape her, Rico!" I interrupted him, "I swear! I swear that I was the one who'd asked Tommy not to come with me to see you that day! If he raped her, then he wouldn't want to come see you, he'd have run away. And furthermore, if he raped her then I wouldn't be defending him. If he murdered someone then yeah, sure, but raping a bird, and getting in trouble with you on top of that?! That shit would come with a heavy price!"

Rico fell silent for a few moments. I was a nervous wreck until he finally spoke up again. "Okay, if that's the case, then I promise that I'll give him a chance to prove to me it didn't happen – just like I gave Nicole a chance to prove to me that nothing happened. I promise to check everything he says until I get to the bottom of this, just like in court! I can't promise you that he'll be found innocent, but until we figure out the truth, I'll treat him as no more than a suspect. I expect to see you two tomorrow at eight sharp!"

"Give us two days, we're pretty far by now and it'll take us a while to get back," I asked him.

"You got it," he replied, "And no fucking about – think about your future, and Angel's too."

My blood boiled within a split second. I suddenly realized what was going on. "We'll be there!" I said, but the moment he hung up, I told Tommy, "Listen to me, he's full of shit! The second he sees you, you're a dead man! He doesn't really care if you raped Shirley or not, he's got it in for you because of Nicole, and Shirley's just his cover."

Tommy gave me a surprised look and shook his head to the sides, "Iggy, what do you think that fucker did to her?"

"Tommy," I sighed, "That sort of thinking ain't gonna help us right now! Listen, I came up with a brilliant idea, and I even planted something about it during the phone call, so that Rico will think there's an actual chance of me going along with him – and he took the bait! The chances of it working depend on my acting skills and how believable I am… If I fail, I'll be the first one to be taken out… The plan goes like this – we continue driving tonight until we get as close to Ireland as possible, and we find a motel where you can stay. I'll head back to London, get to Rico's place all frantic and tell him that when I told you what he'd said on the phone, you panicked and refused to go along with it. Remember how I told him that if you really raped her and got me in trouble with him then I'd make you pay a heavy price for it? I said that on purpose. I'll say that when I told you that he gave me his word about checking your story until he gets to the truth, you hesitated at first, but I eventually persuaded you and you agreed to come with me to meet him – or at least that's what I'd thought, until we reached London and stopped for petrol. That's when you said that you needed the loo and then you just disappeared. I'll convince him that I did exactly what he'd told me to do, and I'll tell him that if you ran away then he must be right, and my trust in you is broken. I'll even remind him that I'd said that over the phone, and I'll say that for all I care, you're on your own now and it's between you and him, and that I'll do whatever it takes to win back his trust."

Tommy looked at me in fright and opened his mouth to say something, but I continued saying my piece. "Listen, in the meantime, just wait for me – don't call anyone, don't go anywhere, don't let a fucking fly into the room, just wait there for a week. Today's Sunday. By next Sunday, I'll get us new identities, plane tickets, and visas. Andy will take care of it all. I'll come back to you next Sunday and we'll head straight to the airport and fly to Brazil, and no one will know about it – just you, me, and Angie! We have to be one step ahead of Rico at all times. All we need is to stall, trust me!"

"That's a wicked idea, if it actually works." Tommy's eyes were filled with fear. "But what if Rico doesn't fall for it? Then what?"

"Then I'm screwed, and you are too," I tried to gather whatever courage I had left to maintain a confident tone, "But we can't stay like this. We have to try and get closer to him, turn the tables and be brave! That's the only way we'll manage to fuck him up and finally be free!"

"Iggy, why overcomplicate everything?" Tommy suddenly piped up, "Let's drive over to his place together. We'll go there with weapons, shoot everyone down – worst case, we'll die too, but at least he'll be dead by then!"

"You're tripping, bruv," I tried to calm him down, "He's got bodyguards and they're armed too; we'll never get a chance to shoot him down and then we'll have died for nothing. Let's just try my plan, odds are fifty-fifty, and if it works, then we'll even have the money to live wherever we fancy, plus we'll have fucked him over, and if we're lucky, we'll have taken him down altogether."

Tommy nodded and we headed out to try my plan. I drove and he occasionally cut us a few sweet lines to stop our minds from coming up with safer ideas than my plan. Even though we constantly came up with new ideas, none of them led to anything worth mentioning.

"You need to come prepared for your meeting with him, just in case…" he said at some point.

"What do you mean?" I asked.

"A gun, Iggy!" he looked at me as though I were an idiot, "You have to be carrying when you get there. We don't trust him, and you can't just waltz in there like a lamb to the slaughter. A gun will make you feel secure. I know where we can get one without a hitch. Once you get back to London, first thing you do is go to that minging pub – the Backrub – and look for Dirty Harry. He's always there and he knows everyone, he'll tell you who to speak to."

"Okay, I will," I said. I tried to sound determined, but despite my best efforts, I let out an old man's sigh and added, "How did it even come to this? Last week we didn't have a care in the world. All we wanted was some dosh and a better life."

"Money's a tricky fucker," Tommy smiled, "It ruins people. Imagine never needing money, or better yet, imagine a world where money has no value… Remember when we were kids and we met that homeless man in the square and he taught us how to whistle at bats?"

"Yeah, I do, and they came to us and all! He was a top man … rich … a businessman."

"That was before he was homeless," Tommy said, "And remember the story he told us?"

"No, remind me."

"He said that the life he'd had as a rich businessman was intense and stressful. He explained that it may have looked like a good life, with the perfect penthouse and lush cars and a different bird every week, but he was always stressed. And then he got into some debt and the whole world turned against him. He stopped paying his mortgage, he couldn't afford his bills or his loan payments, and all of his businesses went bust. And then, all of his mates suddenly abandoned ship, the birds vanished into thin air, and his family turned its back on him after the debt collectors came to see them. He tried to hang in there, but he eventually collapsed, and decided to give everything up and live out on the streets, with no cares or debts and without having to account for anything to anyone. You told him back then that if he made it once then he could do it again. But he replied that he didn't even want to go back to his old life. He said that his life might seem shitty to an outsider, but he felt like the happiest man alive. He ate whenever he was hungry, enjoyed the little things, chose where to lay his head down, and had good mates, the kind that he connected to without any masks or hidden agendas, and he felt as free as could be. Remember what he said in the end?"

"No, what did he say?"

"He said, 'You two make sure to keep that friendship going – especially if you make it big one day. Don't forget each other, because at the end of the day, a second before you leave this world, the important thing won't be your bed or your bank account or some bird wanking you off, it'll be a familiar face holding your hand and looking at you lovingly until you close your eyes for good.' I think I understand that now more than I ever have before."

We made a few pit stops along the way, but that was it. It was important for us not to leave any tracks or be seen. We arrived at a godforsaken town with a roadside motel, and decided that it would be a good place for Tommy to stay and wait – first of all, because we were dead tired, but also because it was right at the entrance to the town so you could see every car coming in. Before that, we stopped at a shop and bought a week's worth of supplies for Tommy – fags, food, and a few basics. That way, he wouldn't have to leave the room and he could keep a low profile.

I went into the reception and registered for the room under my name, paying for a week and a half upfront. Tommy waited in the car so no one would see him. Then we took the car right up to the room. I came out to unlock the door, Tommy ran in, and I quickly locked the door behind us.

I had a shower and collapsed onto the bed. I had to get some sleep for a couple of hours so that I could get through the drive back on my own. I downed a couple more painkillers and was counting on the gear to keep me up during the drive. I split the gear so that Tommy would get most of it, and left myself just enough until I got to London, where I could sort out some more.

I booked a wake-up call because I was scared I'd sleep in, but as knackered as we both were, we couldn't fall asleep.

"I don't know where you get all that courage from, Iggy," Tommy mumbled, "And after what you've been through."

"Bruv, I'm more of an idiot who has to pay for his mistakes than I am courageous."

Tommy laughed. "Aren't you scared that something will go wrong?"

"I am, yeah," I said, "But what they did to me at the parking lot made me realize that I'd only suffer for a few minutes and then I wouldn't feel a thing. A few minutes, get it? They kicked the shit out of me, and all I remember is the pain of the first few kicks and then nothing. We make a big deal out of dying, but when you die, you don't feel anything anyway. No fear, no longing, no pain, nothing – you'll be a soul. So what have we got to lose? Either we make it work and start living the good life, or we keep rotting away and trying to survive. And to be honest, I don't want to live in survival mode anymore, I've had enough of it! Rico and his crew, they're just people, aren't they? Rico's main advantage is that he has no fear…"

"That and his money," Tommy added.

"Yeah, but he made all that money because he's fearless," I explained. "We're scared right now, but if we overcome our fear and use our brains, we'll make it work! And after we fuck him over, then we'll have money too, and then no one will have anything on us! So isn't that worth a try?"

At that point, I felt so tired that my eyes went heavy. Tommy said something, but it mixed in with exhaustion-hallucinations and I couldn't understand a thing. I was sure that we were still having a conversation when the phone suddenly rang and I jumped up in fright. It was the wake-up call I'd booked. I looked at Tommy – he was sound asleep. I tried to get up but my body felt like it had fossilized, so I took some more painkillers, cut a few lines, and then woke Tommy up. He got up and started getting dressed.

"What are you doing?" I asked.

"I ain't waiting around, Iggy, I'm coming with you. I don't think it's right, me staying here. You go up to his office alone, but I'll wait in the car or nearby somewhere, just in case you need my help."

I looked at him and he suddenly seemed like an insecure child. "Do you know why plans fail?" I asked in the most assertive tone I could summon within me, "Because they get last-minute changes and then everything turns to shit. We have a solid plan, so stop worrying!"

Tommy nodded tiredly and collapsed onto the bed as I quickly got my things together. I pulled out some money and left it for him on the dresser, just in case. Before I left, I said, "Remember that it's all about fate – no matter what happens, it's meant to be. But don't worry, I have a good feeling about this. We'll be on that plane to Brazil in no time, bruv, think positive and everything will turn out fine!"

"Just do your best to make it work!" he said in a stifled tone.

I opened the door and deliberated whether to tell him what I had in mind. I finally turned to him and said, "If – and only if, yeah? Chances are a hundred to one – but just in case ... if anything goes wrong, find a way of telling Angie that she was the most precious thing I ever had. Tell her that when I thought about joy, I thought about her. When I thought about success, I thought about her. When I was sad, I thought about her, and when I thought about life it was with her and her alone!"

"Don't worry, I'll even tell her that when you shagged other birds, you only thought about her."

"You tosser!" I cussed him and we burst out laughing. But deep down, I silently thanked him for lightening up the mood for me even though he was scared shitless.

CHAPTER 21

When they say, "What doesn't kill you makes you stronger," they probably mean that time I drove back to London on my own. That was actually when I felt the most connected to my roots – empowered, strong, and determined to make it.

I didn't stop for a second on the way back, except for petrol. I couldn't afford to waste any time. Once I got back to the city, I headed straight to the Backrub pub to get a gun, just like we'd agreed. That bar was the world's lowest point – there were two types of people there, the kind who'd lost hope, and the dodgy wheeler-dealers.

I parked the car behind the pub next to a vehicle with a cover on it. I couldn't stop myself – I lifted the cover and peered at the car. It was a gorgeous black Lamborghini, and it sent all sorts of thoughts and worries rushing through my mind. I was paranoid that maybe it belonged to one of Rico's lot, or that maybe it was Rico's own car – but I had no other choice but to go into the pub. It was the only place I could get a gun on the lowdown. I pulled myself together and walked in, immediately coming across the smell of putrid sweat from the local drunks, probably from the night before. It actually played to my advantage considering that even if there were people there who might know me, they were probably too wasted to notice me. In fact, even if a naked, Native-American Chief walked in with a spear in hand, no one would pay him any attention – or no one would care, to be more precise.

I approached the bar. Within seconds, I spotted Dirty Harry sitting at the edge of the bar, completely and utterly wasted. His real name was Arie Barbash, but everyone called him Dirty Harry, like that Clint Eastwood film – not because of any resemblance to the actor, but rather because of how filthy he always was. Ever since he'd moved to our neighborhood, years back, he never showered – not even once. They say he used to be a top accountant and was happily married to a woman that he loved. They lived in London's most prestigious area and were considered the elite of the business world. On his fortieth birthday, his wife – who was five months pregnant – planned a surprise party for him with their closest mates. Everyone showed up and waited for him, and about half an hour before he was supposed to show up, his wife drove by to pick up his parents, who'd flown in especially and were waiting for her at the airport. They say that before she left the house, his wife turned the oven on to keep the food warm, and she made sure to shut the windows so that it would seem like no one was home, just in case Arie decided to get there early.

No one really knows what happened. Some say that she'd forgotten to turn the gas off and that the oven caused a short. Others say that one of their closest mates was madly in love with the wife and had planned the whole thing – even though the coppers had questioned him for days and ended up letting him go a week later due to lack of evidence. In any case, when she came back home with his parents and opened the front door, a sudden explosion shook up the entire neighborhood. The house burned down, including everyone inside it. Within a split second, Arie had lost all of the people he'd ever loved. When he arrived and turned into his street, he could already see the crowd gathering outside his house. He ran there frantically, but they wouldn't let him near it. He saw his home go up in flames, and he saw his loved ones' bodies being carried out on gurneys, one after the other. He went wild and the coppers eventually had to cuff him so that he wouldn't harm himself.

fter that, they hospitalized him at a mental asylum by court order. He was there for a good few months and tried to commit suicide numerous times, until he happened to meet Rabbi Shulman who was visiting someone there. The rabbi explained to him that if he ever wanted to reunite with his loved ones in heaven, he couldn't kill himself. He claimed that the souls of suicide victims end up in a different dimension and lose their loved ones for all eternity. Two weeks after that, Arie was discharged and he moved into our neighborhood, right near the rabbi's house.

I walked up to him. He looked at me and smiled, but his eyes looked wet, as though he'd been crying all that time.

"What's your story, son?" he asked.

"I'm looking for someone who sells weapons," I replied. He nodded his head in silence. "Know of anyone?"

"What do you need that for?"

"Protection," I said and caused him to burst out laughing.

"Protection from what? You really think that'll do you any good?" he asked and pointed upwards, "It all depends on him! If he wants you to live then you will, if he wants you to die then…"

At that point, he neared his face to mine and looked deep into my eyes. His stare made me uneasy. He then got up and started walking away from me, but I followed him and whispered, "I need it to try and protect my family and my best mates."

Harry stopped and turned to face me. "Did you really think I'd fall for that, son?"

"No…" I answered hesitantly.

"Wrong! It did!" he said and added, "Buy me a drink, will ya?"

"Whatever you want," I replied.

He ordered a full bottle of vodka and two shots of tequila. He put the bottle next to him and handed me one of the shot glasses. I downed the shot and got right to it. "I need a gun, Arie. I'm in trouble with some really bad people who want to take everyone I love away from me, and I have to save them."

"I wish I could turn back time and save my loved ones, son." His voice had so much pain in it that my heart almost broke. "A gun won't really help you, but what do I care, eh? Each to his own. Now tell me, if I help you out, will you help me out too?"

"Of course, gladly," I replied.

"All right, so I'll get you a gun to save your loved ones, and you promise to help me out and send me to my loved ones."

Shivers ran down my spine. "I can't promise you that."

"Then I ain't gonna help you!" he said. I could see the torment in his pained stare. The tears kept streaming from his droopy eyes, but he wasn't the one weeping – it was his soul. It must be true what they say about the eyes being the window to the soul. I felt sorry for him.

"Arie, I'm begging you, please help me," I pleaded with him.

"See the man with the brown jacket over there?" he pointed towards the loo, "The one talking to that little doll?"

I looked to the side and saw a huge, bald man with a threatening look in a brown leather jacket. He was talking to a bird who looked like a teenage runaway. "The bald one?" I asked to make sure we were on the same page.

"That's right," he replied.

"How should I approach him?" I asked, steadying myself on my feet.

"Depends on what you're after," he said.

"A gun!"

"Then you'll need to talk to her – the little doll, she's got the works."

I was stunned. I didn't really believe him. I thought he was just wasted and hallucinating. "Arie, focus for a minute," I said, "Are you sure? That bird, who looks like a kid, she's the one that's going to sort me out – not the bald fella?"

"As sure as I am that I'll wake up tomorrow morning," he said gloomily.

"Thanks, Arie," I said and rose from the barstool.

"Don't thank me with words," he said and mulled his fingers together to signify cash. I took out a ten-quid note and put it in his hand, then hesitantly walked over to the bird. I was expecting a bloke, I wasn't planning on buying a gun from some Barbie doll. As I neared her, I felt even more uncomfortable, I had no idea how to talk to a bird about bloke stuff.

I came closer and stared at her until she noticed me. I motioned to her that I wanted to have a word, she whispered something in the bald fella's ear and walked up to me. The closer she came, the more surprised I felt. The bird was tiny and incredibly slim, a blonde with braids and huge, baby-blue eyes. 'What on earth does she have to do with weapons? How did she even get into that?' I wondered.

"Hiya," she said.

"Hi," I replied, "I'm Iggy, nice to meet you."

"So you fancy me so badly that you couldn't wait another minute?"

"No!" I replied.

"No?!" she repeated, baffled.

I felt completely confused. "Yeah ... no ... I mean, it's not about that ... I wasn't trying to pull you."

"Got a light?" she asked and gently pulled out a pack of fags from her pocket.

"Sure," I said and lit her cigarette.

"I'm all ears," she whispered delicately yet assertively.

"I'm friends with Harry," I pointed in his direction.

"Great, what about it?"

"I'm looking for a gun..." That was all I'd managed to say, and immediately, from an innocent, 'Year Ten' teenager, she turned into a South American drug cartel dealer ... full-blown white trash. She flicked her fag in one swift move and reached her hand to my throat. Before I even managed to blink, she shoved me up the wall with one hand and pressed a blade against my bollocks with the other.

"Now listen here, you little shit, this time, I'll just cut off your bollocks and send you back to Marcus for you to deliver them so he can finally have a pair of his own. What's the matter? Has he run out of men that he's sending little boys over now?"

I was hysterical! She was as strong as Bruce Lee. Even in my worst nightmares, I'd never imagined I'd lose my bollocks over a mistake, and on top of that, Rico would finish the job and have me killed.

"Wait, this is a mistake…" I wheezed, "I'm not who you think I am, and I don't know any Marcus… I'm not lying, ask Arie…"

She looked at me for a moment, then turned her face back towards the bar and shouted, "A-r-i-e! Oi, Arie!"

Harry turned around, as did the rest of the punters. I felt as humiliated as could be and just prayed to God that this would end soon.

"You know this fella?" she asked.

Harry got up and slowly walked towards us. "Yeah, I sent him over to ya," he confirmed.

She let go of me and resumed her Year Ten appearance. Needless to say, her innocent look no longer worked on me. "Sorry, I have to be careful. I'm Martine," she said and reached her hand out to me. I cooperated and shook her hand, but I was still in shock. "No offense," she went on, "If you really were who I thought you were and I didn't do what I did, then I'd be in real trouble by now."

"Right…" I replied.

"Follow me," she said and started walking out of the bar. I stayed right behind her. "Gave you a fright, eh? Did I surprise you?" she asked as she walked.

"Yeah, you're a bird," I mumbled in embarrassment, "It's confusing … I couldn't react the way I would with a fella."

"Of course," she smiled, pleased with herself, "That's one of the advantages for women doing men's work."

"And what are the disadvantages?"

"I'll have to tell you some other time, when you buy me a drink."

"See? Another thing that couldn't happen between two blokes!"

"That's right, another little advantage," she laughed.

We came out and walked behind the pub, straight to the black Lamborghini. She took the cover off and got in the car. I stood there frozen, shocked by the fact that it was her car. "Are you coming or what?" she rolled the window down and revved the engine. I quickly got in and she tossed a blindfold at me. "Here, put that on, don't want you seeing the way."

I covered my eyes with it, she stepped on the gas and we sped away. "Guess it's worthwhile, being a weapons dealer," I said.

"Depends, I went through quite a lot to get to where I'm at, it's not for just anyone."

"How did you even get into it?"

"That's a sixth date kind of story. What gun are you after?"

"I don't really know much about guns. I need something simple and good."

"What's your budget?"

"What's the price range?"

"You know, anywhere between ten and two hundred, depends on the quality."

"Ten quid? You sell toy guns too?" I jested.

"Funny! For someone who doesn't really know much about guns, you're quick!"

"I'm actually surprised at the prices, I thought you'd say it starts at a grand and goes up to hundreds of thousands. Let's go for fifty," I suggested.

She halted the car with a screech and roared, "Are you fucking shitting me?!"

I didn't understand what was happening and automatically started taking off the blindfold, but she screamed at me, "Blindfold stays on at all times, mate!"

"All right, all right, what happened? What am I missing?"

"When I said it starts from ten, I meant ten grand, crystal?"

I was shocked! I felt like such an idiot!

"Oi," she continued, "If you ain't got the dosh then just say so and we'll head back. I ain't got the time or the temper for this sort of shit!"

"Sorry, I really don't know much about any of this," I mumbled submissively, "Please don't be angry with me, just give me a minute to think."

I tried to figure out how to get myself out of this mess. 'How can I come up with that kind of sum, and what was I even thinking? And how do I get a gun and show up at Rico's prepared?'

"Are you serious? What planet are you from, thinking you could get a gun for a tenner? You want a ten-quid gun?" she was getting angrier by the minute, "Go to a bloody toy shop, you can get fireworks and a coloring book too while you're at it. Get the hell out of my car! I ain't got time for freaks!" The door opened automatically and I was still blindfolded.

"Okay, okay, wait a minute," I pleaded with her, "Listen, I'm in serious trouble and I really need your help. I'm not a criminal and I couldn't hurt a fly, but my loved ones' lives are in danger and I don't have any time to waste. I'm asking you to help me. Please."

She fell silent, probably considering my plea. Then, she shut the car door and revved the engine again. I sighed with relief.

"So what's your budget?" she asked in a calmer tone. "And don't say it's ten quid cuz that won't float! I wouldn't even help my baby brother for that – this ain't Jobseekers you know!"

"Got anything for a grand?" I asked hesitantly.

I heard her taking a deep breath and muttering, "How the fuck did you even find me?!" Her pitch kept rising. "Look, you don't seem like the kind of scum I usually deal with, so you've clearly gotten caught up in something too big for your own good, and I really want to help you, but I can't give you something that'll put me at risk, there's a limit to what I can do. But I can offer you … you know … a smoking."

"A smoking? A smoking what?" I asked, baffled.

"A smoking gun," she explained patiently, "The kind that has already fired and is being searched for – a marked gun. Like a gun that was used during a robbery and shot a copper down, get it?! If you get caught with it then you're fucked for life! That's the sort of gun I can sell you for a grand."

"Okay, I don't care." I said, "Either way, if things get messy, I don't think I'll make it out alive."

CHAPTER 22

Martine parked the car and told me I could take the blindfold off. We'd arrived at a rundown, abandoned house and went inside. The whole place looked demolished, as though someone had scattered rubbish around instead of furniture.

"This is where you live?" I asked.

"No mate. This is where I do business."

"It's proper dirty here," I noted.

"It's dirty business too, don't worry," she laughed dryly, "Wait here."

Martine went into the next room and came back after a few seconds with a crate. She dragged it over and opened it in front of me. There were a few nice-looking weapons in there, and then she pulled out one of them and handed it to me.

"This is your man, a 0.38 Beretta. Fit, simple, smart, but smoking – like I said."

"What about bullets?" I asked.

"That's not included, they're a hundred quid per bullet, how many do you need?"

I reached my hand into my pocket to check how much I'd have left after paying her the grand for the gun, when suddenly my coke baggie fell to the floor. Martine's eyes gaped open. "Oh hello, what have we here?"

"It's nothing, just a bit of fuel, fancy some?"

"I'd never say no to the good stuff," she said, "But, if you want, I know some people who have the best gear. I can sort you out."

"Really?" I smiled, "I know everyone, try me."

"I ain't namedropping, mate," she hissed at me, "If you want it, I'll get it."

"From who? Daniel? Blacky? Cuba?"

"I see you're knee-deep into it. Blacky's got some things that only I can get my hands on."

"Then I've got news for you," I announced proudly, "You might have the final say on weapons, but drugs are my turf. True, Blacky gets good gear, but he doesn't compete with what I get, and trust me – I know his finest products. Try my stuff out, I'll cut you a couple of lines in return for two bullets." I immediately opened the baggie and cut her two beautiful lines.

She looked at me with intrigue and sniffed the gear. "Oh that's good, mate, can you get any more?" she asked as she pulled out two bullets from a little box and popped them in the cartridge.

"As much as you want!" I replied confidently, "Let me just finish my urgent matter first, and if I'm still alive, then I'll sort you out with as much as you fancy."

"You better stay alive because I want a lot."

I felt like I was on top of the world. I'd just found us another source of income to sort us out faster than I'd even imagined. "I'll come by the Backrub once I'm done," I promised.

"Okay," she said determinedly, "The gun's loaded, do you know how to use it?"

I shook my head and she instructed me until I got the gist of it. "Remember," she said, "When you shoot, there's always recoil, you have to hold it steadily, otherwise you'll fly backwards and miss your mark."

"You're a real pro," I flattered her.

"And you're a good kid," she smiled, "Take the bullets out of the gun and only load it when you get to where you're going." As she spoke, she dragged the crate into the other room.

We got out of the house and back in the car, I put the blindfold on and we drove back to the Backrub. I felt like I was in a spaceship again. She parked the car exactly where she'd parked it before, right next to my car. I thanked her, got in my car, and quickly started the engine.

"Good luck!" she called out.

"Thank you. Any other bit of advice before I take off?"

She thought for a second and then said, "When you put your jeans in the washer, turn them inside out – keeps the color from fading."

"Yet another one of your advantages!" I said and we laughed.

I headed towards Rico's office. My heart was racing and my stress levels rose as I neared the building. I stopped a few feet away because I wanted to hide the gun somewhere. I suddenly started trembling, as though my mind and body had disconnected and stopped transmitting on the same wavelength. I couldn't find a comfortable spot for the gun, let alone think clearly. I felt like I was burning up and I kept shaking, and my entire body was covered in cold sweat, so I took the baggie out and sniffed a couple of fat lines in one go. Within a couple of minutes, I felt like my body was now the spaceship. The adrenaline and the gear were merging beautifully, as were my sense of fear and confidence, and I finally felt prepared for my suicide mission. I shoved the gun deep into my shoe and tied the shoelace around my ankle a few times. It hurt, but I knew that it was the safest place – whenever Don frisked me, he always started from the ankles and worked his way up.

CHAPTER 23

I got out of the car and walked towards the building. With every step I took, I could feel everything coming up. I was nauseous and had a terrible headache. I tried to pull myself together, but suddenly it all burst out of me and I puked my guts out. I cleaned my mouth, took a few deep breaths, and walked in. Don was standing at the entrance along with two other fellas, as though they were waiting for me. He looked at me and then glanced outside and surveyed the surrounding area.

"You here alone?" he asked.

"Yes."

He took a deep breath and shook his head, as though saying – you're in trouble now, mate. "Wait here," he muttered and walked over to the phone, lifted the receiver and reported, "He's alone… All right…"

After hanging up, he motioned to the two blokes and they approached me. At first, I was sure they were going to beat me up, but they motioned for me to spread my legs and lift my arms up so they could frisk me. I felt anxious because I'd expected Don to frisk me, not someone else. 'They'll probably be more thorough and find the gun,' I thought. I had to do something to interfere with the frisk. One of them stood behind me and started feeling my groin and my legs, and the other one stood in front of me and asked me to unbutton my jacket. I immediately resisted.

"Hold still," he told me, but I kept resisting and he got more and more aggressive. Naturally, I continued resisting fervently. At this point, the bloke frisking my legs stood up to help his mate as Don approached us. I got a bit wilder and the three charged at me. They held me tightly and Don peeled the jacket off me. He rummaged through the pockets and found the baggie with the bit of gear I had left. He chuckled. "That's what this is about? This is what you worked yourself up for? You think anyone here gives a shit that you're a filthy junkie?"

The phone rang and Don picked it up as the other two continued holding me, making sure I couldn't budge. It was most likely Rico on the phone, having watched the whole thing on CCTV.

"Yeah, just a bit of gear," Don reported. He then hung up and motioned for the blokes to let me go. They complied and he gestured with his hand for me to go ahead, but I waited for him to give me back my jacket and the baggie.

He looked at me for a few seconds and smiled, put the baggie in the jacket's inner pocket, and handed it to me. I was ecstatic about having managed to turn their attention to the gear and keep the gun hidden. 'If everything goes this smoothly then we'll be home free, mate!' I thought as I got into the lift.

The lift's doors opened and I walked down the hallway to the office, praying to God again. 'Please, God, please, I've never complained about the life I was born into, and it hasn't been easy, to be fair. I know that you look after the good guys, and I know that I'm one of them, so please help me get through this, I swear that once it's all over, I'll do all the good deeds I possibly can.'

I had a feeling that my prayers reached Him. I got to the door and stood in front of it. I felt like I needed a few more seconds because I knew that once I got in, anything could happen. The shoelace was tied so tightly around my foot to secure the gun that it stopped the blood flow, and it hurt so badly that I wanted to die, but I suffered in silence.

Once I felt ready, I knocked on the door. Russ opened it with a chilling stare. "You're here alone?!" he whispered to me in shock.

Rico was sitting on his chair behind the desk and didn't get up to greet me this time. He just stared at me, and I could swear that he looked like the devil incarnate.

"You've managed to surprise me yet again. Sit down, Iggy!" he said and got into one of his famous monologues. "You know, there's a tribe in Africa called the Bubi, and what's special about them is that they have thirty-inch bollocks. I swear! I haven't seen yours, but either they're that big or you have some sort of magnificent explanation, because for the life of me, I don't get how you dared show up here without Tommy! I can't wait to hear this."

'*I guess I have both*,' I thought and took a deep breath. "All right, well, after I spoke to you, I confronted Tommy again. You see, we grew up together, I know him better than I know myself! And he swore to me that nothing happened with Shirley – nothing like what she's saying, anyway. I believed him, and frankly, I decided to mug you off and continue our escape, but then, later on, he started saying that on the day when he came to the club, he met this bird and they started a love affair. I put two and two together and realized that it was Nicole, the waitress you have a thing with. At that moment, I knew that no matter what…" I noticed Rico's face had gone bright red but I still went on, "You see, he didn't know about you and her… but I did, I mean, it was clear to me that you had known about it for a while and that you wouldn't let it fly, and that you wanted him to come here because of that. You wanted revenge. And then I thought about what you'd told me, about the good and the bad – it really stuck with me. So I told him that she was your girlfriend and explained that he had to come back with me and confront you like a man and accept whatever lesson you were going to teach him, just like you'd taught me – you know, to take the good along with the bad."

"Is that right?" Rico retorted sarcastically, but I maintained a serious tone.

"Yeah, I swear that I quoted you on that! I told him that if he didn't do it, then he'd be getting me in trouble. I emphasized how he needed to learn his lesson and check before he pulled his cock out, and to be honest, I was surprised by how helpful it was! He eventually agreed. I won't lie, I promised him that if you didn't go through with what you'd promised, I'd take his side. So we got to London at five o'clock this morning, having said we'd be at yours at eight. We stopped to freshen up at a petrol station and Tommy said he was going to the loo, and then he just disappeared! I checked his parents' place, our mates' houses – nothing, he ran away. He fucking chickened out and left me hanging! Now, I had two choices – either I wouldn't show up here at all and try to run away, or I'd come here and tell you the truth. As you can see, I chose the second option. If I were guilty then I'd have never come here. My bollocks ain't that big, and I know that you can't be fooled. Tommy fucking betrayed me. He abandoned me without thinking about anything but his own ass. So, right now, I'm choosing to kick him out of my life, he can deal with you and his actions all on his own. He's made his choice and I've made mine. And you will too. That's the truth."

As I told him the story, I remembered that whenever someone lies, they avoid eye contact, play with their lips, scratch their face, and swallow a lot because they feel thirsty, so I made sure to look him right in the eye and restrained myself when I started feeling itchy.

Rico stared at me silently and seemed pensive. Russ looked at him, awaiting his reaction. You could cut the air with a knife. I was sure that Rico was going to pull out a gun and shoot me in the face, but after a few moments of silence, he sighed and said, "I believe you!" He then turned to Russ and added, "I believe him!"

At that moment, a thousand bits of confetti exploded in my mind. I wanted to get up and scream as though I'd just won an Oscar, but I maintained my tormented exterior. "So what now? What are you going to do with me?" I asked.

"Look, it's not that simple. I believe you, but I know how people work," he explained, "You're angry now, but in a few days' time you'll calm down, Tommy will find you and apologize... and a long friendship like yours isn't something that just ends in a day! You'll find yourself unsure again and then you'll make another mistake, and then what?"

"That's not going to happen!" I said in an assured tone, "I mean, say Tommy reappears and apologizes and I decide to forgive him instead of turning him in. I can still promise you that I won't help him out, I won't interfere in what you have going on with him. You two should settle your score. I'm not an idiot, I know that Tommy and I are as insignificant to you as fleas on a dog – annoying, yeah, but not dangerous. And it ain't the dog that gets it in the end – the fleas do! All I can do is ask you for another chance. Do whatever you think is right!"

Rico seemed pensive again. I felt the gun barrel cutting through the flesh at the end of my foot and I wanted to scream with pain, but I maintained my steady, calm appearance.

And then Rico said, "You look like shit, Iggy. Go home and get some rest, I need to figure out where we're going from this point on. We have a lot to talk about – like the fact that I don't employ junkies."

"What?" I asked him, confused.

"Drugs, Iggy," he clarified, "You lied to me – you're a junkie!"

"I do a bit of coke, I won't lie," I confessed, "But I don't think you'd call that a junkie. In any case, ever since I started working for you, I just do a line here and there, just to calm down a bit."

"Iggy, you're an addict!" he exclaimed, "And I need to decide what to do about it. I reckon I'll send you to rehab, and then we can talk about work again."

"No, no, I'm not an addict," I quickly explained, "I don't need rehab! I just dabble here and there, and if it jeopardizes my work here then I'll stop. I just went a little crazy lately, you know, suddenly getting all that dosh, partying, and the last few days were stressful so I overdid it a bit, but it's under control, it's all good."

Rico wasn't impressed by my little speech. "Go home and get some rest, Iggy," he muttered, "I have some thinking to do, I'll see you tomorrow."

I left the office with my head held high, but every step I took felt like I was dunking my foot in fiery water. I got to the lift, and the second the doors closed, I started panting with pain. All I wanted was to get to the car and untie that bloody shoelace. I was proud of myself and I wanted to call Tommy so badly, just to tell him how talented his best mate is. I also wanted to call Angie and tell her how brilliant I was, then call Manu and Andy and update them – but I knew that I couldn't afford any more mistakes at that point. Rico had asked me to go home and rest, and that's exactly what I needed to do. I was back in business and I had to stick to the plan, because from that moment on, it was only a matter of time before it worked!

The lift opened and I stepped out and walked towards the exit. I was walking tall and relaxed. Don and the two blokes stared at me, and I played calm and kept my face forward, making sure not to taunt them.

I got in the car, let out a sigh of pain, and drove away. After passing a couple of traffic lights, I stopped on the side of the road, untied the shoelace and pulled out the gun. I put it in my jacket's inner pocket and allowed myself to ache freely.

My mind was buzzing. 'What do I do first? And how do I get everything done without anyone noticing?' The longing for Angie was burning a hole in my soul and I wanted to do a line, just out of habit, but I stopped myself. I knew that I needed to take a step back from the drugs, or at least hide my daily use, so I decided that booze could do the job for a while. 'I'll just drink a bit more – better off drinking than doing coke.'

I was exhausted by the pain, the worries, the hunger, the longing, and the exhaustion, but it was nothing compared to my huge desire to have a proper chat with my mum so she could clarify everything about my dad and Rico. I wanted to stop by Cuba to get some gear, but I knew that it could come with a heavy price.

I felt like something within me had changed. I'd never calculated my moves or worried about the next day before the last few days' events, and even the anger towards my mum felt different. Usually, whenever I was angry, I'd take it out on myself, I'd feel like a failure and have zero confidence, but on that day, it felt different – I was no longer angry with myself for her mistakes and her behavior. I guess that all those little victorious achievements empowered me. I had come out of my comfort zone and I did things that made me feel like I could really make something of myself.

Alice, my teacher, told me once that life is composed of a sequence of memories, and our self-confidence surfaces when a collection of achievements starts assembling within that sequence. For example, if you get a good grade on an exam – that's an achievement. If you score a goal for the team – that's an achievement. If you manage to get a date with the bird you fancy – that's an achievement, and if you manage to save up and buy something you've always dreamed of having – that's also an achievement. That's why people always have to set challenges for themselves – little ones at first, and then as time goes by and our confidence grows, the challenges grow too. That's what really builds our stamina to be able to handle anything that comes our way. "And when that finally happens to you," she summarized, "Then you'll realize that no one has the power to control your feelings, not even your parents."

And then, the penny finally dropped – my current achievements had distanced me further away from my mum's bitter umbilical cord.

When I got home, she was already waiting for me in the kitchen. We skipped the niceties and she just stared at me with a sort of calmness that was very unlike her. "Shall we sit down and talk?" she asked.

I didn't reply. I just took a seat in front of her and looked her right in the eye. Her gaze was vacant. I couldn't figure out if she'd had a lot to drink or if she'd taken something.

"Well?" I said.

"What do you want to know?"

"Everything! Tell me about Dad, about Rico – what went on there? What happened?"

"All right, well, your dad and Rico were partners – mates first, actually, then partners," she began. "They got a fair bit done together and they made it big, until they finally decided to do something that was way over their heads and they ended up crashing and burning. They were both arrested and sent to prison, but your dad decided to snitch on Rico and turn state witness. That's how he managed to save his own ass, and he left me to fend for myself while I was pregnant with you. I had to do whatever it took in order to save us."

"What?" I asked, "So just like that, one sunny morning, he decided to betray his best mate and partner, the woman he loved, and his unborn son?"

"You think your dad was a good man?" her voice rose sharply, "Well he wasn't! He was a piece of shit! He betrayed everyone, he cheated on me all the time, his nickname was the Fox – so you can imagine what he was like! And it was only a matter of time before he betrayed Rico too, and that's precisely what happened. Your dad loved money and he made a ton of dosh, but he was a tight bastard! At least with me! I was always last on his priority list. We fought all the time! He used to give me a pathetic allowance, 'So you don't go all wild on me,' that's what he'd tell me, 'So no one asks any questions and blows our cover' – he gave me all sorts of excuses, but he spent hundreds of pounds on random birds without even batting an eyelid. Hotels, gifts, trips abroad. When he and Rico first got together, the big bucks started coming in, and within a few months, he was going crazy with drugs, booze, prozzies, and gambling! Your dad went through anything and everything that could ever be addictive, and that was bad for business. Rico warned him, and he even tried to get him into rehab, but he always fell back off the wagon."

"But there was a time when he was clean, when he was still Rico's partner, right?"

"No! He wasn't off the drugs and booze at any time. The parties and the prozzies – yeah, for a while," she said. "And then at some point, they started a rumor saying that he was clean and sober, just so they could get in with the mob! They were planning a huge sting operation and he promised to come off everything for it, and he really seemed to be doing well. He was drinking less and he cut down on the drugs, started working out too, and he was completely focused on that. It was a major operation involving a number of businesses all around Europe, and I was in on it too. We planned everything, down to the very last detail, and we contacted people from various fields to help us out. But your dad, as always, with his weak character … he got a bit stressed and started with his nonsense all over again. At first, it was just a few little slips because I'd 'pissed him off,' that's what he told everyone, but as things progressed and we neared the deadline, he was getting much worse. Some of the partners started getting cold feet. You see, it was such a huge operation that either you made it big time, or you lost big time, and there was no room for mistakes! Rico tried to sort things out and he kept putting out fires for your dad. Do you know what it's like when your lives depend on each other and you realize that your partner – the only person you genuinely trust – is lying to you and ruining everything?! We were all in a bloody pressure cooker for a long time, and all we had was one another. Rico had no one to share his frustration with except for me – we couldn't talk to any outsiders, and we obviously couldn't tell the other partners because they'd step back straight away. One of them actually walked out right before the end."

"Richie," I said.

"Yeah, Richie. He abandoned ship at a critical stage, and we almost gave up on the whole thing."

"So you and Rico had an affair?"

"I don't even know how it happened," she said and looked down at the floor, "I felt lonely and Rico felt suffocated, and we vented to each other, but we knew that it was just temporary and that when everything was over, we'd have to put that behind us too. But then, one day, your dad just took off. He left me on my own for a few days and I had too much to drink. When Rico came looking for him, one thing led to another and we found ourselves in each other's arms, and that was when your dad decided to show up. We were in the kind of situation that left little to the imagination, and it caused an outright explosion. Your dad went mental, and he'd arrived with one of the operation's partners, who was supposed to be watching him. I was wasted, and Rico had been drinking too but he tried to apologize, and your dad jumped him so Rico beat the shit out of him, and our partner got so stressed that he ran out of the house. He probably wanted to call for help but he ran straight into the road and got run over. An ambulance came by to take him to the hospital and Rico sent me away to a hotel until everything calmed down. He somehow managed to pacify your dad and continue with the operation as planned. In the meantime, I was at the hotel and I felt really weird, in a bad way, so I got a pregnancy test and it came out positive. Your dad flipped out and disappeared again! Rico tried to persuade me to get an abortion but I didn't want to! So they decided that Richie would take my place, but we were still missing a replacement for the bloke who'd gotten run over. Rico was losing it! The entire operation had cost them an arm and a leg and they were in serious debt, and on top of that, your dad was gone and we were missing a partner! Rico was seeing red, and he decided that no matter what, they'd stick to the plan! And then your dad came back, along with another fella, who turned out to be an undercover copper... Long story short, everyone involved got nicked. I almost did some time too, but we somehow managed to convince the detectives during questioning that I was only his wife – just a weak, pregnant woman who had nothing to do with any of it."

"Did my dad know that the bloke was undercover?" I asked, "I mean, were they cooperating, or did he get screwed just like everyone else?"

"We'll never know."

"But he went to prison, same as everyone," I recalled, "And if it wasn't for that whole mob thing, then he wouldn't have gotten released, so he didn't have anything to do with the undercover fella, it was just bad luck and rash decisions, innit?"

"Look, your dad did all sorts of things," she replied, "I told you – he betrayed everyone, he was a crook and he had everyone wrapped around his little finger. When the whole thing went off and there were articles about it in the papers, your dad was automatically a dead man walking, considering the sting operation he and Rico had planned wasn't even his idea to begin with – this Costa Rican criminal had happened to tell them about his plan when they were staying at Mullner's – the Jewish mobster. The mobsters were fuming when they heard he'd planned the whole thing behind their backs and never told them about it. Your dad, who wanted to save his own ass and was still pissed off with me and Rico, decided that as far as he was concerned, it wasn't even his baby I was carrying. That's why he wanted to get back at us, and he must have realized that the only way for him to stay alive was to turn state witness, blabbering not only about Rico but literally about everyone. What do you reckon that sort of thing does to someone like me – a pregnant woman, wife to the most hated person there was? I was shattered and scared to death. During the first few days, all I did was try to calm the fear of getting caught and skinned alive, so I started drinking like crazy, just to manage to fall asleep at night. I'd been a drinker beforehand, but from that point on, it became a full-on addiction. Rico went mental. He was certain that the baby was his, so he did what he had to do and made sure I was out of the picture. He even told people that he was the one who's gotten me knocked up, and that your dad had snitched about everyone as a shitty act of revenge. Now, mind you, the way the crime world works, having an affair with your partner's wife is punishable by death, but considering the fact that your fucking dad blabbered about everyone just because of a lousy affair, the mobsters put aside Rico's misgivings and even made him their ally."

"How do you know for a fact that I'm not Rico's son?" I asked with intrigue, "After all, you were with both of them at the same time."

"Unfortunately, we did a test after you were born, and you're not his son," she explained. "Rico was devastated. And trust me, in your case, even if I didn't go through with the paternity test, anyone could tell that you were Ethan's son within a few years ... the apple didn't fall far from the tree. You're a spitting image of him!"

"But Richie said…" I tried to argue but she interrupted me.

"Richie's scared and jealous. He dropped out of the operation a second before the deadline and did time in the same prison as your dad. He was fuming about Ethan leaving him and about Rico not helping him out when everything went to shit. He was released long before Rico, but he couldn't get anything right. When Rico was finally released, he got situated in no time, and he refused to cooperate with Richie on anything. That drove Richie crazy, and his jealousy got out of control. Regardless of you, lately he's screwed up one too many times, and there was no other option but to punish him for all of it."

"What do you mean?" I asked.

"Iggy, focus on what you wanted to know," she said in a harsh tone, "Don't stick your nose in other people's business, understand?"

Oh, I understood – I understood everything! I had no idea what to do with all these pennies dropping about my life. "Wait, so if my dad abandoned you when you were still pregnant – then the man I used to think was my dad back when I was a kid was actually Rico?" I asked. "Was he the one who used to come by at night? The one who beat you up? Is that why you didn't leave a trace of him or my dad anywhere – so that I'd think that Rico was my dad?"

"There was no reason for you to remember the pathetic man who called himself your dad!" she replied, "I wanted to forget him too! I thought that you and Rico would bond with time, but that didn't happen because you're so much like your dad! You should be thanking your lucky stars that Rico kept you alive. I think that to this day, the man Rico had bonded with the most was your dad, he genuinely loved him. He went mental when Ethan betrayed him, but he always felt tormented about being the shitty mate who'd had an affair with me. That's why he always swayed – he'd love me one minute and hate me the next. Right now, you remind him of Ethan, but between you and me, you're not Ethan, and what's done is done. So my suggestion is for you to forget about the whole thing and do what he tells you, including laying off the drugs and staying loyal to him and no one else! Otherwise, the moment he realizes he's made a mistake, you're a goner!"

"Goner? I'm your son!" I shouted at her, "Is that what you did? Swore your allegiance to Rico and Rico alone, and not to your son? Not to yourself? You've just become Rico's pawn, another one of his little soldiers! You're sitting here and telling me everything because he asked you to, not because you want to or because I asked you to. He's orchestrated the whole thing. He didn't send me home to rest – he sent me here to talk to you! And you were sitting here waiting for me. You two planned what to tell me! You're both sick! And me – I'm nothing, he could make me disappear off the face of the earth in a second! But the way I see it, Rico's a hunter – he doesn't go around the woods shooting deer, no, he just likes the foreplay. He's playing with me, but he's playing with you too, and you're nothing but a weak woman!"

"Rico was there for me when you were still in my tummy!" she answered defensively, "He always supported me! He literally saved me! So let's see, what was I supposed to do? Stay loyal to this thing growing in my tummy as a result of a relationship with a man who'd walked out on me, or stay loyal to the man who stayed with me all along and saved my life? That's a real dilemma right there ... wait a minute, how about this – stay loyal to the one who came out of me with all the treacherous traits of the man who'd ruined my life, or stay loyal to the one who stuck around even when everything had turned to shit? God, which do I choose?!" she said sarcastically.

"You could have raised me differently," I matched her bitterness, "You could have shown me love! I didn't choose to come to this world and I'm nothing like my dad! I don't love a bunch of women – I only love one woman. And true, I do drugs, and my dad did too, but so do you! You think like an addict! Maybe it's you that I resemble, and you just can't stand me cuz I'm your own fucking reflection staring back at you?!"

"I started drinking because I felt like I couldn't handle the death sentence that was coming to me," she stared at me with her hollow eyes.

"It doesn't matter, I was in your tummy, remember?" I said defiantly, "I got the addiction gene from you, not from him!"

"And what about Tommy? You've betrayed him," she retorted, hoping to have the final say and win the argument.

I almost let it slip that there was no way I'd ever betray Tommy, but I managed to hold it back. I knew that it could ruin everything. It didn't matter what I said anyway, I knew she'd always take Rico's side, so I kept my mouth shut, which got her looking all victorious and full of contempt, but I knew deep down that everything she said was a big fat lie that she was telling herself so that she could feel better about the twisted choices she'd made in life. But still, I couldn't let her feel like she'd won! I didn't want her to be happy or feel good, so I went back to something I was able to tell her, and hoped that it would seep through one day.

"Rico wasn't there for you – it's you who were there for him!" I muttered viciously. "He wasn't saving a pregnant woman; he was using you to save himself. Your relationship only continued because of your blind loyalty to him. After all, if a woman's ready to give up her own bloody son in order to be with her man, then she'd clearly die for him too, and that kind of loyalty is hard to come by. So, just so you know, you gave up your own life for someone who's been taking advantage of you this whole time."

"Whatever, but you're just like me!" she shouted back, "You didn't run away, you surrendered and came back like the coward that you are. You gave up on your mate – who was like a brother to you – just so you could keep your miserable life for a bit longer. How exactly are we any different?"

I couldn't find the words to explain it to her, but I knew that we were nothing alike. At that point, I felt like the umbilical cord had completely ripped. I was freed from the burden I'd carried all that time, freed from the desire to be loved by someone who didn't love me, freed from the desire to have a mother's love just because she was my mum, and freed from feeling like I was alone in this world. At that moment, more than ever before, I was filled with a sense of love and appreciation for everything that I did have – everything that was unlike what anyone else had except for me.

"Will there be anything else?" she asked in a victorious tone – which seemed to me like the Hunchback of Notre Dame winning the world's ugliest man competition.

"No."

"All right then." She got up, went into her room and closed the door.

I stayed sitting there and thought about everything. For some reason, the conversation with her had calmed me down. Maybe she didn't tell me the whole truth, but it didn't matter to me – what does it matter when the truth is completely subjective? No matter the situation, we can never know the truth, because it's always told by someone who experiences things and tells them from their own point of view, and that's their truth. We can know the general facts, but in this life, we have the ability to turn the page and create a new reality every day without having to go back to the past – because it wouldn't help us anyway. We'll always make the same mistakes, even if we've made them before, and we'll always learn new things from our mistakes and move on.

I looked at the clock, it was eleven in the morning, and I didn't have enough time to rest. I had to keep going and get my things in order for my escape. I missed Tommy and I was dying to talk to him. I missed Angie so badly, and I realized that our love was the truest thing I had going for me. I went in the shower to concentrate on what I needed to do in chronological order:

1. Go to Andy and ask him to make us the passports.
2. Buy flight tickets to Brazil.
3. Go see Angie, get everything out in the open, and persuade her to come with us.
4. Contact Tommy and set a day and time for us to meet at the airport.

When I got out of the shower, I knew that I had to get to Rico looking as clean and tidy as I possibly could, so that he'd think I'd managed a rest, so I shaved and spruced myself up as best I could. I did a couple of little lines so I wouldn't start flipping out, and popped a few more sedatives to help me calm down, but I still looked great.

I grabbed a photo album and took out some photos of me, Angie, and Tommy. I called Andy and he told me to come to his house and not the shed, because the place was too risky ever since we'd been there. He also told me that his parents were away for a few days and he had the house to himself. I hung up and left my place.

I was paranoid the whole way there. I kept feeling like I was being followed. Anyone that happened to look at me seemed suspicious, and I was proper stressing out. I immediately thought that I should try to trick the enemy – if there even was one – and disappear amongst the crowds of people, or start running all of a sudden and turn into alleyways or climb walls, anything that could interfere with the surveillance. It made the way there longer, but I felt safer.

I got to Andy's place and quickly climbed the stairs to his flat. I rang the doorbell, and the moment he opened the door, I stormed into the flat and slammed the door behind me. I told him the whole story – including what I thought had happened to Richie.

"You reckon they killed him?" he asked.

"Dunno, bruv, that's a bit harsh," I replied, "But they definitely confronted him, maybe sent him away, or maybe he just decided to do a no-show on us."

Andy was busy with an urgent job. I watched him meticulously forging each and every detail in the passport he was making, and I was seriously impressed. I made sure not to divulge Tommy's location so that he wouldn't be in danger.

"You've changed, Iggy," he gave me an examining look. "You look much more collected, radiant, and confident. It's strange that now, of all times, is when you got some self-confidence," he said while cutting us some lines on the table.

Andy sniffed a couple and then handed me the rolled-up note, but I decided to wait a bit more before my next lines. He didn't make an issue out of it and just sniffed the other two lines and summarized, "So, I'm making three new identities for you, Tommy, and Angie, and then you're off to Brazil?"

"Yeah, that'll be our first stop," I said and placed our photos on the table. "How long will it take you?" I added.

"A few days," he replied, "I need to sort out fictitious identities in order for the passports to look credible. I reckon that within four to five days, you'll be ready to go. In the meantime, go to a travel agent and see how much the flight will cost you."

"By the way, what's happening with Manu?" I asked.

"Well, he's gotten chummy with some French Jew who inherited the building they live in," Andy said. "The fella really took a shining to him and offered Manu to become a partner in some of his projects and run them for him. He's on cloud nine! We spoke yesterday and he told me that in a few days, they'll be flying out to France and it's all paid for, because the fella's itching to get him into the business already. Life is full of surprises, bruv!"

"That's wicked, I'm so chuffed for him!" I said excitedly, "I guess it's our time to shine, there must be some good energy in the air, and we're all on the same wavelength so we're getting all the good stuff. Tommy, Angie, and I will be in Brazil, Smiley's in Israel, Manu's going to be a businessman, and you – what about you?"

"Dunno, mate," he said and stroked his chin, "I'm thinking about joining you lot. What do you say?"

"Brilliant!" I exclaimed, "I thought about suggesting it, but I assumed you'd turn me down, what with all of your clients and that."

"Nah, Iggy, I can't be bothered with all of this anymore," he said and sighed, "Getting nicked every week, having people on my case all the time! Now that the shed's no good anymore, I really fancy getting the hell out of here! I reckon I'll find a lot of opportunities to grow and develop in Brazil."

"Sweet, bruv, then make yourself a passport too. And speaking of Smiley, have you heard from him at all?"

"No, but I met his nan and she said he was really happy there and refused to give me his number. She told me she's happy he's far away from it all, that now he has a real chance at life, and that she doesn't want us jeopardizing that for him."

"Yeah, I can understand her," I said with a heavy heart, "But don't worry, once we get somewhere safe and settle ourselves down, we'll try to get in touch with him. He said he was at a kibbutz, and Israel's tiny, so finding him shouldn't be an issue. I miss that fucker."

"Me too, bruv, me too," he sighed.

"I have to go," I said, "Gotta get home as quickly as possible in case Rico's looking for me – he can't find out that I was here."

"I need to go out for an hour too, got a little job I need to finish. Help me take all this crap over to the hideout, will ya?" he asked.

We gathered the equipment and went to the hideout behind Randell's shop. We waited until the coast was clear and quickly pulled out the bricks and shoved everything in the hole in the wall.

"Iggy, be careful with this whole thing," Andy suddenly said, "It seems a bit strange that everything's going smoothly, something feels dodgy to me. Rico's not an idiot, and he has a lot of experience with people. Remember what Richie told us? He's a hunter. Keep your guard up so that you don't have to deal with any surprises. I'll go back home in the evening and start working on our passports."

"Listen, make another female identity for Tommy's girlfriend, just in case. She's twenty-three or twenty-four years old, I think. Black hair, blue eyes, tall and slim."

"I need her photo, Iggy, can't do it without one."

"I'll try to get you one, then," I said, and we went our separate ways.

I sprinted back to my place. It suddenly dawned on me that if Manu was flying to France with that fella, then he probably knew a trusted travel agent, so I found a phone box and called him, but he wasn't home.

I kept going when I suddenly noticed a long, black Mercedes slowly driving past me. It stopped a few feet ahead of me. I kept walking calmly, and as I passed it, one of its windows rolled down.

"Oi, can I offer you a ride, son?"

I immediately recognized Rico's voice and my heart was pounding. I tried to think up an excuse and in the meantime, I said, "Oh, hi Rico, wow! Wicked car!"

"Where are you off to?" he asked.

"Nowhere, I just popped out to get some fags and a few bits and bobs, and I'm on my way back home…"

"Get in, I'll take you there."

"Nah, it's cool, it's just a minute away," I said.

"What do you need to do at home?" he persisted.

"Gotta keep resting like you asked me to, so that I'm ready to get back to work."

"Jump in and come with me to a gathering I've organized. I was going to invite you earlier, but I couldn't get you at home."

"Really? That's crazy timing, I just got held up talking to a mate."

"Want to bring him along too?"

"No, no, he doesn't like parties," I replied and got in the car. There were two men sitting there with two stylish-looking birds, the kind you only see in films. I immediately recognized one of them – it was Nicole. She looked at me, and I could see the distress hidden underneath her glamorous appearance.

Rico handed me a glass of scotch. Everyone was drinking so I couldn't turn it down. He continued refilling my glass until we reached our destination, and it did help me loosen up, but my mind was constantly occupied with figuring out a way to talk to Nicole and get the hell out of there. The car stopped outside a mansion in a posh neighborhood and we all got out. We went into the mansion, which was filled with beautiful people. I felt completely out of place there – everyone was mingling, and I was the only one standing on the side and praying for the minutes to pass by quickly.

Suddenly, Nicole came up behind me and whispered, "We're surrounded by wankers!"

"Yeah, totally! But you look like a proper film star."

She smiled, even when she muttered to me, "You have to trust me! You need to warn him, tell him to get out of wherever he's at, right now! He's not safe there, he needs to leave immediately!"

"What are you on about?" I asked.

"Tommy!" she said, and my heart started racing so badly I thought I was going to faint. "He's in serious danger," she added.

"And how are you two lovebirds?" I heard a voice behind us and turned around. My mum was standing there, dressed in expensive designer clothes. She looked completely different, beautiful and ten years younger, and her face was glowing. 'She looks so strange,' I thought.

"Surprised?" she asked.

"It's been a good while since you've last managed to surprise me," I told her. My mind was still preoccupied with what Nicole had told me, and all I wanted was to get out of there and warn Tommy. I was stressing, and Nicole motioned to me with her eyes to calm down.

"Nicole, you look as stunning as ever," she said and kissed her politely.

"I need a wee," I muttered and headed towards the exit, but my mum called out, "Iggy, the loo's in the other direction."

"Oh, okay," I said and turned around.

"Not there," she shouted to me.

"I'll show him where it is," Nicole said and walked me to the loo. On the way there, she managed to quickly say, "Meet me tomorrow morning at eight o'clock sharp at Amber Café, number 12 Homer Street. It's over here."

"The café?"

"The loo! I have to get back, number 12 Homer Street, remember!"

CHAPTER 24

I opened the door and looked back. I saw that my mum hadn't taken her eyes off me the whole time, so I went into the loo and shut the door behind me. I felt like I couldn't breathe and I was panting heavily. I had a feeling that things were starting to get tricky, but I didn't quite know what was going on, and that drove me crazy. I wanted to get the hell out of there. I took two pills out of my pocket and swallowed them with some tap water. I then examined the luxurious toilets and noticed that there was a window. I immediately thought that this would be the best chance I had at running away. I opened it and… bingo! It looked so easy. But first, I went back to the door and opened it a bit, peering out to check if my mum was still keeping watch. She was standing in the same spot, but she seemed focused on a heated argument with Nicole. I quickly took the opportunity and jumped out the window, running as fast as I could to the main road.

My head was exploding with thoughts and I tried to figure out how to get in touch with Tommy. All of the possible scenarios ran through my mind – maybe this was just another one of Rico's tricks and he'd sent Nicole to make me contact Tommy and flush him out? Maybe they'd found out his location and they were on their way to him already? And maybe Nicole didn't even know that she was serving as bait… But why was she so certain that I knew Tommy's location? I was going mental! I tried to calm down and decided to go with my gut feeling, which led me to believe Nicole.

I realized that there was no time to waste and that I had to urge Andy to finish the job as quickly as possible. After all, the entire plan depended on those passports. So I hailed a cab and drove over to his place.

I climbed up the stairs and knocked on Andy's door, but he wasn't home. I went over to the shed to look for him, but he wasn't there either. I went back to his place, thinking maybe I hadn't knocked loudly enough and maybe he was high, sprawled out on his sofa and unable to hear anything – after all, he was home alone.

I went upstairs again and knocked as loudly as I could, rang the doorbell, and shouted his name. The neighbor across the landing peered out and said, "No one's home, they're away for a few days."

"But Andy's supposed to be here, he didn't go with them."

"Oh, that's right," he recalled, "I saw him going down the stairs with two nice-looking girls about an hour ago."

"Fuck!" I exclaimed and ran back down to the street and towards my house. On my way, I saw someone locking up a travel agent's office. I'd been passing through that street for years and I'd never noticed there was a bloody travel agent there!

"Excuse me, are you shutting shop for the day?" I asked the man.

"That's right, we're done for the day, come by tomorrow."

"Do me a favor, mate," I pleaded with him, "I want to buy plane tickets to Brazil, there's five of us going on holiday, any chance you could help me out?"

"Of course, gladly! Come by tomorrow."

"It has to be today," I insisted, "Seriously, it would be a shame – this can't be a coincidence, me catching you here right now... Do us a solid, will you? I'm begging you!"

The fella made a face and then opened the door. He turned the lights on, and I surveyed the office – just a few desks with phones on them. I immediately thought that this would be the perfect opportunity for me to call Tommy.

"It'll take a moment for the computer to start running," he said.

"No prob, mate. Say, could I make a quick phone call in the meantime?" I asked, "Just to make sure that one of my mates is definitely flying with us."

"Of course."

I thanked him and ran over to the furthest desk, took out the motel's business card and dialed the number.

"Room 513, please," I whispered to the receptionist and he transferred the call. I prayed for Tommy to pick it up.

"Hello?" I heard his voice.

"Tommy, bruv!" I almost shouted.

"Iggy, you're alive!" he called out excitedly.

"I am! For now," I replied, "Can't elaborate right now, but listen – I met Nicole, she said you need to get out of the motel as soon as possible."

"Why? What did you tell her? What happened?"

"I'm not sure, but something's definitely up. Just take the money I left you and look for a new place for the next couple of days," I instructed him, "I'm meeting her tomorrow morning to find out more details. In the meantime, get the fuck out of there!"

"All right," he said.

"I have to go."

"Iggy!" he exclaimed.

"What?"

"How will you know where I am?"

"Once you get to the motel, call Angie and tell her to pass me a message and give her a telephone number," I thought as I spoke, "Make up some story with the motel's name encoded into it, and give her a phone number where the last three digits are the same as your room number. Crystal?"

"Clear! To be honest bruv, I'm a bit scared," he said.

Truth be told, my stomach was cramping with fear, but I wanted to encourage him, so I said, "Bruv, it's all under control, we're practical people, problem-solvers, don't get scared on me now. Just a few more days and we'll be reclining under a coconut tree, sipping on margaritas before group therapy at some shaman's temple. And don't worry, Nicole's coming with us too, so get yourself together mate, be brave. All right?"

"All right! And Iggy…"

The travel agent was giving me a look but I ignored him. "Yeah?" I replied.

"Tell her I love her."

"Tell her yourself when you see her," I told him and hung up.

I sat down in front of the travel agent and booked five one-way tickets to Brazil on a direct flight, leaving in a week's time at 06:30 in the morning. Each ticket cost 1200 quid.

I knew that I had to get some more money together, but I'd been counting on the sting I'd planned on Rico, so I wasn't particularly worried. 'Worst case scenario, I'll just rob a place,' I thought.

"I'll need your passports, please," the agent said.

"I'll bring them by in a couple of days," I told him.

"That won't be possible, I need them now I'm afraid," he insisted.

"Then I'll put a down payment on the tickets and just keep them on hold for me, will you?" I asked him.

The agent explained that he couldn't do that, but he promised that once I brought the passports over, he'd sort out the tickets for me. He gave me a business card so I could get in touch with him.

It was ten at night, and I hoped Tommy had already managed to sort something out. I now had to do the hardest thing on my list – go talk to Angie. I was scared of being followed, scared she'd refuse to talk to me. I was stressing like mad and thought that maybe I'd just do a line or two to take the edge off, so I drove over to Andy's place, making sure I wasn't being followed. I knocked on the door again but there was still no reply, so I went over to the shed, but he wasn't there. I started feeling like something really bad was going on. It wasn't like Andy, disappearing like that for such a long time, especially at this point, when he was supposed to be making our passports as quickly as possible. I decided to call Manu, hoping he was hanging out at his place. Manu's mum answered the phone and said he'd gone away with a mate and hadn't come back or gotten in touch for two days.

'What's going on here?' I thought, 'How have we suddenly become this separated? Where's everyone when I need them?'

Even though I knew that I was risking it, I went over to my place, got in the car and drove over to Cuba's digs. I bought a tiny bit of gear off him, just to calm my nerves before meeting Angie, and then I drove straight to her place.

I parked the car two streets away from her and ran through the yards, just in case I was being followed. When I reached her building, I didn't turn the stairwell lights on. I went up to the third floor as silently as I could and stood in the dark hallway outside her door. I couldn't breathe and I was sweating like crazy. I didn't even tremble that bad before meeting Rico. I knocked on the door.

"Who's there?" I heard Angie's voice and my heart exploded like fireworks.

"Angie, it's me, Iggy," I said, but she fell silent and didn't open the door. "Please, open up, I have to talk to you, please…" I pleaded with her. I prayed to God she'd open the door and at least hear me out, and He must have heard my prayer, because the door suddenly opened.

Angie was standing there, more beautiful than ever. She looked radiant, but distant too, which scared me. I felt mucky and embarrassed. I wanted to tell her I love her, I wanted to say – let's stop with this phony pretending game. I wanted to tell her I was strong and ready, and that I really am everything she thought I was. In short, I wanted to show her that I was her man, but the moment I opened my mouth, I choked, and everything just came up. The man I wanted her to see started crying like a little boy. I couldn't stop the tears, they just streamed like a breached dam. It caught me by surprise, as though my brain had started giving out orders of its own accord, without consulting me first, and my body was just doing whatever it wanted. I recoiled and my hands covered my face in shame.

I suddenly felt her hands stroking my head, and then the warmth of her body. She enveloped me in her arms and it was so calming. The trembling subsided, and she caressed my head gently and softly, and gave me little kisses. I felt protected.

"This is so good…" I whispered.

"This is so good…" she replied.

I wanted us to stay that way forever, but the stairwell lights suddenly came on and ruined the moment. I jumped in fright, thinking that maybe it was one of Rico's men, but it was just a neighbor walking up to the top floor.

"We should go inside," I told Angie.

"My nan went to visit a friend in the countryside yesterday," she said.

"What is it with everyone going away all of a sudden? Andy's parents are away too!"

"You're funny, aren't you? It's Passover, the Jewish holiday."

I'd forgotten all about Passover. We never celebrated any holidays at my house. But to me, being alone with Angie was as festive as humanly possible. I felt like the happiest man in the world.

We sat down on the sofa and Angie looked at me with a soft gaze. She stayed quiet and waited for me to speak.

"I'm in trouble Angie, and Tommy's in trouble too," I said. I told her the whole story and didn't leave anything out – including my victorious achievements. When I finished, she looked shocked and didn't say a word.

"Come with me, Angie," I pleaded.

"I dunno, Iggy, it all sounds dangerous, shouldn't we go to the police?"

"By the time we get to the station they'll already have me killed," I explained, "And besides, let's say I make it work and they arrest

Rico and crew and put them in prison, do you really think that we'll be able to live in peace and quiet? That they won't want revenge and send their people after us? Or do you think I'll turn state witness, just like my dad? If you tell me that you're with me on this, I'll do it."

"I don't know, Iggy, I can't just disappear on my nan like that," she said gloomily, "It'll break her heart, and it'll break mine too."

"Then my plan definitely makes more sense."

"Yeah, but your plan still means we have to disappear."

"True, but we'll disappear in style. That's why it's so urgent for Andy to sort out our passports! That way you'll have a new identity, and you'll be able to get your nan to join us – we'll find a way," I said excitedly. "I promise you, we'll be everything that you dreamed we'd be, I'm sure of it, more than anything in this world! Say yes, Angie, follow your heart, please, I'm begging you, don't let the past dictate anything anymore. What's done is done, I'll be everything you've ever wanted. And you … you're already everything I want."

"I love what you've become."

"It's all thanks to you!"

"Really?" she asked in a childish, soft tone.

"Really!" I replied without taking my eyes off her, praying she'd say yes.

She took a deep breath. I was stressed for a moment, and then she said, "I'll come with you, my love."

I'll come with you, my love!!! That sentence echoes in my mind to this day. I'll come with you, my love… It was the most beautiful combination of words I'd ever heard. I was floating like a feather, I loved her so much that it genuinely hurt.

Everything felt as though it were the first time – the first kiss, the first touch. We made love all night long. It was like we were colors on a canvas and God was the painter. He mixed, drew, and merged us in harmony, and after we came, we cuddled and fell asleep together.

"Iggy, did you forget about our meeting?" I suddenly heard Nicole's voice in my dream and jumped out of bed, giving Angie a fright.

"Shit, shit, shit!" I cussed and quickly got dressed.

"What's the matter?" she asked.

"I have to meet Nicole at eight o'clock at Amber Café on number 12 Homer Street, what's the time now?" I asked as I put my jacket on when suddenly – the gun fell out of it. I quickly put it back in the inner pocket.

Angie got out of bed and checked the time. "It's quarter to eight, Iggy. Maybe you should leave the gun here? I'll keep an eye on it for you."

"I have to take it with me, but I promise I'll be careful," I replied confidently, "Don't worry, gorgeous, and stay home – don't go anywhere, don't talk to anyone, and if my mum calls and tries to snoop around, then just tell her that you've been blossoming ever since we broke up, and that you have no intention of ever seeing me again! Promise me, Angie?"

"I promise," she looked into my eyes. "You know where Homer Street is, right? Remember that little café by the laundrette where we stole the clothes from that time?"

"Oh, yeah," I recalled.

"That's Amber Café," she said and walked me to the door.

"You're a lifesaver," I said. I kissed her hard and then ran as fast as I could. As a precaution, I circled round the building instead of leaving through the front, just in case I was being followed. On the one hand, I was stressing like crazy, but on the other hand, I felt like Angie had charged my batteries. It was like she'd taken seven tons of worries off my back. I felt focused and sharp.

I reached my car and hoped I'd make it there in time. After all, I knew where I was heading now, thanks to Angie. I took all the shortcuts I could, but I was still twenty minutes late by the time I got to the café. I rushed inside to look for Nicole but she wasn't there. I hoped that she was running late so I sat down to wait for her. I ordered a coffee and put my hand in my pocket to take out a fag and a couple of pills. I noticed there was only one fag in the pack, and there was also the baggie with the bit of gear I'd bought on my way to Angie. I went to the loo, swallowed two pills and did a couple of little lines, just to calm my racing mind. The minutes crawled by and I grew impatient. My mind wouldn't stop thinking up challenging questions – what if she doesn't show up? Or if she was followed here? Or if she's just part of Rico's plan?

Eventually, I decided that no matter what, I wouldn't tell her where Tommy was hiding. I didn't want to take even the smallest of chances, just in case she was in on it with Rico. When an hour had passed and she still hadn't shown up, I started worrying, but I had no way of checking up on her. I asked for the bill and paid up, and the moment I got up to leave, a hefty fella wearing smart clothes approached me and asked, "Are you Iggy?"

"Depends who's asking," I gave him a smart-ass reply.

"Rico sent me, he wants to see you."

"Really?" I pretended to be surprised, "Well, I just need to finish up a few things and then I'll come over to his office."

"No, he wants to see you now; you're coming with me."

"Sorry mate, my mum won't let me go with strangers…" I tried the smart-ass tactic again when I suddenly realized that either I was being followed – or Nicole was in trouble.

His next reply confirmed my suspicions. "Look, you can either come with me on your own two feet, or I can break them and carry you to the car. Your choice."

"Are you threatening me?"

"Have it your way," he said impatiently and inched closer to me.

"All right, all right, I'll come with you," I said. He nodded and seemed pleased with himself.

We walked out quietly. I remember hardly even managing to swallow. I tried to keep cool and not show him how badly I was stressing, but it was tricky considering the amount of sweat covering my entire body.

I looked to the sides. I thought about running away, but he seemed pretty skilled at what he was doing, and it wouldn't be the first time he'd have to deal with that kind of situation. "Don't even think about it," he cautioned me, "I won't hesitate to pull a gun on you."

I suddenly recalled that I had a gun too, but I decided to keep it for the right moment. Once we got to his car, he opened the door for me, fastened my seatbelt, and quickly got in the driver's seat. We started driving away, but he wasn't going to Rico's office.

"Where's Rico waiting for me?" I asked.

"At his new office."

I felt just like in that film I'd seen, where the hitman took the traitor to a quiet place where he could kill him. I tensed up, and after a long silence, I asked him, "Do you mind if I smoke? Got a last one in the pack."

"No prob," he said and pulled a fag out too.

I kept thinking about the moment that he'd take his gun out and I'd surprise him and be the first to shoot. We reached the entrance of an abandoned building – it definitely wasn't a new office building, but I played along and didn't ask any questions. We went inside and it was clear that there was no one there, not even Rico. There was a set of stairs and he stayed behind me. "After you," he said. I started going up, one floor after the other.

"Stop and turn into that hallway," I heard his voice behind me, along with the sound of a gun being cocked. My heart froze. "Keep walking to door number 32," he muttered and tossed a key on the floor.

I hesitated at first, but followed his instructions. I unlocked the door and he shoved me in. The office was small and vacant, and there was a putrid scent of an animal carcass. At the other end of the room, there was a rolled-up rug and another one spread open on the floor.

"I gather Rico's not coming, then," I started turning my head back.

"Oi!" he shouted, "Turn your head to where it was, keep your back to me at all times!" I did as he said and turned away, but that wasn't enough for him. "Walk over to the rug, slowly lean down and take your shoes off," he continued instructing me.

"Why do I need to take my shoes off?" I asked.

"Because you won't be needing them anymore," he replied and added, "Over to the rug, now."

I started losing my shit. I knew exactly what was happening, and I knew that this was my last chance to do something and come out of there alive and in one piece.

"Before you pull the trigger, can you pass a message to Rico for me?" I asked him as I leaned down and slowly took my shoes off.

"Whatever you want, I'm all ears." He sounded like he was smiling devilishly. I quickly put my hand in my jacket and ran through Martine's instructions in my mind.

I discreetly pulled the gun out as he asked, "Well, are you gonna say something, or have you changed your mind?"

I tried to figure out where to aim, since he was standing behind me. I knew that if I turned my head to him, I'd be a dead man, so all I could do was take a wild guess, reach my hand back and shoot. My dilemma was which shoulder to aim to, so I tried to get him to talk. "I'm trying to find the words, give me a minute."

"Well hurry up then, don't try stalling like some knob-end coward," he said, "It's a done deal, there's no hope for you."

That was enough for me to realize that I needed to aim the gun above my left shoulder, and that's what I did. I just lifted it up, squeezed the trigger and took a shot behind me. The recoil flung me to the side, and then I heard another gunshot. I crouched and closed my eyes tightly. My entire body cramped up and I waited to feel the pain. I was sure I'd missed and that he shot me. I thought I was just in shock and too flooded with adrenaline to feel anything.

There was complete silence, and I suddenly felt a warm current flowing down my legs. I was certain that it was my blood, so I started feeling my body with my hands, and I put my hand down on the blood gushing over the floor. I was surprised by how watery it felt, and when I finally opened my eyes, I looked down at my trousers and realized I'd pissed myself. I turned my head to the side and saw the fella's body – his head was shot into smithereens. There were bits of skin, flesh, and blood all over the room, including the walls. I felt like the madness was taking over me and I got up, hysterical. I paced back and forth across the room and the only thing going through my mind was – where do I go from here? What do I do?!

I accidentally bumped into the rolled-up rug and felt like there was something inside it. I rolled it open and realized – it was Nicole. I was so overtaken by fear that I wished he'd killed me when he had the chance. I knew that the moment I got out of there, the first thing I needed to do was make sure Angie was all right and then drive over to Tommy and figure out how to proceed from there.

As my mind struggled with all those thoughts, Tommy's image suddenly appeared before me – as though he were really there, talking to me. "Iggy, you bloody hero, look at you – everything happens for a reason. Who'd have ever thought about doing what you just did? You're the messenger of all things good, and God takes care of the good guys, remember? You're one of those people who always see the light at the end of the tunnel, so just go all the way!"

'I'll go all the way, Tommy,' I replied in my mind, 'That man's the bad guy, and I'm the good guy, and I won't let you down – and I sure as hell won't let God down!'

I made an active switch in my mind, just like that, and felt more empowered and focused than ever before. I started surveying my surroundings calmly, calculating my moves as I took the baggie out and cut a few lines on the windowsill. 'Fuck getting off the gear now! We'll just all do it together once we're in Brazil,' I thought as I sniffed the lines and lit a fag. I looked at the fella's dead body, and without overthinking it, I swapped my wet trousers for his. I also took the set of keys that was tossed on the floor next to him. I felt through his trouser pockets and pulled out a pack of cigarettes and a wallet. I took the money out and shoved it into my pocket. I didn't want to leave any traces behind, so I took his jacket off him and collected all the pieces of flesh scattered around the room. I then pulled the body onto the rug and placed everything I'd collected onto it too. I gave Nicole a goodbye glance – my heart ached for her, and for Tommy too, I knew he was going to be broken up about it. I rolled up the two rugs, pressed them together, and lit them up. I waited to make sure that the fire caught and spread, and then I rushed out of the building.

I got into the dead fella's car and drove straight to Andy's place. I figured that I had a good few hours before anyone realized that it wasn't my body going up in flames. On the way, I stopped to call Angie and let her know what had happened.

"Iggy, I was waiting for you to call," I heard her voice enveloping me, "Tommy called me and asked to write down a message for you, he said that someday soon, when the days get warmer, you'll go catch some waves at California Beach's clear blue waters, and he left a phone number too – 9756863. Is everything all right with you?"

"I'm fine, gorgeous," I replied. My heart was so full that it nearly exploded. "I'll update you the moment I can, in the meantime just keep a low profile and wait for me, okay?"

'California Beach room 863, Tommy's the best!' I thought.

"Wait, Iggy, don't hang up! I have to tell you something important!" she said.

"What is it?"

"I'm still purging…" she confessed.

"It's okay, gorgeous, we'll take care of ourselves once we get to Brazil, promise."

"I love you!"

"I love you too!"

I reached Andy's building and quickly went upstairs. I knocked on the door and his mum came to open. She told me they'd returned from their Passover getaway and hadn't seen him yet. She thought that he was with me and the lads, and she said he hadn't been in touch with them for a few days.

I had a terrible feeling that something bad happened to Andy. At the same time, I hoped that it was just me being paranoid because of everything that was happening, and that he was just doing a major job for a mobster at some posh mansion. I didn't want to get his mum worried so I told her that he had been with me and the lads the previous day, and that he was probably now at Manu's.

"But Manu flew out to France with a mate a few days ago – that's what his parents told me," she said.

"Oh, yeah, I meant Manu Applebaum," I fibbed, "He's a mate of ours, a nice Jewish lad. His family organized a very festive Seder dinner and he invited Andy over, so you have nothing to worry about."

Andy's mum calmed down and I said goodbye and went back downstairs. I felt completely broken up. I couldn't understand how all of my mates had just disappeared – and at such a critical time! I couldn't find any of them, time was running out, and all I could do was stick to the plan and try to save Tommy and Angie – but without the passports, we'd most likely get caught before even managing to get on the plane. 'And that's only if I manage to sort out enough dosh to buy the bloody tickets!'

I suddenly had the idea of trying to forge the passports myself. After all, I'd seen Andy doing it a million times. 'Maybe I'll make it and maybe I won't, but it's our only hope of getting out of here and finding a safe place. I'll figure out how to pay for the tickets later.'

I went to the hideout and grabbed all of the equipment. I rummaged deep inside the hollow wall to find the plastics which were wrapped around the paper but I couldn't find them, so I closed the nook back up and went over to the shed. I opened the door and to my surprise, our passports' spines had been laid out on the table. Andy must have started working on them and never got to finish the job. I had most of what I needed in order to get the job done, and I remembered what I needed to do, more or less, but I knew for a fact that I had to find the plastics. I searched through the drawers and under the mattress and bingo! I found them in a shopping bag. There were two other little bags there – one had a wad of cash in it, and the other had a baggie of coke and a few uppers. I was shocked, so the first thing I did was crush the uppers into a fine powder and sniff them.

Within ten minutes, I felt the pills kicking in and started working on the passports. It took me three hours to finish all four of them. I compared them to the originals and felt pleased with the end result. To be honest, Andy had already done the hard part, but what I did wasn't that easy either.

I cleaned everything up and burned anything connected to the four of us, then gathered the equipment, grabbed a pen and paper, and wrote Andy a note saying I'd finished the job myself and that he needed to call me or Angie. I deliberated on what to do with the money, and a voice inside my head told me – 'It's your only option now, Iggy, Andy will understand, he'd have given it to you himself, and one of the tickets is his anyways. It's not like you're doing a runner on him. Just take the money and pay him back once you all get settled down in Brazil.' I grabbed the wad of cash and stuffed it in my trousers, but I left the coke baggie and the rest of the uppers there.

I ran to the travel agent's office and anxiously handed him the passports. He inspected them and I watched him, trying to see if he noticed something wrong with them. He started filling out the paperwork, and then he got up and made a few phone calls. I was as tense as a hunter crouching in the woods. After a few moments, he came back to the desk holding an envelope with tickets inside it. "After the deposit you left here, you now have four thousand three hundred pounds left to pay," he told me.

I took out the bag with Andy's money in it, which was filled with fifty-pound notes. I counted out the sum he'd asked for – which still left me with half the wad. He handed me the envelope with the flight tickets and said, "Have a nice holiday, Edgar."

For a second there, I got confused and almost corrected him, but I quickly came to my senses, thanked him, and left the office. I noted to myself that I had to get used to our new names.

On the one hand, I was ecstatic! I could already envisage Tommy, Angie, and me on a plane on our way to true freedom. 'Just a few more steps and this nightmare ends,' I thought. But then I thought about Andy disappearing on me, and about how he'd eventually discover that I'd taken all the money he'd saved up. I hoped he'd understand, and I promised myself that once we got settled down in Brazil, I'd find a way of paying him back – with interest. 'If he comes back in time, that is… Otherwise it'll be quite a predicament – stay here and look for him or go on without him.' I suddenly remembered that Nicole's life ended in a rolled-up rug, and I tried to figure out how I was going to tell Tommy about it.

'This is such a crazy journey we're on, when will this nightmare finally end?!' I wondered as I got back in the car. I decided that I needed to get to Tommy as fast as possible. After all, it wasn't like I could walk around London all carefree, I couldn't risk Rico finding me. I planned to stop on the way and call Angie, ask her if Tommy had left me another message, and prep her for the great escape. While that whirlwind of thoughts was going through my mind, a police car suddenly sped past me and stopped right in front of my car, blocking my way. A copper came out of it and stood a few feet away from me. He shouted over the megaphone for me to turn my engine off and step out of the car with my hands in the air.

"No, this isn't happening to me, this can't be real!" I mumbled to myself. I quickly pulled out the gear and the gun from my pocket. Then I grabbed my jacket and wrapped it around them. The second I opened the door, I raised my hands, dropping the rolled jacket to the ground and shoving it beneath the car with my foot.

The copper ran over to me and shouted, "Don't move, stay right where you are!" In the meantime, I noticed another copper coming out of the car, and the two stood in front of me.

"What's the matter?" I asked.

"I'll tell you what's the matter," one of them said as he motioned for me to turn around and started frisking me, "You're driving a stolen car."

"What? No way! It's a mate's car."

"So you stole your mate's car?" he asked as he cuffed me.

"No, he let me borrow it."

"He let you borrow it and then he reported it stolen?" he asked cynically, "And what's your mate's name?"

"Andy Greenberg," I lied, hoping they'd manage to find out where he was.

"Andy Greenberg?" the copper repeated, "That's odd, the car's registered to someone else's name. Maybe Andy Greenberg stole it and then let you borrow it? How about you come to the station with us and we can figure it all out."

"Yeah, that's a great idea! Just find Andy and we'll get to the bottom of this!" I agreed.

"Don't worry, we know how to do our job," he told me as the other copper grabbed the jacket from the ground.

"Can I just put my jacket on? I'm cold," I said, but he started rummaging through the pockets and pulled out the envelope with the flight tickets. "Four tickets to Brazil... Carnival time, is it? Well, I'm afraid you won't make your flight."

"I don't mind that personally, but I have to deliver the other three tickets today," I explained to him. I was stressing. "Otherwise they won't make the flight either," I added.

"Don't worry," he replied, "How about you start by coming in for questioning, and if we find you guilty, then we'll make sure to call the other passengers and get them to collect their tickets. Now, you don't have to say anything, but it may harm your defense if you don't mention when questioned on something which you later rely on in court. Anything you do say may be given in evidence. Is that clear?"

I nodded my head and he got me into the police car. The other copper got in the car I'd driven and followed us.

"Oi, he can't do that! He can't take the car! He's in uniform, he can't drive a regular car wearing uniform!" As I shouted, I turned my head back and spotted the gun and the coke baggie on the road. The copper at the wheel ignored me. To say that I was frustrated would be an understatement – I felt like the end was nearing, and I had a strong feeling that this whole thing had something to do with Rico, but being taken in the police car made me realize that I had to let go. 'You did everything you could,' I thought, 'From here on in, it's out of your hands.'

We reached the police station, and I was taken into a dark interrogation room. A detective sat down in front of me, but he didn't say a word, he just looked me up and down. There was a clock hanging on the wall behind him, and I stared at the dials and imagined that once it reached twelve o'clock, my life would end. The uppers I'd sniffed were wearing off, my eyes grew heavy, and I felt like I couldn't stay awake for a moment longer.

All of a sudden, Rico walked into the room along with a uniformed officer. They stood there with the detective, whispering amongst themselves, and Rico didn't take his eyes off me the whole time. All I wanted was to open my mouth and tell the coppers everything about Rico, but I knew that if I did that, I'd be the one getting it. Who would ever believe a junkie who'd just lied through his teeth to the police? Rico would probably pin the murder and arson on me too, I'd be put in prison, and he'd definitely have me killed once I was in there. And then my mates would be goners too – especially Tommy. So I kept my mouth shut.

After a few moments, Rico finally addressed me. "What am I gonna do with you, eh? From the moment you started working for me, I treated you like my own son, but you just keep getting yourself in trouble! How many more chances do you want?"

I looked at him, fuming. *'If that's how he wants to play, I'll show him something he's never seen before! That way he'll know that I'm different from any victim he's ever had before!'*

"I've already gotten to know you, Rico," I muttered, "And we both know that no matter what I say, you'll do what you want, so let's get this over and done with. So there you have it – you won, I lost."

Rico looked at the coppers, motioned with his head and they left the room. It was just the two of us – Rico and me. He sat down in the chair in front of me, looked at me for ages, and then said, "You know, if I wanted to end you, I'd have done that a long time ago. I know you're hiding Tommy, and I know all about your little plan. I don't need you in order to find him, I was just curious to see how far you'd go, and how many more rabbits you'd pull out your hat in order to save your shitty little mate's ass. You know what? Me and your mum have a bet going – she said you're just like your dad, but I wasn't sure about it, so I decided to test it and see if you'd end up betraying Tommy, meaning your mum's right, or if you'd stay loyal and fight for him till the end. And to be honest, Iggy, you surprised me – I wasn't expecting this. So, here's what's gonna happen. Once I get my hands on Tommy, I'll start by castrating him. My great-granddad was born in Iraq, and in the olden days, whenever someone stole something there, they'd cut off his hand, just like that, with a butcher's knife, so that he could never steal anything again. So, I'll cut Tommy's dick off, so that he can never fuck anyone again…"

"You're a liar and you're full of shit," I told him, "Go write a book instead of all this bloody heritage story-time. You wanted to have me killed! You sent someone to take me out!"

"I don't know what you're on about," he said and smiled viciously, "You've hoovered way too much gear up that nose of yours, son… You need to cut that shit out; I told you that already."

"Don't bullshit me!" I fumed, "I saw Nicole, she was dead and rolled up inside a rug, you killed her because she had an affair with Tommy. I wonder if you killed Shirley too, or any of the other girls that someone else shagged instead of you. To be fair, I'm sure I'd get frustrated too if all the girls I was shagging were looking for some other cock all the time. But how is that Tommy's fault? Maybe you should take some responsibility, realize that you have a problem and start learning to fuck properly, because even if you kill Tommy, your problem won't be solved – you'll still be a shit shag, and whoever your next girl is, she'll still look for some other cock."

I don't know where I got the balls to tell him all of that. Maybe it was because I'd realized that I had nothing left to lose at that point. Everything was already doomed, and I was about to get a bullet in the head. I knew that the end was nearing, and at the point where I felt that there was nothing left for me to say or do to change things, I decided to let go. I always used to tell Angie that once you reach the end of the road, you have to let go. Whenever we were in a rush to get somewhere and only had five minutes left, I'd go mental, grab her by the hand and run as fast as I could. I'd try my best to get there on time, and I never called it quits until the clock hit the deadline – and at that very moment, I'd let go all at once, because we'd tried everything we could and there was nothing left to do, we'd be late either way, so all there was left to do was arrive and deal with it. That was exactly what I felt at that moment with Rico – everything was lost and there was no need to rush anymore, no point in doing anything. The only thing left was to accept my sentencing in the hope that Tommy, Andy, and Manu would come out of it in one piece.

"Wow, Iggy," Rico maintained his devilish grin, "You've got quite the pair of bollocks, don't you?"

"It's just like Richie said – you enjoy playing with your prey," I ignored him and tried my best to keep a brave tone, "You filled my head with all those stories about second chances, and all the while you already knew that you were gonna take me out, and you thought that it would work – but you were sorely mistaken!"

"We learn from our mistakes," he said.

"All right, well just get on with it then, leave the nattering out of it. I won't give you the pleasure of watching me squirm and beg for my life. I'll choose how to die, and I'm going to die with my dignity intact!"

"Quite the speech! You're a tough one, you are!" he announced, "You're giving me a proper fight here, son, you're a real challenge. That's where you're the spitting image of your dad – he always did challenge me, and that's what I loved about him. You've really surprised me!"

"That's what I'm like, surprising!" I told him, pleased with myself. Even though I knew that these were my last few moments of being alive, I thought that at least when it came to comebacks, he remained a loser. I'd die, and he'd stay with the knowledge that this kid was wittier than him.

"I just had a brilliant idea," he suddenly wiped the smile off his face, "How about this – you're gonna judge a competition called the Shagging Master."

"I hope you won't partake in it, because we both know you'll definitely lose," I replied. All these quick, witty comebacks made me feel a whole lot better.

"Is that right? Even though you don't know who's competing and what the prize is?" he smiled again. "That's not very nice – or fair, for that matter."

"Life's not fair." Another point scored!

"You're right about that!" he said and laughed.

I felt alert and sharp, as though Tommy's spirit had landed on my tongue, and I just shot every which way without giving a shit anymore.

"I like the way you think," he added. "Let's keep going, this is wicked! Listen to this – in light of everything that happened with Tommy, you know, him shagging two of my lovers… well, he raped one of them, that is."

"He didn't rape her!" I exclaimed.

"Whatever you say, just focus on the gist of it," he said, sounding pleased with himself. "Imagine a live studio audience, a huge stage with a posh-looking bed smack in the middle of it. The judges are you and the audience – the majority decides, and you have fifty votes to give out, which means that you can influence the outcome. And the contestants are – Tommy versus Rico King."

'Where's he going with this? He's such a psycho!' I thought, sensing my enthusiasm starting to die down. "What are you competing for?" I asked.

"Who's the best shag!" he replied.

"Okay, but how's it all going to work?"

"Ah, now that's where you come in – with Angie."

Boom – that was the knockout I'd awaited. I didn't know where that came from, but at that very moment, he'd managed to turn everything around. My blood was boiling – I wasn't ready for that.

"You fucking cunt!" I screamed at him, "If you touch her, I'll skin you alive! I'll tell the coppers everything right now!" Rico burst out laughing. "Listen to me," I then pleaded, "I made a mistake, Tommy made a mistake, but Angie? What did she ever do to you? This isn't fair!"

"Life's not fair," he presented his payback.

"I'm sorry, from the bottom of my heart, really," I continued pleading, "I'm just a stupid, smart-ass kid, I'm nothing, worthless, what am I even capable of? Nothing! I was just jealous of you because you're so successful, Rico. I'll beg and I'll squirm, and all you have to do is choose how to end me." Rico listened but kept quiet. "Take Tommy, you want him?" I continued, "Should I tell you where he's hiding? He deserves it! And I deserve it too! But what has she got to do with any of this? She's not even my girlfriend anymore, she dumped me ages ago! I'm begging you, Rico, I'm begging, she's never harmed a fly, ever. She doesn't even want me anymore." Rico stayed silent. "My mum loves her; she won't let you do anything to her. I'm such a fuck-up, I'm so messed up!"

My imagination was running wild – images of Angie all tied up flooded through my mind and I burst into tears like a crushed little boy. I closed my eyes and prayed to God. 'I'm talking to you, God Almighty, I know you can hear me. Take me, take Tommy, we're the ones who've sinned, but Angie? She never did anything except love. Please, please.'

"Oi! Wake up, what's the matter with you, had a little nightmare? And wipe that drool off, it's disgusting. Come on, we're going," the detective said, towering over me in the interrogation room.

I slowly came to my senses and realized that it was all a dream! I must have fallen asleep, and everything that had just happened with Rico was a nightmare! "Thank God!" I shouted.

The detective and the copper standing next to him looked at me as though I'd completely lost it. They led me out to the hallway. I felt strange – my muscles were cramping, everything felt heavy, and my body was itching so badly that I wanted to peel my skin off. "What's going on? When are you questioning me? Am I under arrest?" I asked.

"You're free to go. The owner of the vehicle decided not to press charges," the detective told me, "Run along now, and get those flight tickets delivered before the plane takes off!"

"All right," I replied. I didn't ask any more questions and I just started walking as fast as I could, but I felt so confused. My body was acting strangely, and on top of the muscle spasms and the itching, my jaw had started cramping and I felt like my teeth were about to fall off. My pulse was racing and I was sweating in places I didn't even know could sweat, but I kept going until I got to the front desk. The copper sitting there gave me some papers to sign. Everything looked blurry and I wasn't sure I'd signed in the right places. In the meantime, he handed me the envelope with the flight tickets, as well as my fags and the keys to the house.

"What about the money I had in my pocket?" I asked.

"What money? I don't know what you're talking about."

"I had money! A lot of money!"

"You're more than welcome to file a complaint!" he said and chuckled.

I was in no mood to argue. I could barely stand straight, and I had to get the hell out of there and sort myself out. I was shaking! The dream was still roaming through my mind, as though it had really happened, as though my prayer was the reason that everything had worked out all right.

I started walking towards my house – no car, no money, no mates, nothing but the flight tickets and a mad craving buzzing through me. My stomach turned and I tried my best to keep walking. "How do I get myself out of this?" I mumbled. I had to stop every few minutes because I had the worst diarrhea ever. 'I can't pray to God to get me some gear because that's a bad thing,' I thought as I marched in some random direction – anything, anywhere, just to get away.

A car suddenly appeared behind me and the window rolled down. It was Don. "Oi, get in, Rico wants to see you."

"Hi Don, tell Rico he was right and I was wrong, I never stood a chance. He's the king, and I mean it," I said.

Don gave me a baffled look, but I didn't care anymore. I wasn't going to repeat my mistakes, surely not after praying to God for help and actually getting it. I was a total mess.

"Get in the car Iggy, Rico wants to talk to you now. Here," he added and handed me a baggie with some gear in it.

I immediately grabbed it, made a little hole in it and sniffed right out of the baggie, four whiffs. Within a minute, I was already feeling better. My mind slowly cleared up, and when I realized that all of my chances had turned into risks, I got in the car and sat next to Don.

"What is that horrid smell?" he made a face, "Did you shit yourself?"

I didn't reply. He hit the gas and rolled all the windows down. I looked out at the view as though this were the last time I'd ever see it. I started envisaging the people I wanted to say goodbye to before leaving this world, one by one, until I finally reached Angie. In my mind, there could never be a more beautiful goodbye than that final night we'd had – when we merged, body and soul, in the most immaculate way possible.

We reached Rico's building – the real one, this time. Don told me that Rico was waiting for me upstairs.

I got in the lift and felt just like I did on my first time there, but I wasn't as stressed or excited as I was back then. I knew that I needed to stay calm and accept whatever Rico said. 'If he asks me to get on all fours, that's what I'll do. If he asks me to jump up and bray like a donkey, that's what I'll do. Whatever he says, just so he doesn't think up any creative ways to crush me and somehow get to Angie.'

I reached the door to his office, took a deep breath, and walked in. Rico was sitting behind his desk and my mum was sitting in an armchair. The moment she saw me, she gave me this compassionate kind of look, which seemed strange.

"Sit down, Iggy!" Rico commanded. I took a seat in front of him. I was prepared for any and all forms of degradation, and just repeated again and again in my mind, 'Iggy, listen carefully before you open your big mouth.'

And then Rico said, "I'm disappointed, Iggy." I stayed quiet. "Do you mind your mum being here? Do you want her to go out?" he asked.

"Whatever you prefer," I replied.

"Sarah," he turned to her, "Give us some privacy, will you?" My mum got up and left the room. "Now it's just the two of us, Iggy," he began. "I've been thinking about you a lot these last few days. What happened with Sebastian made me realize that maybe I was too rash with you. You shot his bloody head off. You acted like a pro and finally learned to keep your mouth shut. That got me thinking, and it took me back in time. You were only little, so you probably won't remember this, but there's a moment that's stayed with me all this time – call it a defining moment."

I suddenly realized that maybe I could connect him to his feelings, because I knew the exact moment he was talking about. This was my chance at softening him and making him change his plans regarding me, and Tommy too.

"The day I called you Dad?" I asked. Rico's eyes gaped open with surprise, he didn't think I'd remember. "You tucked me in and hugged me tightly," I kept going, "I think you even cried."

"Wow! Your memory's spot on, son!" he said, impressed, "And I'll have you know, I'm not usually an emotional person. When you go through the kind of harsh things that I had to endure in life, when everyone betrays you, you end up turning into concrete, because you realize that emotions are the thing that gets you into trouble. But no matter how many walls you build around you, and no matter how much you try to run away, there are moments in life when someone manages to sneak in through the cracks and plants himself or herself right in your heart! And that's what happened to me with you. Trust me, I really did have the best of intentions when it came to you and me."

"Then what happened? What did I do?"

"Look, what happened with your mate ain't the sort of thing that you can just forget about and move on. Do you agree?" he asked.

"I agree that it wasn't cool, and that he's a knob and needs to check before he goes in, but Rico, you're a bloody rottweiler, and Tommy's a chihuahua! It's not a fair match," I said.

"Well then, someone needs to teach that chihuahua not to touch the rottweiler's bowl."

"True, but still, it's a chihuahua, it only took a grain or two and sufficed – the rottweiler's bowl is still full."

"All right, but today it's a chihuahua, tomorrow it'll be the labrador who saw the rottweiler ignoring the chihuahua." He seemed exceptionally pleased by all the metaphors. "Do you get it? It's the food chain, that's life, sometimes the chihuahua has to pay a heavy price so that the other dogs learn not to touch the rottweiler's bowl – no other way about it!"

"And me, what am I?" I asked.

"Good question. You're not a chihuahua, that's for sure – actually, you're not even a dog. You keep escaping right at the very last minute, each and every time," he said pensively. "Maybe you're a cat. Cats have nine lives, so the question is – how many lives have you used up?!"

I was so surprised that I burst out laughing, even though I should have been stressing about the way in which he'd ended his metaphor-laden speech. Rico joined in and we laughed for a good long while.

CHAPTER 25

Rico looked at me with a fatherly gaze. "You know, before you came by here today, I wasn't in a mood at all, and look at me now – I can't remember the last time I enjoyed talking rubbish this much, and laughing on top of that, really laughing, a cathartic kind of laugh, you know? There's something different about you, son, something true and pure, and I recognized that the moment you first set foot in my office. That's it, I've made my decision!" he announced and slammed his hand on the desk. "We're going for a truce, everything's on halt for four days, that way everyone can calm themselves without having to make any decisions! After that, we'll meet up again for a calm conversation and discuss what's next."

"Wait, what do you mean 'everything's on halt?' Tommy too?" I asked.

"Tommy too."

"And Andy?" I asked hesitantly.

"Everything, Iggy!" he declared, "We're both giving our word here that neither of us will do anything – from the moment you leave this office until we meet again. I won't look for anyone, and you won't get in touch with anyone – not even Tommy. We'll rebuild our trust in each other. Deal?"

"Four days? Deal," I said.

"Excellent! In the meantime, I'm sending you off on a job," he continued, "That way you won't be tempted to get into any more trouble, and you'll even make a nice bit of dosh. What do you say?"

I was stunned. "And what about the money we owe Shirley?"

"That's the last thing you need to worry about, it's been taken care of."

Everything was going so smoothly that I felt like something was off. He didn't try to deny anything when I'd asked about Andy, and there was no way that I wasn't going to check up on Tommy and Angie. 'What's his real plan?' I wondered. 'And how can it be that every time I get to the end of the road and I'm sure I'm finally about to move on to the next life, God sorts everything out and keeps me alive?'

I had no intention of honoring my pact with Rico since I didn't really trust him, but it was as though my plan had rewound right to where I wanted it to be – win his trust, get a few more days to sort everything out, do a final delivery job and execute my sting plan on him. "Well then, I'll be going home for a kip in the meantime," I said, "Just call me when you need me, all right?"

"Look, in a few hours' time, there's a delivery leaving this building, and this time you'll be on your own," he said, "And like I told you, I don't employ junkies, but I'll make an exception so that you can have another go. So, how about you do something to keep me sweet and just stay here, put your head down on the sofa for a few hours, that way you'll be able to rest without any distractions. We've already sorted out everything you'll need – toothbrush, soap, towel … a change of clothes. And I even got you this," he said and pulled out a little baggie, placing it in front of me, "Just so you don't flip out on me. You don't mind doing that for me, do you?"

That's when the penny finally dropped – this whole thing was one big manipulation act. Rico had slipped up without noticing. After all, if the idea of a four-day truce had only just come to him, then how could it be that he'd already sorted out supplies for me so that I could hit the road straight away? Toiletries, a towel, and clothes, even a bit of gear! Anything for me to not leave his office and do a runner on him. *'Of course it was all planned!'*

"Iggy, where did you drift off to? Are you with me?"

"Yeah, that's fine, I'll stay here," I replied.

"I know that there were a few issues with Don – but we said truce, right?" he added, "And I need to make a move and sort a few things out. Trust me, it's been a challenging week. The job you're about to do is very personal, I'll tell you about it before you leave, but in any case, Don's here if you need anything or go hungry or run out of bog roll. Feel free to ask him for anything you fancy, and try to rest for a few hours, you've got a long drive ahead of you. I'm off," he said and left the office.

The last thing on my mind was resting. I thought that with the amount of adrenaline gushing through my body at that point, I could have stayed awake for the rest of my life. My brain started processing everything quickly: Rico had in fact imprisoned me in his office – elegantly, but imprisoned nevertheless – without any way of contacting the outside world. He'd hinted that if tried to leave, Don would be waiting right outside.

'What's he planning?' I thought, 'After all, if he wanted to kill me, then he could have done it right there and then.' I paced around the room like a madman, trying to figure out what he was up to. "Think, Iggy, think," I commanded myself.

I couldn't make a phone call since all the telephones were connected to the same line, and Don would surely listen in. I opened the baggie with the gear and cut a couple of lines, and then I surveyed the room to try and figure out my escape options.

'Maybe I can climb out the window,' I thought as I approached it to check the height and look for something to grab onto. I peered outside and realized that I was way too high up and it would be too dangerous to try and get out through the window.

I had to think of a creative way of getting my plan back in motion, and when I recalled that I was about to leave for a job in a few hours' time, I suddenly had an idea – Rico had said I'd be traveling alone, which meant that I'd be free to stop on the way, get an envelope full of dosh, drive over to the Backrub and buy another gun from Martine. Then I planned to stop on the way and call Angie to tell her to get ready and let Tommy, Andy, and Manu know that they needed to head to the airport. In the meantime, I'd make the delivery, take the suitcase full of money, and drive to the airport. Then we'd buy tickets to a new destination, now that Brazil had been flushed out, get on a plane, and fly all the way to freedom.

A sudden knock on the door gave me a fright. "Yeah?" I said and the door opened. Russ was standing there. "All right, son, what's happening? I just came by to see how you're doing. Can I come in or are you trying to rest?"

"No mate, come in, it's all good," I replied.

Russ walked in and sat down on the sofa. I could see his gun peering from his trousers, underneath his unbuttoned jacket. I thought to myself that if only I had another ecstasy on me, then everything could have worked out and I'd persuade him to help me.

"You lot are in a bit of trouble, aren't you," he said.

"That's putting it lightly," I replied.

"You can say that again! I tried to tell you that money wasn't everything in life, I told you to go learn something, a trade or a craft, because this world ain't everyone's cup of tea. I could tell from the word go that this wasn't the life for you."

"Yeah. It hasn't been that long, but you could say that I was young and innocent back then."

"You grow up real fast in this life, don't you?" he said.

"Now I understand why you said that you never get attached to people."

"When did I say that?"

"When we were in the car, you probably don't remember. I hope you didn't get attached to me."

"Oh, I see what you're doing. You're trying to figure out if there's some sort of plan to take you out."

"Is there?" I asked, intrigued.

"Not as far as I know," he said, "But if there was, why would you want to know about it?"

"So that I could do some final soul searching, for example, say goodbye to the people that I love, have a proper last meal and a drink."

"That's precisely why you should live every day as though it's your last. It's funny, you know, you're worrying about something external, when the most dangerous thing – the thing that can actually kill you – is that baggie on the table right there. But, as usual, people only heed advice in hindsight. You're traveling alone tonight, try not to fuck it up this time."

Russ got up to leave. As he walked towards the door, I was dying to ask him to help me, but I knew that it was pointless and would only come out as a pathetic last attempt. "Adios, son, see ya when I see ya," he said and walked out.

I was losing my mind. I wished Rico had killed me a few hours back, when I'd lost all hope, because now that I'd regained it, the fear came back too.

But me being me, as long as there was still time, there was always a little light at the end of the tunnel, and I wasn't going to give in. So I repeated the plan in my mind and waited for Rico to come back and send me out on my delivery.

I washed my face and brushed my teeth, changed my clothes, and tidied myself up a bit. I wanted to feel refreshed so that I'd be ready for my meeting with Angie at the airport. Rico walked in with Don, who was carrying a bag with a burger and chips.

"I brought you some food," Rico said, "It's never a good idea to drive on an empty stomach – it's a good few hours' ride, and you won't be able to make any pitstops because I need the delivery to get there right on time, otherwise it'll reek."

"Reek? What am I delivering?"

"We had a bit of a mess with one of the deliveries this week," he explained, "And our family lost a few of the boys. It wasn't easy, dealing with their poor parents and that, and if we waited for the authorities to clear out the bodies, then they'd be rotting for weeks until they'd finally get taken to their hometowns. So, I took it upon myself to personally deliver them to their grieving parents, who want to bury them at the Little Britain Cemetery. I promised they'd get there by six in the morning, so you've got all night to drive there, and there won't be any traffic to hold you back. And, as a gesture of sympathy and compensation – it was a work accident after all – I'll be sending them quite a bit of money with you. On the way back, I'll need you to pick up a suitcase for me and bring it over here. So, you'll be alone on the road, with a lot of cash – both on your way there and back, and the road's pretty secluded, so the moment you get out of the city, it won't be safe for you to make any stops. We wouldn't want you running into any dodgy fuckers trying to rob you, you see. Let's go downstairs, I'll show you what I'm on about."

I was glad that Rico said I'd have loads of cash on my way there and back – it meant more money for our new flight tickets. It also calmed me down because I assumed that if he wanted to harm me then he'd never leave me in charge of that much dosh.

We went downstairs to the parking lot. A few laborers were shoving coffins inside the truck – four closed caskets. Rico put his arm around my shoulder and took me aside. "Iggy, that talk we had earlier, it really did something to me, I won't lie," he said, "I hope I can trust you, and that this'll be a fresh start for you."

"Yeah, you can trust me," I said, noticing the laborers placing the last coffin in the truck from the corner of my eye. Something inside me was still uneasy, I had no idea why. I had a feeling that the caskets had a huge amount of gear in them, and that if I got pulled over by the coppers and they checked the load, I'd be put in prison for life without parole.

"Hey, Rico, if I get pulled over at any point, what am I allowed to show them? If you know what I mean."

"You've got all the papers you'll need; it's all written down so you have nothing to worry about – it's all legal. Come here, have a look," he said and took me to the back of the truck. He asked the laborers to open the door and lower the casket that was closest to us. They lowered it to the ground and he told them to open it. I was surprised by his willingness to show me the delivery, especially considering there was a dead fat man in the coffin, which scared the hell out of me.

"See? Just a coffin, nothing special about it. Show me some trust, eh?" he said and patted my back firmly. "If you come across any issues, anything, you can call me anytime. In any case, I've installed a tracking device in the truck – so if heaven forbid something goes wrong on the way, I'll send you some backup in no time. Don't worry, everything will be fine."

My heart plummeted. I didn't know whether to laugh or cry. 'How do I get out of this now? Every move on the road, any diversion and he's on my tail.' I had to think of a creative solution, and what I really needed in order to think straight was to get the hell away from that place. We went back to the front of the truck as the laborers closed the back door. Rico handed me a map and an envelope with cash.

'More dosh,' I thought, but there was no time to waste. 'It'll be a five-hour drive with a stop or two for petrol and freshening up, so I can afford to take my time without raising any suspicion for an extra hour, say. And if the truck really does have a tracking device installed, then the whole drive has to be in the same direction – heading towards the final destination.'

I revved the engine and hit the gas. I looked through the rearview mirror and saw Rico waving goodbye to me, but then I suddenly saw my mum standing next to him with dark glasses covering half her face. He grabbed her hand and they stood there, watching me until I was out of sight. I didn't understand what she was doing there and why she hadn't come over to say anything to me before I'd left.

'And why was she wearing those glasses? Maybe he hit her again?' I thought, but the moment I left the parking lot, I forgot all about her and focused on figuring out how to pop by to see my mates without raising suspicion and still reach my destination within five or six hours at the most.

I suddenly recalled a film I'd seen where the criminal had to get rid of the coppers who were waiting outside his house. They saw him coming out, getting in the car, and driving away, and they chased after him for hours. He finally halted the car with the coppers right behind him, got out, and walked close enough to their car for them to realize that it was actually someone else that whole time. Long story short – I realized that I needed someone to drive the truck instead of me and get to the delivery point. That way, Rico would see that the truck was heading the right way and stopping at the right place, and I'd be free for at least five hours to plan everything in a nice, calm manner.

But there was another suitcase that I needed to pick up – and it wasn't like I was about to forgo all that money. So, I thought that I could tell the driver to wait for us somewhere half-way on his inbound journey. Angie and I would buy an old, battered car, pick up Manu and Andy, and then head to the meeting point, getting there right on time for the driver to swap with me – he'd take the old car and I'd get in the truck. They'd follow me at a safe distance, I'd then pick up the suitcase, and the driver would swap with me again and head to Rico's office, which would leave us at least three hours before he got there, and that would be plenty of time for us to get to the airport and buy the new flight tickets. By the time Rico realized that someone else was driving, we'd already be on the plane with suitcases full of dosh, heading towards our ultimate freedom.

'I'm a genius!' I thought. All I needed in order to set the plan in motion was to find the right driver for the job.

I drove slowly, trying to figure out how to make the plan work. I prayed to God for a foolproof idea. 'After all, there's no way that such a genius plan won't work,' I thought.

"Think, Iggy, think," I urged myself as I passed by the Backrub and immediately halted right outside the front door. I was sure that I could find someone mad enough or hungry enough in there who'd be willing to do the job for some dosh. I parked the truck on the pavement and went in. Luckily, I immediately spotted Martine. "All right doll," I said.

She seemed happy to see me. "I see you managed to stay alive, then."

"For now," I replied, "And I need a favor."

I explained the gist of what I was after, and she went over to someone sitting by the bar and whispered into his ear. He got up and they both approached me. He seemed pretty out of it, but I was in no position to be fussy – and on top of that, I was running out of time.

"Nothing to write home about, but that's as good as it'll get at such short notice," Martine said and introduced us.

I explained to the bloke exactly what I needed him to do, and said I'd pay him 500 quid now and 500 more when he got back. He seemed pleased as punch about it and we walked out to the truck. He sat down on the driver's seat and I instructed him on how to drive the truck. I was a bit worried that he was too wasted and would mess things up, so I told him that if everything went smoothly and he didn't drink on the way, I'd treat him to a huge bonus. I pulled the map out and marked the exact route he needed to take to the destination, explained what he needed to offload there, and emphasized that if anyone asked, his name was Iggy. Then I marked the route he needed to take on the way back and the meeting point half-way through, and made sure he understood everything I'd said. I obviously asked him to repeat everything back to me to make sure he'd got it all before I paid him the first 500 quid.

"And remember, if everything goes smoothly," I fibbed, "I promise that once you get back here, you'll get 500 quid from me plus a 500 quid bonus." I knew that by the time he got back to London, I'd no longer be there to give him the rest of the dosh, but I didn't feel guilty about it. *'Five hundred quid's a lot of money – the kind of dosh he wouldn't even get for a few months' work,'* I thought.

I told him to hit the road and checked the time, which was slowly but surely running out. I added that I'd get off later because I wanted to make sure that he was all right with driving the truck. I planned for him to let me off at the exit from the city, and that I'd head over to Angie's on foot from there.

Once we started the drive, I realized that he was way more wasted than I'd thought. He couldn't even hold the steering wheel steadily. "Listen," I said in a worried tone, "Let's stop for some coffee to wake you up a bit, eh? You're out of focus, and that's a major problem! If you fuck this up, then I won't be able to pay you the money once you get back. You know what, I'll do you one better – go with me on this and I'll give you 1500 quid, and that's a lot of money, mate. It would be a shame to miss out on that kind of dosh."

"Yeah, coffee might really help, good idea," he replied. "It's a shame, you know, if you just got there five minutes earlier … I was still pretty with it at that point…"

"It's all good," I told him, "See the café after the traffic lights? Stop on the pavement next to it and I'll go get you a coffee."

My eyes nearly popped out of their sockets when I saw the light turning red and he just kept on driving, not even batting an eyelid. The cars crossing the junction honked at us and a passing vehicle nearly crashed into us. The drunk turned the wheel and I felt like the truck was about to flip onto its side, but right at the very last second, the truck steadied itself and he halted right outside the café. We were both in shock and it took us a few seconds to shake it off.

Without saying a word, I hopped out of the truck and ran over to get him a coffee with loads of sugar to help him sober up. I even bought him a sandwich to make sure he was on a full stomach. I looked at the time and realized that we were risking it. He looked pretty stressed as he sipped his coffee and took a few bites of the sandwich. "Dunno, mate," he said, "I'm a bit scared that it'll happen again. Why don't you find someone else? Don't wanna get into trouble, me." He pulled the money out of his pocket and handed it to me.

"No, no, no, please, I'm begging you! Please, please, do this for me, mate, I'll pay you 2000 quid when you get back, maybe even more."

"What do you even have in here? Drugs?" he asked in a suspicious tone.

"No mate, I swear, it's all legal," I replied, "No drugs, nothing illegal, I promise."

"I wouldn't mind if it were drugs, you know," he chuckled and started driving again – real slowly this time, too slowly, even. I thought that maybe I'd be better off letting him drive away so I could finally get to Angie's place, but before I managed to tell him to stop, we suddenly heard a police siren behind us, and I saw the red flickering lights through the rearview mirror.

'Shit, shit, shit! Now of all times! This is the last thing I need!' I thought. *'They'll ask him for his license – which doesn't cover this type of vehicle – and then they'll realize he's drunk and arrest us, and it'll be over for me! Finished!'*

"Pull over, Sir," the coppers called out through their megaphone.

I couldn't take any risks. "Come on, swap with me," I instructed him and hopped over him onto the driver's seat. Luckily for me, the truck was pretty tall, so the coppers couldn't see what we were up to. "Listen," I said, "No matter what I tell them, just back me up. Let's get rid of them and hit the road as quickly as possible. We're way behind and we can't fuck this up!"

The fella just nodded, and I looked up to the sky. "What else can go wrong? If someone's trying to tell me something then just make it clear, please," I said out loud.

The copper approaching us had a badge on his chest stating that he was a sergeant. He motioned with his hand for me to roll down the window. "Evening, Sir," he said.

"Evening, Sergeant, is there a problem?" I asked politely.

"I noticed that you were swerving a little," he replied in a cynical tone. "Have you been drinking?"

"No, Sir, not me. My mate over here had a few too many… You see, his family was killed in a car accident and we're transporting their coffins for the funeral… Poor dear."

The sergeant made a face. "You seem a tad stressed," he noted.

"I just want to get this over with," I sighed, but it didn't help – he insisted on seeing my papers. I presented everything to him, but that still wasn't enough.

"Why don't the two of you come out for a moment," he insisted.

"Sergeant, Sir, I'm begging you, just let us get on with it, everything's fine and you're holding us up for no reason! We have to get to the Little Britain Cemetery in time, we have funerals to get to."

"Open the back door, please, I want to see what this is all about."

"Why?" I exclaimed, "What on earth could be so special about bloody coffins? What do you think, that we're some sort of Columbian drug smugglers? Give me a break!"

"You're a smart-ass, aren't you – one more word out of you and you'll be spending the night in a cell!" he said.

I quickly apologized and escorted him to the back of the truck. I unlocked the door and the Sergeant's face contorted as he grabbed his nose with his fingers. He then immediately came to his senses, aimed his flashlight at the coffins, and counted them. "Now, Sir," he said as he examined the papers, "It states here that there should only be four coffins, but you have five. Can you explain why you have a fifth coffin?"

"I don't understand what you mean, I've only got four coffins. Just four," I said.

"I see, but here, look," he pointed at the papers, "It clearly states that there should only be four coffins – and you quite clearly have five in your truck."

"Maybe there's some sort of mistake with the papers," I said and thought to myself, 'Why's there another coffin? Why didn't Rico say anything about it...?'

I recalled that first day when Rico had asked me to count the goods going into the truck until the laborers shut the doors – and I hadn't done it this time. *'Could it be that he snuck another coffin in there just to get me into trouble? After all, he explicitly said that there were four coffins. Maybe he put another one in with some incriminating stuff inside it?'* I started stressing like crazy and sweating all over. *'If anything bad happens now, then my plan will go to shit.'* I prayed for God to help me again.

"Listen, mate, I'm sorry but I'm going to need you to open the coffins."

"Yes, of course, no problem, Sir," I said. We both went into the truck and looked at the coffins. The smell was unbearable, and I hoped that it would deter him and make him leave us alone, but he didn't flinch and just shone his flashlight over the coffins. At that point, I noticed that four of the coffins had a lock on them, and only the fifth one was unlocked – the one Rico had shown me.

The copper asked me to open a coffin and I hesitated for a moment. On the one hand, I was curious to open one of the locked ones. On the other hand, I was scared of taking the risk and finding something incriminating in there – and then the whole of London Met would show up and everything would be ruined. My plan was so perfect that I didn't even want to think about it crashing and burning like that.

"So, should I open it?" I asked, reaching my hand towards the unlocked coffin, but the copper had already noticed that the other coffins were locked, so he shifted my hand aside and shone his flashlight on one of the locked coffins.

"That one, if you don't mind," he said.

"All right," I turned my head to look for the keys.

The moment I turned, I heard the drunk fella's voice as he peered into the truck. "What's the deal, mate? Are we making a move soon?"

"Get back in your seat, bruv, just a few more minutes and we'll be heading out," I replied. He looked at me and paused. *'What a mess,'* I thought. *'If the tracking device shows us staying here for too long, then Rico will send his people over and they'll see the drunk – and then I'm a goner!'*

"I don't want him to be here when I open the coffin so let me just help him back to his seat, all right?" I asked the sergeant. He nodded his head, and I got out and led the drunk back to the front. "You can't get out of the truck," I clarified to him, "I don't want us getting in trouble because of your drinking, get it?"

"It's a bit hard for me to just sit and wait," he moaned, "I wanna go back to the Backrub."

"I'm asking you to stay, have some patience. Even though you're the reason they stopped us to begin with, I'll pay you way more than I'd promised if you just stay." This time, I was using my most desperate tone. I felt like I was about to crack under all that pressure, and I was dying for a few lines to calm me down.

I took the baggie out, punctured a hole in it, and sniffed some right into my nose – there was no time to cut any lines. The drunk's eyes gaped open, but I didn't care. "Want some too?" I asked.

"I'd love a drink, actually."

"No worries, the second we finish with the coppers, I'll go buy you a bottle of whatever you fancy!"

"All right, now you're talking. Let's go for some 18-year-old scotch, whichever one I choose, yeah?" he clarified.

"Done, I swear on my mother's life!"

"Okay then," he agreed.

I ran back to the sergeant. "I dunno where the keys for the locks are, Sir. We're gonna need something sharp, or maybe a hammer, so we can break the lock."

He put his hand in his pocket and pulled out a Swiss Army knife. Then he aimed his flashlight, inserted the knife between the lock and the coffin, and pressed until the chain's loops loosened. We opened the coffin, and the truck immediately became filled with the sort of stench that digs deep into your bones. We felt like we were suffocating. For a second there, I didn't even notice the body inside the coffin because the smell was killing me, but another glance at the rot covering it made my whole body twitch. I felt like my blood had frozen stiff and I couldn't breathe. I swayed and stumbled. The Sergeant tried to lift me back up, but my body had stiffened and I could literally feel the blood leaving me.

"You all right?!" he asked and shouted for his partner to come over.

The other copper ran over to us with his baton drawn. "What's the matter?" he asked as he peered inside, "Should I call for backup? What's that God-awful smell?"

"No, no need for backup," the sergeant replied, "The fella just saw a body and shriveled up, come on, help him down and I'll close the coffin back up."

The other copper came in and helped me get out, trying to calm me down, but I was completely mental – everything was coming up, and I finally puked my guts out. They were stunned by my reaction, and the sergeant ran over to their car and brought back a canteen of water for me.

"Cheer up, lad," he said after they got some water in me, "I know it can be unsettling, seeing a dead body – we've seen our fair share."

He had no idea that I hadn't lost it because there was a dead body in there, or because of the smell. I'd lost it because the body was Manu's. I had tears in my eyes and I felt my stomach going up and down in a kind of whirlpool sensation, and then, all at once, everything burst out again.

"Jesus, you're a real sensitive one, aren't you, lad. Maybe we should get you some help?"

"No! I'll be fine," I said in a stifled tone, "Really, I'm fine, thank you."

"Are you sure? We can come with you if you'd like."

"No! No, no, no, I'm fine," I said.

The coppers' radio started making sounds. "We have to go," the sergeant said, "Wait here for a bit longer and make sure to calm down before you head back out – don't want you driving in your current state, all right? Once you feel better, then just make sure and drive carefully."

The coppers got in their car and drove off. I rose up from the pavement and went to check on the drunk, but he wasn't in the truck anymore, and I didn't care. I started trembling, as though I were standing naked in minus twenty degrees. I checked that the coast was clear, closed the truck's back door behind me and went back to the coffin – I wanted to make sure that I wasn't imagining things. I lifted the lid up again and realized – it was really happening. The body lying there wasn't Rico's mate or some stranger's – it was Manu.

"God, no!" I said, full of terror. Seeing him lying there like that was the harshest thing in the world. I burst out crying. I felt completely helpless and scared. "I'm so sorry," I told him, and then I looked at the rest of the coffins and thought, 'If Manu's in this coffin, then who the hell are in the other ones?!'

"Please, God, don't do this to me," I fell onto my knees and pleaded, "I can't take it." I looked around and saw the sergeant's Swiss Army knife on the floor. It was as though God had replied, "Yes you can!"

The smell in the truck was putrid, and I felt the sour stomach juices coming up my throat. I couldn't stop crying and I felt completely choked, but I was determined, and nothing could stop me anymore. I picked up the knife and walked over to the second coffin, trembling with fear. I opened it, and Andy's lifeless body was lying inside it.

"Now I see where you've disappeared to," I told him and then walked over to the third coffin. Tommy was there, a shopping bag wrapped around his head. "They didn't even bother taking the bag off you. Breathe, bruv, please, breathe," I cried and hugged him.

I walked over to the fourth coffin in a frenzy. There was no fear left inside me anymore, nothing but despair, frustration, and wickedness – I wanted revenge!

I opened the fourth coffin, looked inside, and found Richie in there. 'What's going on? What's happening to me? Someone wake me up from this crazy nightmare!'

The fifth coffin was left slightly ajar. I remembered Rico showing me a body inside it that I hadn't recognized, but then I recalled having to always check and lock the truck doors myself with each and every delivery, so I approached the coffin, shaking with fear. 'If that coffin has my Angie in it ... I won't handle it.' With trembling hands and a crushed heart, I opened the coffin – but to my surprise, it was empty. 'What's that supposed to mean?' I wondered, but immediately realized that the empty coffin was meant for me. This ride was supposed to be my very last one. Everything suddenly added up. 'Fuck! The hunter really does enjoy playing with his prey, and God keeps letting me live each and every time. Why? What am I supposed to do?'

I closed my brothers' coffins with a sense of determination I'd never experienced before – I knew exactly what I had to do. I quickly got in the driver's seat and started driving like a maniac to Angie's place. I kept imagining myself getting there right in the nick of time to save her.

I drove well over the speed limit all the way there. Strangely enough, there were hardly any cars on the road, and even though I'd gone through a number of traffic violations, there wasn't a copper in sight. It was as though God himself had cleared the path for me, as though that's what he had wanted me to do this whole time – because if we really did come to this world to make amends, then I guess my way of doing it was through mine and Angie's love. I looked up to the heavens and told my mates, "I hope you lot are watching out for her – do whatever you can!" I'd never felt like that before. I'd reached the most intense level of alertness, of madness.

It was three in the morning by the time I got there, so I parked a few blocks away from her building, and even though I was in a rush, I made sure to stay as hidden and as cautious as possible, just in case – I'd already learned that it was better to surprise than to be surprised.

Once I reached the entrance to the building, I made sure that there was no one around outside. Even though it was quiet, something felt off to me, so I climbed the stairs quietly without turning the lights on until I reached Angie's floor and walked up to her front door. I pressed my ear against the door to see if I could hear anything or anyone inside, and the bloody door just opened on its own – my heart stopped! I froze and peered inside. The house was dark and quiet, but I managed to see a dull light coming through Angie's bedroom door, which was at the other end of the corridor – it was like the light at the end of the tunnel. Her door was slightly ajar. I started walking along the corridor, looking around for something to serve as a weapon if need be. I passed by the bathroom and went in, feeling around for sharp objects. I felt a pair of tweezers, a toothpaste tube, and then a glass – which was exactly what I needed. It would suffice to break it for it to become a useful weapon.

I continued quietly tiptoeing until I reached her bedroom door. I prayed to God that she was asleep and in one piece, but I had a terrible feeling that something bad was happening in there. I felt like there was someone else in there with Angie, and I wondered what I could do to surprise him without endangering her. One option was to make a ruckus, so if someone was really there, then he'd come out to check on the noise and then I'd be able to pounce on him, but it could still be risky – he could kill her before leaving the room, if that's what he was there for, that is. There was also the chance that more than one person was in there, and then we'd be toast, but if that was the case, then she was doomed to begin with. One thing was certain in that scenario – at least we'd die together, and she'd die knowing that I had come to save her, that I hadn't abandoned her.

I took a deep breath. *'Here goes nothing,'* I thought and swung my foot up, kicking the door down. After that, everything happened so fast… I saw Rico putting his trousers on while Angie was lying on her back, naked and bruised everywhere. They both looked at me, but Angie's eyes were swollen and I couldn't see her pupils. I'd surprised him. He had one hand holding up his trousers, and his other hand reached for the gun he'd left by the side of the bed, but Angie beat him to it. She grabbed the gun and tried to aim and fire it, but she missed…

The bullet passed right by Rico and hit me. I felt it going in, piercing through my stomach and internal organs, ripping them apart. All of my blood vessels burst open and my shirt turned red. I fell to the floor and the glass broke.

Angie screamed, "No!!!"

At that moment, I had a strange thought – *'How could it be that the one thing that's been motivating me to live ends up killing me?'* And, with that thought, I no longer felt any pain. My body must have been flooded by adrenaline. I saw Rico bending down to pick up the gun from the floor and I quickly grabbed a piece of broken glass. I leaped up and grabbed onto him. He tried to shake me off and maintain a grip on his gun, but I swung my hand up and stuck the broken glass deep into his throat, twisting it around with all the strength I had left in me, until my own wrist felt like it was about to tear off. Rico's eyes gaped open and fixed onto mine, and I stared back at him without even blinking. We both collapsed onto the floor, but he was lifeless within a few seconds.

In my mind, I felt like I had the strength to get up and check on Angie, but I couldn't physically move. For a moment there, I opened my eyes and felt like I was standing on my feet, but when I blinked, I found myself lying in Angie's arms, enveloped and protected, like a child in his mother's lap. I'd never imagined that this would be the end of everything. I was so sure that we'd beat them all. I truly believed that we'd be lying on some tropical beach somewhere, margaritas in hand, far away from all this mess – Tommy, Andy, Angie, and me. But now, the only thing that mattered to me wasn't the success, or the money, or the drugs. All I wanted was for the one I loved to hold my hand and stay with me during those final moments – just like my teacher and that homeless fella had said.

For some reason, I didn't feel bad about leaving this world. I was even excited about starting afresh. Something strange happens a few moments before you die, like some kind of spiritual preparation, everything gets put on a lower flame – passion, anger, greed, sadness, frustration, even the form of love – the way we experience it here, in this lifetime. Love actually intensifies, but it feels so healthy and beautiful, utterly lacking in fear. All of the feelings that come when we enter this universe change. I knew that Angie felt different about it all, but I had no way of changing it. You should all know – this is bigger than us, and it's the soul's natural course.

"I'm right here with you, Iggy, please try to hold on, for me. Don't leave me here on my own. I love you."

"I love you too."

Fragmented memories flashed before my eyes, and I didn't regret a single one of them. This was my way, this was what my soul was supposed to undergo in this world, just like all the other souls. If I apologized for it then I'd be questioning the Creator's will, and we're nothing but a tiny spark in the universe, after all.

Farewell, mad world, I feel like I'm on the way to the right place … no more pain, nothing but the sensation of a melody accompanying the heart's final path. I came to this world before you, Angie, and I'm leaving before you too, but our souls are destined to be bound together, so I'll wait for you, wherever I'll be. And remember — the kind of love we have is once in a lifetime, and it's forever and ever, in all dimensions.

The strange thing is that even here, in the place I'm fairly convinced is hell, where everything's so complicated, where most things are so very evil, there's still no greater force than the power of love.

The end.

Printed in Great Britain
by Amazon